OXFORD WORLD'S
CLASSICS

UNCLE REMUS
OR
MR FOX,
MR RABBIT,
AND MR TERRAPIN

JOEL CHANDLER HARRIS

AVENEL BOOKS
NEW YORK

Uncle Remus was first published in 1881, and in The
World's Classics in 1930

This edition first published in 1985 by Avenel Books,
distributed by Crown Publishers, Inc

produced by

Chancellor Press
59 Grosvenor Street
London W1

under license from

Oxford University Press
Walton Street
Oxford

ISBN 0 517 60605 4

Printed in Shenzhen, China

h g f e d c b a

INTRODUCTION

I AM advised by my publishers that this book is to
be included in their catalogue of humorous publi-
cations, and this friendly warning gives me an
opportunity to say that however humorous it may
be in effect, its intention is perfectly serious ; and,
even if it were otherwise, it seems to me that a
volume written wholly in a dialect must have its
solemn, not to say melancholy, features. With re-
spect to the Folk-Lore series, my purpose has been
to preserve the legends themselves in their original
simplicity, and to wed them permanently to the
quaint dialect, if indeed it can be called a dialect,
through the medium of which they have become
a part of the domestic history of every Southern
family ; and I have endeavoured to give to the
whole a genuine flavour of the old plantation.

Each legend has its variants, but in every instance
I have retained that particular version which seemed
to me to be the most characteristic, and have given
it without embellishment and without exaggera-
tion. The dialect, it will be observed, is wholly
different from that of the Hon. Pompey Smash and
his literary descendants, and different also from the
intolerable misrepresentations of the minstrel stage,
but it is at least phonetically genuine. Nevertheless, if the language of Uncle Remus fails to give
vivid hints of the really poetic imagination of the
negro ; if it fails to embody the quaint and homely

humour which was his most prominent characteristic ; if it does not suggest a certain picturesque
sensitiveness, a curious exaltation of mind and
temperament not to be defined by words, then I
have reproduced the form of the dialect merely,
and not the essence, and my attempt may be ac-
counted a failure.   At any rate, I trust I have been
successful in presenting what must be, at least to a
large portion of American readers, a new and by
no means unattractive phase of negro character, a
phase which may be considered a curiously sympathetic supplement to Mrs. Stowe's wonderful de-
fence of slavery as it existed in the South.   Mrs.
Stowe, let me hasten to say, attacked the possibili-
ties of slavery with all the eloquence of genius ; but
the same genius painted the portrait of the Southern
slave-owner, and defended him.

A number of the plantation legends originally
appeared in the columns of a daily newspaper,
The Atlanta Constitution, and in that shape they
attracted the attention of various gentlemen who
were kind enough to suggest that they would prove
to be valuable contributions to myth-literature.
It is but fair to say that ethnological considerations
formed no part of the undertaking which has resulted
in the publication of this volume.   Professor J. W.
Powell, of the Smithsonian Institution, who is engaged in an investigation of the mythology of the
North American Indians, informs me that some of
Uncle Remus's stories appear in a number of different languages, and in various modified forms,
among the Indians ; and he is of the opinion that
they are borrowed by the negroes from the red men.
But this, to say the least, is extremely doubtful,
since another investigator (Mr. Herbert H. Smith,
author of *Brazil and the Amazons*) has met with some

of these stories among tribes of South American Indians, and one in particular he has traced to India, and as far east as Siam. Mr. Smith has been kind enough to send me the proof-sheets of his chapter on *The Myths and Folk-Lore of the Amazonian Indians*, in which he reproduces some of the stories which he gathered while exploring the Amazons.

In the first of his series, a tortoise falls from a tree upon the head of a jaguar and kills him ; in one of Uncle Remus's stories, the terrapin falls from a shelf in Miss Meadows's house and stuns the fox, so that the latter fails to catch the rabbit. In the next, a jaguar catches a tortoise by the hind-leg as he is disappearing in his hole ; but the tortoise convinces him he is holding a root, and so escapes ; Uncle Remus tells how the fox endeavoured to drown the terrapin, but turned him loose because the terrapin declared his tail to be only a stump-root. Mr. Smith also gives the story of how the tortoise outran the deer, which is identical as to incident with Uncle Remus's story of how Brer Tarrypin outran Brer Rabbit. Then there is the story of how the tortoise pretended that he was stronger than the tapir. He tells the latter he can drag him into the sea, but the tapir retorts that he will pull the tortoise into the forest and kill him besides. The tortoise thereupon gets a vine-stem, ties one end around the body of the tapir, and goes to the sea, where he ties the other end to the tail of a whale. He then goes into the wood, midway between them both, and gives the vine a shake as a signal for the pulling to begin. The struggle between the whale and tapir goes on until each thinks the tortoise is the strongest of animals. Compare this with the story of the terrapin's contest with the bear, in which Miss Meadows's bed-cord is used instead of a

vine-stem. One of the most characteristic of Uncle
Remus's stories is that in which the rabbit proves
to Miss Meadows and the girls that the fox is his
riding-horse. This is almost identical with a story
quoted by Mr. Smith, where the jaguar is about to
marry the deer's daughter. The cotia—a species of
rodent—is also in love with her, and he tells the deer
that he can make a riding-horse of the jaguar.
"Well," says the deer, "if you can make the jaguar
carry you, you shall have my daughter." Thereupon the story proceeds pretty much as Uncle
Remus tells it of the fox and rabbit. The cotia
finally jumps from the jaguar and takes refuge in a
hole, where an owl is set to watch him, but he flings
sand in the owl's eyes and escapes. In another
story given by Mr. Smith, the cotia is very thirsty,
and, seeing a man coming with a jar on his head,
lies down in the road in front of him, and repeats
this until the man puts down his jar to go back after
all the dead cotias he has seen. This is almost
identical with Uncle Remus's story of how the rabbit
robbed the fox of his game. In a story from Upper
Egypt, a fox lies down in the road in front of a man
who is carrying fowls to market, and finally suc-
ceeds in securing them.

This similarity extends to almost every story
quoted by Mr. Smith, and some are so nearly identical as to point unmistakably to a common origin ;
but when and where ? When did the negro or the
North American Indian ever come in contact with
the tribes of South America ? Upon this point the
author of *Brazil and the Amazons,* who is engaged in
making a critical and comparative study of these
myth-stories, writes :

"I am not prepared to form a theory about these
stories. There can be no doubt that some of them,

found among the negroes and the Indians, had a common origin. The most natural solution would be to suppose that they originated in Africa, and were carried to South America by the negro slaves. They are certainly found among the Red Negroes ; but, unfortunately for the African theory, it is equally certain that they are told by savage Indians of the Amazons Valley, away up on the Tapajos, Red Negro, and Tapurá. These Indians hardly ever see a negro, and their languages are very distinct from the broken Portuguese spoken by the slaves. The form of the stories, as recounted in the Tupi and Mundurucú languages, seems to show that they were originally formed in those languages or have long been adopted in them.

"It is interesting to find a story from Upper Egypt (that of the fox who pretended to be dead) identical with an Amazonian story, and strongly resembling one found by you among the negroes. Varnhagen, the Brazilian historian (now Visconde de Rio Branco), tried to prove a relationship between the ancient Egyptians, or other Turanian stock, and the Tupi Indians. His theory rested on rather a slender basis, yet it must be confessed that he had one or two strong points. Do the resemblances between Old and New World stories point to a similar conclusion ? It would be hard to say with the material that we now have.

"One thing is certain. The animal stories told by the negroes in our Southern States and in Brazil were brought by them from Africa. Whether they originated there, or with the Arabs, or Egyptians, or with yet more ancient nations, must still be an open question. Whether the Indians got them from the negroes or from some earlier source is equally uncertain. We have seen enough to know that a very interesting line of investigation has been opened."

Professor Hartt, in his *Amazonian Tortoise Myths*, quotes a story from *The Riverside Magazine* of November, 1868, which will be recognized as a variant of one given by Uncle Remus. I venture to append it here, with some necessary verbal and phonetic alterations, in order to give the reader an idea of the difference between the dialect of the cotton plantations, as used by Uncle Remus, and the lingo in vogue on the rice plantations and Sea Islands of the South Atlantic States:

"One time B'er Deer an' B'er Cooter (Terrapin) was courtin', and de lady did bin lub B'er Deer mo' so dan B'er Cooter. She did bin lub B'er Cooter, but she lub B'er Deer de morest. So de noung lady say to B'er Deer an' B'er Cooter bofe dat day mus' hab a ten-mile race, an' de one dat beats, she will go marry him.

"So B'er Cooter say to B'er Deer: 'You has got mo' longer legs dan I has, but I will run you. You run ten mile on land, and I will run ten mile on de water!'

"So B'er Cooter went an' git nine of his fam'ly, an' put one at ebery mile-pos', an' he hisse'f, what was to run wid B'er Deer, he was right in front of de young lady's do', in de broom-grass.

"Dat mornin' at nine o'clock, B'er Deer he did met B'er Cooter at de fus mile-pos', wey dey was to start fum. So he call: 'Well, B'er Cooter, is you ready? Go long!' As he git on to de nex' mile-pos', he say: 'B'er Cooter!' B'er Cooter say: 'Hullo!' B'er Deer say: 'You dere?' B'er Cooter say: 'Yes, B'er Deer, I dere too'.

"Nex' mile-pos' he jump, B'er Deer say: 'Hullo, B'er Cooter!' B'er Cooter say: 'Hullo, B'er Deer!

you dere too?' B'er Deer say: 'Ki! it look like you gwine fer tie me; it look like we gwine fer de gal tie!'

"W'en he git to de nine mile-pos' he tought he git dere fus, 'cause he mek two jump; so he holler: 'B'er Cooter!' B'er Cooter answer: 'You dere too?' B'er Deer say: 'It look like you gwine tie me.' B'er Cooter say: 'Go long, B'er Deer. I git dere in due season time,' which he does, and wins the race."

The story of the Rabbit and the Fox, as told by the Southern negroes, is artistically dramatic in this: it progresses in an orderly way from a beginning to a well-defined conclusion, and is full of striking episodes that suggest the culmination. It seems to me to be to a certain extent allegorical, albeit such an interpretation may be unreasonable. At least it is a fable thoroughly characteristic of the negro; and it needs no scientific investigation to show why he selects as his hero the weakest and most harmless of all animals, and brings him out victorious in contests with the bear, the wolf, and the fox. It is not virtue that triumphs, but helplessness; it is not malice, but mischievousness. It would be presumptuous in me to offer an opinion as to the origin of these curious myth-stories; but, if ethnologists should discover that they did not originate with the African, the proof of that effect should be accompanied with a good deal of persuasive eloquence.

Curiously enough, I have found few negroes who will acknowledge to a stranger that they know anything of these legends; and yet to relate one of the stories is the surest road to their confidence and esteem. In this way, and in this way only, I have been enabled to collect and verify the folk-lore included in this volume. There is an anecdote about

the Irishman and the Rabbit which a number of
negroes have told to me with great unction, and
which is both funny and characteristic, though I
will not undertake to say that it has its origin with
the blacks. One day an Irishman who had heard
people talking about "mares' nests" was going along
the big road—it is always the big road in contra-
distinction to neighbourhood paths and by-paths,
called in the vernacular "nigh-cuts"—when he came
to a pumpkin-patch. The Irishman had never seen
any of this fruit before, and he at once concluded
that he had discovered a veritable mare's nest.
Making the most of his opportunity, he gathered
one of the pumpkins in his arms and went on his
way. A pumpkin is an exceedingly awkward thing
to carry, and the Irishman had not gone far before
he made a misstep, and stumbled. The pumpkin
fell to the ground, rolled down the hill into a " brush-
heap," and, striking against a stump, was broken.
The story continues in the dialect : " W'en de pumpkin roll in de bresh-heap, out jump a rabbit ; en
soon's de I'shmuns see dat, he take atter de rabbit
en holler : ' Kworp, colty ! kworp, colty ! ' but de
rabbit, he des flew." The point of this is obvious.
As to the songs, the reader is warned that it will
be found difficult to make them conform to the
ordinary rules of versification, nor is it intended
that they should so conform. They are written, and
are intended to be read, solely with reference to the
regular and invariable recurrence of the cæsura, as,
for instance, the first stanza of the Revival Hymn

" Oh, whar | shill we go | w'en de great | day comes |
　　Wid de blow | in' er de trumpits | en de bang | in' er de
　　　　drums |
　　How man | y po' sin | ners'll be kotch'd | out late |
　　En fine | no latch | ter de gold | in' gate | "

In other words, the songs depend for their melody and rhythm upon the musical quality of *time*, and not upon long or short, accented or unaccented syllables. I am persuaded that this fact led Mr. Sidney Lanier, who is thoroughly familiar with the metrical peculiarities of negro songs, into the exhaustive investigation which has resulted in the publication of his scholarly treatise on *The Science of English Verse.*

The difference between the dialect of the legends and that of the character-sketches, slight as it is, marks the modifications which the speech of the negro has undergone even where education has played no part in reforming it. Indeed, save in the remote country districts, the dialect of the legends has nearly disappeared. I am perfectly well aware that the character-sketches are without permanent interest, but they are embodied here for the purpose of presenting a phase of negro character wholly distinct from that which I have endeavoured to preserve in the legends. Only in this shape, and with all the local illusions, would it be possible to adequately represent the shrewd observations, the curious retorts, the homely thrusts, the quaint comments, and the humorous philosophy of the race of which Uncle Remus is a type.

If the reader not familiar with plantation life will imagine that the myth-stories of Uncle Remus are told night after night to a little boy by an old negro who appears to be venerable enough to have lived during the period which he describes—who has nothing but pleasant memories of the discipline of slavery—and who has all the prejudices of caste and pride of family that were the natural results of the system; if the reader can imagine all this, he will find little difficulty in appreciating and sympathizing with the air of affectionate superiority which Uncle Remus assumes as he proceeds to unfold the mysteries of plantation lore to a little child who is a product of that practical reconstruction which has been going on to some extent since the war, in spite of the politicians. Uncle Remus describes that reconstruction in his *Story of the War*, and I may as well add here for the benefit of the curious that that story is almost literally true.

J. C. H.

CONTENTS

LEGENDS OF THE OLD PLANTATION

I   PAGE

UNCLE REMUS INITIATES THE LITTLE BOY   1

II

THE WONDERFUL TAR-BABY STORY . .   5

III

WHY MR. POSSUM LOVES PEACE . . .   9

IV

HOW MR. RABBIT WAS TOO SHARP FOR MR.
FOX   13

V

THE STORY OF THE DELUGE, AND HOW IT
CAME ABOUT   17

VI

MR. RABBIT GROSSLY DECEIVES MR. FOX .   21

VII

MR. FOX IS AGAIN VICTIMIZED   27

VIII

MR. FOX IS "OUTDONE" BY MR. BUZZARD   33

IX
PAGE
MISS COW FALLS A VICTIM TO MR. RABBIT   37

X
MR. TARRYPIN APPEARS UPON THE SCENE .   43

XI
MR. WOLF MAKES A FAILURE   47

XII
MR. FOX TACKLES OLD MAN TARRYPIN . .   51

XIII
THE AWFUL FATE OF MR. WOLF . . .   55

XIV
MR. FOX AND THE DECEITFUL FROGS . .   59

XV
MR. FOX GOES A-HUNTING, BUT MR. RABBIT
    BAGS THE GAME   63

XVI
OLD MR. RABBIT HE'S A GOOD FISHERMAN .   67

XVII
MR. RABBIT NIBBLES UP THE BUTTER   .   71

XVIII
MR. RABBIT FINDS HIS MATCH AT LAST   .   77

XIX
THE FATE OF MR. JACK SPARROW . . .   81

XX
HOW MR. RABBIT SAVED HIS MEAT . . .   87

XXI   PAGE

MR. RABBIT MEETS HIS MATCH AGAIN . . 93

XXII

A STORY ABOUT THE LITTLE RABBITS . . 97

XXIII

MR. RABBIT AND MR. BEAR 101

XXIV

MR. BEAR CATCHES OLD MR. BULL-FROG . 105

XXV

HOW MR. RABBIT LOST HIS FINE BUSHY TAIL 109

XXVI

MR. TARRYPIN SHOWS HIS STRENGTH . . 113

XXVII

WHY MR. POSSUM HAS NO HAIR ON HIS TAIL 117

XXVIII

THE END OF MR. BEAR 121

XXIX

MR. FOX GETS INTO SERIOUS BUSINESS . 125

XXX

HOW MR. RABBIT SUCCEEDED IN RAISING A

DUST 129

XXXI

A PLANTATION WITCH 133

XXXII

" JACKY-MY-LANTERN " 139

XXXIII

WHY THE NEGRO IS BLACK . . . . . PAGE 145

XXXIV

THE SAD FATE OF MR. FOX 147

PLANTATION PROVERBS 153

HIS SONGS

I

REVIVAL HYMN 157

II

CAMP-MEETING SONG 158

III

CORN-SHUCKING SONG 159

IV

THE PLOUGH-HANDS' SONG 162

V

CHRISTMAS PLAY-SONG 163

VI

PLANTATION PLAY-SONG 165

VII

TRANSCRIPTIONS :

    1. A PLANTATION CHANT 167

    2. A PLANTATION SERENADE . . . 168

VIII

THE BIG BETHEL CHURCH 169

IX PAGE

TIME GOES BY TURNS 170

A STORY OF THE WAR 171

HIS SAYINGS

I

JEEMS ROBER'SON'S LAST ILLNESS . . . 181

II

UNCLE REMUS'S CHURCH EXPERIENCE . . 182

III

UNCLE REMUS AND THE SAVANNAH DARKEY 184

IV

TURNIP SALAD AS A TEXT 187

V

A CONFESSION 188

VI

UNCLE REMUS WITH THE TOOTHACHE . . 189

VII

THE PHONOGRAPH 192

VIII

RACE IMPROVEMENT 193

IX

IN THE RÔLE OF A TARTAR 194

X

A CASE OF MEASLES 196

XI

PAGE

THE EMIGRANTS 198

XII

AS A MURDERER 200

XIII

HIS PRACTICAL VIEW OF THINGS . . . 202

XIV

THAT DECEITFUL JUG 204

XV

THE FLORIDA WATER-MELON 208

XVI

UNCLE REMUS PREACHES TO A CONVERT . 210

XVII

AS TO EDUCATION 211

XVIII

A TEMPERANCE REFORMER 212

XIX

AS A WEATHER PROPHET 214

XX

THE OLD MAN'S TROUBLES 215

XXI

THE FOURTH OF JULY 217

UNCLE REMUS

LEGENDS OF THE OLD PLANTATION

I

ONE evening recently, the lady whom Uncle Remus
calls "Miss Sally" missed her little seven-year-old.
Making search for him through the house and
through the yard, she heard the sound of voices
in the old man's cabin, and, looking through the
window, saw the child sitting by Uncle Remus.
His head rested against the old man's arm, and
he was gazing with an expression of the most
intense interest into the rough, weather-beaten
face, that beamed so kindly upon him. This is
what "Miss Sally" heard:

"Bimeby, one day, arter Brer Fox bin doin'
all dat he could fer ter ketch Brer Rabbit, en Brer
Rabbit bin doin' all he could fer ter keep 'im fum
it, Brer Fox say to hisse'f dat he'd put up a game
on Brer Rabbit, en he ain't mo'n got de wuds out'n
his mouf twel Brer Rabbit come a lopin' up de
big road, lookin' des ez plump, en ez fat, en ez
sassy ez a Moggin hoss in a barley-patch.

1

"'Hol' on dar, Brer Rabbit,' sez Brer Fox, sezee.

"'I ain't got time, Brer Fox,' sez Brer Rabbit, sezee, sorter mendin' his licks.

"'I wanter have some confab wid you, Brer Rabbit,' sez Brer Fox, sezee.

"'All right, Brer Fox, but you better holler fum whar you stan'. I'm monstus full er fleas dis mawnin',' sez Brer Rabbit, sezee.

"'I seed Brer B'ar yistiddy,' sez Brer Fox, sezee, 'en he sorter rake me over de coals kaze you en me ain't make frens en live naberly, en I tole 'im dat I'd see you.'

"Den Brer Rabbit scratch one year wid his off hine-foot sorter jub'usly, en den he ups en sez, sezee :

"'All a settin', Brer Fox. Spose'n you drap roun' termorrer en take dinner wid me. We ain't got no great doin's at our house, but I speck de ole 'oman en de chilluns kin sorter scramble roun' en git up sump'n fer ter stay yo' stummuck.'

"'I'm 'gree'ble, Brer Rabbit,' sez Brer Fox, sezee.

"'Den I'll pen' on you,' sez Brer Rabbit, sezee.

"Nex' day, Mr. Rabbit an' Miss Rabbit got up soon, fo' day, en raided on a gyarden like Miss Sally's out dar, en got some cabbiges, en some roas'n years, en some sparrer-grass, en dey fix up a smashin' dinner. Bimeby one er de little Rabbits, playin' out in de backyard, come runnin' in hollerin', 'Oh, ma! oh, ma! I seed Mr. Fox a comin'!' En den Brer Rabbit he tuck de chilluns by der years en make um set down, en den him en Miss Rabbit sorter dallo roun' waitin' for Brer Fox. En dey keep on waitin', but no Brer Fox ain't come. Atter 'while Brer Rabbit goes to de do', easy like, en peep out, en der, stickin' out fum behime de cornder, wuz de tip-een' er Brer Fox tail. Den Brer Rabbit shot de do' en sot down, en put his paws behime his years en begin fer ter sing:

> " ' De place wharabouts you spill de grease,
> Right dar youer boun' ter slide,
> An' whar you fine a bunch er ha'r,
> You'll sholy fine de hide.'

" Nex' day, Brer Fox sont word by Mr. Mink, en skuse hisse'f kaze he wuz too sick fer ter come, en he ax Brer Rabbit fer ter come en take dinner wid him, en Brer Rabbit say he wuz 'gree'ble.

" Bimeby, w'en de shadders wuz at der shortes' Brer Rabbit he sorter brush up en santer down ter Brer Fox's house, en w'en he got dar, he yer somebody groanin', en he look in de do' en dar he see Brer Fox settin' up in a rockin' cheer all wrop up wid flannil, en he look mighty weak. Brer Rabbit look all 'roun', he did, but he ain't see no dinner. De dish-pan wuz settin' on de table, en close by wuz a kyarvin' knife.

" ' Look like you gwineter have chicken fer dinner, Brer Fox,' sez Brer Rabbit, sezee.

" ' Yes, Brer Rabbit, deyer nice, en fresh, en tender,' sez Brer Fox, sezee.

" Den Brer Rabbit sorter pull his mustarsh, en say: ' You ain't got no calamus root, is you, Brer Fox? I done got so now dat I can't eat no chicken 'ceppin she's seasoned up wid calamus root.' En wid dat Brer Rabbit lipt out er de do' and dodge 'mong de bushes en sot dar watchin' fer Brer Fox; en he ain't watch long, nudder, kaze Brer Fox flung off de flannil en crope out er de house en got whar he could cloze in on Brer Rabbit, en bimeby Brer Rabbit holler out: ' Oh,

Brer Fox! I'll des put yo' calamus root out yer on dish yer stump. Better come get it while hit's fresh,' and wid dat Brer Rabbit gallop off home. En Brer Fox ain't never kotch 'im yit, en w'at's mo', honey, he ain't gwineter."

II

THE WONDERFUL TAR-BABY STORY

"DIDN'T the fox *never* catch the rabbit, Uncle Remus?" asked the little boy the next evening.

"He come mighty nigh it, honey, sho's you bawn—Brer Fox did. One day atter Brer Rabbit fool 'im wid dat calamus root, Brer Fox went ter wuk en got 'im some tar, en mix it wid some turkentime, en fix up a contrapshun what he call a Tar-Baby, en he tuck dish yer Tar-Baby en he sot 'er in de big road, en den he lay off in de bushes fer ter see wat de news wuz gwineter be. En he didn't hatter wait long, nudder, kaze bimeby here come Brer Rabbit pacin' down de road—lippity-clippity, clippity-lippity—dez ez sassy ez a jay-bird. Brer Fox, he lay low. Brer Rabbit come prancin' 'long twel he spy de Tar-Baby, en den he fotch up on his behime legs like he wuz 'stonished. De Tar-Baby, she sot dar, she did, en Brer Fox, he lay low.

"'Mawnin'!' sez Brer Rabbit, sezee—'nice wedder dis mawnin',' sezee.

"Tar-Baby ain't sayin' nuthin', en Brer Fox, he lay low.

"'How duz yo' sym'tums seem ter segashuate?' sez Brer Rabbit, sezee.

5

"Brer Fox, he wink his eye slow, en lay low, en de Tar-Baby, she ain't sayin' nuthin'.

"'How you come on, den? Is you deaf?' sez Brer.Rabbit, sezee. 'Kaze if you is, I kin holler louder,' sezee.

"Tar-Baby stay still, en Brer Fox, he lay low.

"'Youer stuck up, dat's w'at you is,' says Brer Rabbit, sezee, 'en I'm gwineter kyore you, dat's w'at I'm a gwineter do,' sezee.

"Brer Fox, he sorter chuckle in his stummuck, he did, but Tar-Baby ain't sayin' nuthin'.

"'I'm gwineter larn you howter talk ter 'spect-tubble fokes ef hit's de las' ack,' sez Brer Rabbit, sezee. 'Ef you don't take off dat hat en tell me howdy, I'm gwineter bus' you wide open,' sezee.

"Tar-Baby stay still, en Brer Fox, he lay low.

"Brer Rabbit keep on axin' 'im, en de Tar-Baby, she keep on sayin' nuthin', twel present'y Brer Rabbit draw back wid his fis', he did, en blip he tuck 'er side er de head. Right dar's whar he broke his merlasses jug. His fis' struck, en he can't pull loose. De tar hilt 'im. But Tar-Baby, she stay still, en Brer Fox, he lay low.

"'Ef you don't lemme loose, I'll knock you agin,' sez Brer Rabbit, sezee, en wid dat he fotch 'er a wipe wid de udder han', en dat stuck. Tar-Baby, she ain't sayin' nuthin', en Brer Fox, he lay low.

"'Tu'n me loose, fo' I kick de natal stuffin' outen you,' sez Brer Rabbit, sezee, but de Tar-Baby, she ain't sayin' nuthin'. She des hilt on, en den Brer Rabbit lose de use er his feet in de same way. Brer Fox, he lay low. Den Brer Rabbit squall out dat ef de Tar-Baby don't tu'n 'im loose he butt 'er cranksided. En den he butted, en his head got stuck. Den Brer Fox, he sa'ntered fort', lookin' des ez innercent ez wunner yo' mammy's mockin'-birds.

"'Howdy, Brer Rabbit,' sez Brer Fox, sezee. 'You look sorter stuck up dis mawnin',' sezee, en den he rolled on de groun', en laft en laft twel he couldn't laff no mo'. 'I speck you'll take dinner wid me dis time, Brer Rabbit. I done laid in some calamus root, en I ain't gwineter take no skuse,' sez Brer Fox, sezee."

Here Uncle Remus paused, and drew a two-pound yam out of the ashes.

"Did the fox eat the Rabbit ?" asked the little boy to whom the story had been told.

"Dat's all de fur de tale goes," replied the old man. "He mout, en den agin he moutent. Some say Jedge B'ar come 'long en loosed 'im— some say he didn't. I hear Miss Sally callin'. You better run 'long."

WHY MR. POSSUM LOVES PEACE

"ONE night," said Uncle Remus—taking Miss Sally's little boy on his knee, and stroking the child's hair thoughtfully and caressingly—"one night Brer Possum call by fer Brer Coon, 'cordin' ter greement, en atter gobblin' up a dish er fried greens en smokin' a seegyar, dey rambled fort' fer ter see how de ballunce er de settlement wuz gittin' 'long. Brer Coon, he wuz wunner deze yer natchul pacers, en he racked 'long same ez Mars John's bay pony, en Brer Possum he went in a han'-gallup; en dey got over heap er groun', mon. 'Brer Possum, he got his belly full er 'simmons, en Brer Coon, he scoop up a 'bunnunce er frogs en tadpoles. Dey amble 'long, dey did, des ez soshubble ez a baskit er kittens, twel bimeby dey hear Mr. Dog talkin' ter hisse'f way off in de woods.

"'Spozun he runs up on us, Brer Possum, w'at you gwineter do?' sez Brer Coon, sezee. Brer Possum sorter laff 'round de cornders un his mouf.

"'Oh, ef he come, Brer Coon, I'm gwineter stan' by you,' sez Brer Possum. 'W'at you gwineter do?' sezee.

"'Who? me?' sez Brer Coon. 'Ef he run up onter me, I lay I give 'im one twis',' sezee."

" Did the dog come ? " asked the little boy.

" Go 'way, honey ! " responded the old man, in an impressive tone. " Go 'way ! Mr. Dog, he come en he come a zoonin'. En he ain't wait fer ter say howdy nudder. He des sail inter de two un um. De ve'y fus pas he make Brer Possum fetch a grin fum year ter year, en keel over like he wuz dead. Den Mr. Dog he sail inter Brer Coon, en right dar's whar he drap his munnypus, kaze Brer Coon wuz cut out fer dat kinder bizness, en he fa'rly wipe up de face er de earf wid 'im. You better b'leeve dat w'en Mr. Dog got a chance to make hisse'f skase he tuck it, e'en w'at der wuz lef' un him went skaddlin' thoo de woods like hit wuz shot outen a muskit. En Brer Coon, he sorter lick his cloze inter shape en rack off, en Brer Possum, he lay dar like he wuz dead, twel bimeby he raise up sotter keerful like, en w'en he fine de coas' cle'r he scramble up en scamper off like sumpin was atter 'im."

Here Uncle Remus paused long enough to pick up a live coal of fire in his fingers, transfer it to the palm of his hand, and thence to his clay pipe, which he had been filling—a proceeding that was viewed by the little boy with undisguised admiration. The old man then proceeded :

" Nex' time Brer Possum meet Brer Coon, Brer Coon 'fuse ter 'spon' ter his howdy, en dis make Brer Possum feel mighty bad, seein' ez how dey useter make so many 'scurshuns togedder.

" ' W'at make you hol' yo' head so high, Brer Coon ? ' sez Brer Possum, sezee.

" ' I ain't runnin' wid cowerds deze days,' sez Brer Coon. ' W'en I wants you I'll sen' fer you,' sezee.

" Den Brer Possum get mighty mad.

"'Who's enny cowerd?' sezee.

"'You is,' sez Brer Coon, 'dat's who. I ain't soshatin' wid dem w'at lies down on de groun' en plays dead w'en dar's a free fight gwine on,' sezee.

"Den Brer Possum grin en laff fit to kill hisse'f.

"'Lor', Brer Coon, you don't speck I done dat kaze I wuz 'feared, duz you?' sezee. 'W'y I want no m' 'feared dan you is dis minnit. W'at wuz dey fer ter be skeered un?' sezee. 'I know'd you'd git away wid Mr. Dog ef I didn't, en I des lay dar watchin' you shake him, waitin' fer ter put in w'en de time come,' sezee.

"Brer Coon tu'n up his nose.

"'Dat's a mighty likely tale,' sezee, 'w'en Mr. Dog ain't mo'n tech you 'fo' you keel over, en lay dar stiff,' sezee.

"'Dat's des w'at I wuz gwineter tell you 'bout,' sez Brer Possum, sezee. 'I want no mo' skeer'd dan you is right now, en I wuz fixin' fer ter give Mr. Dog a sample er my jaw,' sezee, 'but I'm de most ticklish chap w'at you ever laid eyes on, en no sooner did Mr. Dog put his nose down yer 'mong my ribs dan I got ter laffin', en I laft twel I ain't had no use er my lim's,' sezee, 'en it's a mussy unto Mr. Dog dat J wuz ticklish, kaze a little mo' en I'd e't 'im up,' sezee. 'I don't mine fightin', Brer Coon, no mo' dan you duz,' sezee, 'but I declar' ter grashus ef I kin stan' ticklin'. Git me in a row whar dey ain't no ticklin' 'lowed, en I'm your man,' sezee.

"En down ter dis day"—continued Uncle Remus, watching the smoke from his pipe curl upward over the little boy's head—"down ter dis day, Brer Possum's bound ter s'render w'en you tech him in de short ribs, en he'll laff ef he knows he's gwineter be smashed fer it."

IV

HOW MR. RABBIT WAS TOO SHARP FOR MR. FOX

"UNCLE REMUS," said the little boy one evening,
when he had found the old man with little or nothing
to do, "did the fox kill and eat the rabbit when
he caught him with the Tar-Baby?"

"Law, honey, ain't I tell you 'bout dat?"
replied the old darkey, chuckling slyly. "I 'clar'
ter grashus I ought er tole you dat, but ole man
Nod wuz ridin' on my eyeleds 'twel a leetle mo'n
I'd a dis'member'd my own name, en den on to
dat here come yo' mammy hollerin' atter you.

"W'at I tell you w'en I fus' begin? I tole you
Brer Rabbit wuz a monstus soon beas'; leas'ways
dat's w'at I laid out fer ter tell you. Well, den,
honey, don't you go en make no udder kalkalashuns,
kaze in dem days Brer Rabbit en his fambly wuz
at de head er de gang w'en enny racket wuz on
han', en dar dey stayed. 'Fo' you begins fer ter
wipe yo' eyes 'bout Brer Rabbit, you wait en see
whar'bouts Brer Rabbit gwineter fetch up at.
But dat's needer yer ner dar.

"W'en Brer Fox fine Brer Rabbit mixt up wid
de Tar-Baby, he feel mighty good, en he roll on
de groun' en laff. Bimeby, he up'n say, sezee:

"'Well, I speck I got you dis time, Brer Rabbit,'
sezee; 'maybe I ain't, but I speck I is. You been

13

runnin' roun' here sassin' atter me a mighty long
time, but I speck you done come ter de een' er
de row. You bin cuttin' up yo' capers en bouncin'
roun' in dis naberhood ontwel you cum ter b'leeve
yo'se'f de boss er de whole gang. En den youer
allers some'rs whar you got no bizness,' sez Brer
Fox, sezee. 'Who ax you fer ter come en strike
up a 'quaintence wid dish yer Tar-Baby? En
who stuck you up dar whar you iz? Nobody
in de roun' worril. You des tuck en jam yo'se'f
on dat Tar-Baby widout waitin' fer enny invite,'
sez Brer Fox, sezee, 'en dar you is, en dar you'll
stay twell I fixes up a bresh-pile and fires her up,
kaze I'm gwineter bobbycue you dis day, sho,' sez
Brer Fox, sezee.

"Den Brer Rabbit talk mighty 'umble.

"'I don't keer w'at you do wid me, Brer Fox,'
sezee, 'so you don't fling me in dat brier-patch.
Roas' me, Brer Fox,' sezee, 'but don't fling me
in dat brier-patch,' sezee.

"'Hit's so much trouble fer ter kindle a fier,'
sez Brer Fox, sezee, 'dat I speck I'll hatter hang
you,' sezee.

"'Hang me des ez high as you please, Brer
Fox,' sez Brer Rabbit, sezee, 'but do fer de Lord's
sake don't fling me in dat brier-patch,' sezee.

"'I ain't got no string,' sez Brer Fox, sezee,
'en now I speck I'll hatter drown you,' sezee.

"'Drown me des ez deep ez you please, Brer
Fox,' sez Brer Rabbit, sezee, 'but do don't fling
me in dat brier-patch,' sezee.

"'Dey ain't no water nigh,' sez Brer Fox,
sezee, 'en now I speck I'll hatter skin you,' sezee.

"'Skin me, Brer Fox,' sez Brer Rabbit, sezee,
'snatch out my eyeballs, t'ar out my years by
de roots, en cut off my legs,' sezee, 'but do please,

Brer Fox, don't fling me in dat brier-patch,' sezee.

"Co'se Brer Fox wanter hurt Brer Rabbit bad ez he kin, so he cotch 'im by de behime legs en slung 'im right in de middle er de brier-patch. Dar wuz a considerbul flutter whar Brer Rabbit struck de bushes, en Brer Fox sorter hang 'roun' for ter see w'at wuz gwineter happen. Bimeby he hear somebody call 'im, en way up de hill he see Brer Rabbit settin' crosslegged on a chinkapin log, koamin' de pitch outen his har wid a chip. Den Brer Fox know dat he bin swop off mighty bad. Brer Rabbit wuz bleedzed fer ter fling back some er his sass, en he holler out:

"'Bred en bawn in a brier-patch, Brer Fox— bred en bawn in a brier-patch!' en wid dat he skip out des ez lively ez a cricket in de embers."

V

THE STORY OF THE DELUGE AND HOW IT CAME ABOUT

"One time," said Uncle Remus—adjusting his spectacles so as to be able to see how to thread a large darning-needle with which he was patching his coat—"one time, way back yander, 'fo' you wuz borned, honey, en 'fo' Mars John er Miss Sally wuz borned—way back yander 'fo' enny un us wuz borned, de anemils en de beastesses sorter 'leeshuneer roun' 'mung deyselves, twel at las' dey 'greed fer ter have a 'sembly. In dem days," continued the old man, observing a look of incredulity on the little boy's face, "in dem days creeturs had lots mo' sense dan dey got now; let 'lone dat, dey had sense same like folks. Hit was tech en go wid um, too, mon, en w'en dey make up der mines w'at hatter be done, 'twant mo'n monehun'd 'fo' it wuz done. Well, dey 'lected dat dey hatter hole er' sembly fer ter sorter straighten out marters en yer de complaints, en w'en de day come dey wuz on han'. De Lion, he wuz dere, kaze he wuz de king, en he hatter be dere. De Rhynossyhoss, he wuz dere, en de Elephent, he wuz dere, en de Cammils, en de Cows, en plum down ter de Crawfishes, dey wuz dere. Dey wuz all dere. En w'en de Lion shuck his mane, en tuck his seat in
17

de big cheer, den de sesshun begun fer ter commence."

"What did they do, Uncle Remus?" asked the little boy.

"I kin scacely call to mine 'zackly w'at dey did do, but dey spoke speeches, en hollered, en cusst, en flung der langwidge 'roun' des like w'en yo' daddy wuz gwineter run fer de legislater en got lef'. Howsomever, dey 'ranged der 'fairs, en splained der bizness. Bimeby, w'ile dey wuz 'sputin' 'longer wunner nudder, de Elephent tromped on wunner de Crawfishes. Co'se w'en dat creetur put his foot down, w'atsumever's under dere's bound fer ter be squashed, en dey wuzn't nuff er dat Crawfish lef' fer ter tell dat he'd bin dar.

"Dis make de udder Crawfishes mighty mad, en dey sorter swawmed tergedder en draw'd up a kinder peramble wid some wharfo'es in it, en read her out in de 'sembly. But, bless grashus! sech a racket wuz a gwine on dat nobody ain't hear it, 'ceppin may be de Mud Turkle en de Spring Lizzud, en dere enfloons wuz pow'ful lackin'.

"Bimeby, w'iles de Nunicorn wuz 'sputin' wid de Lion, en w'ile de Hyener wuz a laffin ter hi'se'f, de Elephent squashed anudder one er de Crawfishes, en a little mo'n he'd er ruint de Mud Turkle. Den de Crawfishes, w'at dey wuz lef' un um, swawmed tergedder en draw'd up anudder peramble wid sum mo' wharfo'es; but dey might ez well er sung Ole Dan Tucker ter a harrycane. De udder creeturs wuz too bizzy wid der fussin' fer ter 'spon' unto de Crawfishes. So dar dey wuz, de Crawfishes, en dey didn't know w'at minnit wuz gwineter be de nex'; en dey kep' on gittin madder en madder en skeerder en skeerder, twel bimeby dey gun de wink ter de Mud Turkle en de Spring Lizzud, en den dey bo'd little holes in de groun' en went down outer sight."

"Who did, Uncle Remus?" asked the little boy.

"De Crawfishes, honey. Dey bo'd inter de groun' en kep' on bo'in twel dey onloost de fountains er de earf; en de waters squirt out, en riz higher en higher twel de hills wuz kivvered, en de creeturs wuz all drownded; en all bekaze dey let on 'mong deyselves dat dey wuz bigger dan de Crawfishes."

Then the old man blew the ashes from a smoking yam, and proceeded to remove the peeling.

"Where was the ark, Uncle Remus?" the little boy inquired, presently.

"W'ich ark's dat?" asked the old man, in a tone of well-feigned curiosity.

"Noah's ark," replied the child.

"Don't you pester wid ole man Noah, honey. I boun' he tuck keer er dat ark. Dat's w'at he wuz dere fer, en dat's w'at he done. Leas'ways, dat's w'at dey tells me. But don't you bodder longer dat ark, 'ceppin' your mammy fetches it up. Dey mout er bin two deloojes, en den agin dey moutent. Ef dey wuz enny ark in dish yer w'at de Crawfishes brung on, I ain't heern tell un it, en w'en dey ain't no arks 'roun, I ain't got no time fer ter make um en put um in dere. Hit's gittin' yo' bed-time, honey."

VI

MR. RABBIT GROSSLY DECEIVES MR. FOX

ONE evening when the little boy, whose nights with Uncle Remus are as entertaining as those Arabian ones of blessed memory, had finished supper and hurried out to sit with his venerable patron, he found the old man in great glee. Indeed, Uncle Remus was talking and laughing to himself at such a rate that the little boy was afraid he had company. The truth is, Uncle Remus had heard the child coming, and, when the rosy-cheeked chap put his head in at the door, was engaged in a monologue, the burden of which seemed to be—

> " Ole Molly Har',
> W'at you doin' dar,
> Settin' in de cornder
> Smokin' yo' seegyar ? "

As a matter of course this vague allusion reminded the little boy of the fact that the wicked Fox was still in pursuit of the Rabbit, and he immediately put his curiosity in the shape of a question.

" Uncle Remus, did the Rabbit have to go clean away when he got loose from the Tar-Baby ? "

" Bless grashus, honey, dat he didn't. Who ? Him ? You dunno nuthin' 't all 'bout Brer Rabbit ef dat's de way you puttin' 'im down. W'at he

21

gwine 'way fer ? He mouter stayed sorter close twel de pitch rub off'n his ha'r, but twern't menny days 'fo' he wuz lopin' up en down de naberhood same ez ever, en I dunno ef he wern't mo' sassier dan befo'.

"Seem like dat de tale 'bout how he got mixt up wid de Tar-Baby got 'roun' 'mongst de nabers. Leas'ways, Miss Meadows en de girls got win' un' it, en de nex' time Brer Rabbit paid um a visit Miss Meadows tackled 'im 'bout it, en de gals sot up a monstus gigglement. Brer Rabbit, he sot up des ez cool ez a cowcumber, he did, en let 'em run on."

"Who was Miss Meadows, Uncle Remus ? " inquired the little boy.

"Don't ax me, honey. She wuz in de tale, Miss Meadows en de gals wuz, en de tale I give you like hi't wer' gun ter me. Brer Rabbit, he sot dar, he did, sorter lam' like, en den bimeby he cross his legs, he did, en wink his eye slow, en up en say, sezee :

"'Ladies, Brer Fox wuz my daddy's ridin'-hoss fer thirty year ; maybe mo', but thirty year dat I knows un,' sezee ; en den he paid um his 'specks, en tip his beaver, en march off, he did, des ez stiff en ez stuck up ez a fire-stick.

"Nex' day, Brer Fox cum a callin', and w'en he gun fer ter laff 'bout Brer Rabbit, Miss Meadows en de gals, dey ups en tells 'im 'bout w'at Brer Rabbit say. Den Brer Fox grit his toof sho' nuff, he did, en he look mighty dumpy, but w'en he riz fer ter go he up en say, sezee :

"'Ladies, I ain't 'sputing w'at you say, but I'll make Brer Rabbit chaw up his words en spit um out right yer whar you kin see 'im,' sezee, en wid dat off Brer Fox marcht.

" En w'en he got in de big road, he shuck de dew off'n his tail, en made a straight shoot fer Brer Rabbit's house. W'en he got dar, Brer Rabbit wuz spectin' un 'im, en de do' wuz shut fas'. Brer Fox knock. Nobody ain't ans'er. Brer Fox knock. Nobody ans'er. Den he knock agin— blam! blam! Den Brer Rabbit holler out mighty weak:

" ' Is dat you, Brer Fox? I want you ter run en fetch de doctor. Dat bait er pusly w'at I e't dis mawnin' is gittin' 'way wid me. Do, please, Brer Fox, run quick,' sez Brer Rabbit, sezee.

" ' I come atter you, Brer Rabbit,' sez Brer Fox, sezee. ' Dere's gwineter be a party up at Miss Meadows's,' sezee. ' All de gals'll be dere, en I promus' dat I'd fetch you. De gals, dey 'lowed dat hit wouldn't be no party 'ceppin' I fotch you,' sez Brer Fox, sezee.

" Den Brer Rabbit say he wuz too sick, en Brer Fox say he wuzzent, en dar dey had it up and down, 'sputin' en contendin'. Brer Rabbit say he can't walk. Brer Fox say he tote 'im. Brer Rabbit say how? Brer Fox say in his arms. Brer Rabbit say he drap 'im. Brer Fox 'low he won't. Bimeby Brer Rabbit say he go ef Brer Fox tote 'im on his back. Brer Fox say he would. Brer Rabbit say he can't ride widout a saddle. Brer Fox say he git de saddle. Brer Rabbit say he can't set in saddle less he have bridle fer ter hol' by. Brer Fox say he git de bridle. Brer Rabbit say he can't ride widout bline bridle, kaze Brer Fox be shyin' at stumps 'long de road, en fling 'im off. Brer Fox say he git bline bridle. Den Brer Rabbit say he go. Den Brer Fox say he ride Brer Rabbit mos' up ter Miss Meadows's, en den he could git down en walk de balance er de way. Brer Rabbit 'greed,

en den Brer Fox lipt out atter de saddle en de
bridle.

"Co'se Brer Rabbit know de game dat Brer Fox
wuz fixin' fer ter play, en he 'termin' fer ter outdo
'im, en by de time he koam his ha'r en twis' his
mustarsh, en sorter rig up, yer come Brer Fox,
saddle en bridle on, en lookin' ez peart ez a circus
pony. He trot up ter de do' en stan' dar pawin'
de ground en chompin' de bit same like sho' nuff
hos, en Brer Rabbit he mount, he did, en dey amble
off. Brer Fox can't see behime wid de bline bridle
on, but bimeby he feel Brer Rabbit raise one er
his foots.

"'W'at you doin' now, Brer Rabbit?' sezee.

"'Short'nin' de lef stir'p, Brer Fox,' sezee.

"Bimeby Brer Rabbit raise up de udder foot.

"'W'at you doin' now, Brer Rabbit?' sezee.

"Pullin' down my pants, Brer Fox,' sezee.

"All de time, bless grashus, honey, Brer Rabbit
wer puttin' on his spurrers, en w'en dey got close
to Miss Meadows's, whar Brer Rabbit wuz to git
off, en Brer Fox made a motion for ter stan' still,
Brer Rabbit slap de spurrers inter Brer Fox flanks,
en you better b'leeve he got over groun'. W'en
dey got ter de house, Miss Meadows en all de gals wuz
settin' on de peazzer, en stidder stoppin' at de
gate, Brer Rabbit rid on by, he did, en den come
gallopin' down de road en up ter de hoss-rack, w'ich
he hitch Brer Fox at, en den he santer inter de
house, he did, en shake han's wid de gals, en set
dar, smokin' his seegyar same ez a town man.
Bimeby he draw in long puff, en den let hit out in
a cloud, en squar hisse'f back en holler out, he
did:

"'Ladies, ain't I done tell you Brer Fox wuz de
ridin'-hoss fer our fambly? He sorter losin' his

gait' now, but I speck I kin fetch 'im all right in a mont' or so,' sezee.

"En den Brer Rabbit sorter grin, he did, en de gals giggle, en Miss Meadows, she praise up de pony, en dar wuz Brer Fox hitch fas' ter de rack, en couldn't he'p hisse'f."

"Is that all, Uncle Remus?" asked the little boy as the old man paused.

"Dat ain't all, honey, but 'twon't do fer ter give out too much cloff fer ter cut one p'ar pants," replied the old man sententiously.

VII

MR. FOX IS AGAIN VICTIMIZED

When "Miss Sally's" little boy went to Uncle Remus the next night to hear the conclusion of the adventure in which the Rabbit made a riding-horse of the Fox, to the great enjoyment and gratification of Miss Meadows and the girls, he found the old man in a bad humour.

"I ain't tellin' no tales ter bad chilluns," said Uncle Remus curtly.

"But, Uncle Remus, I ain't bad," said the little boy plaintively.

"Who dat chunkin' dem chickens dis mawnin'? Who dat knockin' out fokes's eyes wid dat Yaller-bammer sling des 'fo' dinner? Who dat sickin' dat pinter puppy atter my pig? Who dat scatterin' my ingun sets? Who dat flingin' rocks on top er my house, w'ich a little mo' en one un em would er drap spang on my head?"

"Well, now, Uncle Remus, I didn't go to do it. I won't do so any more. Please, Uncle Remus, if you will tell me, I'll run to the house and bring you some tea-cakes."

"Seein' um's better'n hearin' tell un um," replied the old man, the severity of his countenance relaxing somewhat; but the little boy darted out, and in a few minutes came running back with his pockets full and his hands full.

"I lay yo' mammy'll 'spishun dat de rats' stummucks is widenin' is dis naberhood w'en she cum fer ter count up 'er cakes," said Uncle Remus, with a chuckle. "Deze," he continued, dividing the cakes into two equal parts—"deze I'll tackle now, en deze I'll lay by fer Sunday.

"Lemme see. I mos' dis'member wharbouts Brer Fox en Brer Rabbit wuz."

"The rabbit rode the fox to Miss Meadows's, and hitched him to the horse-rack," said the little boy.

"W'y co'se he did," said Uncle Remus. "Co'se he did. Well, Brer Rabbit rid Brer Fox up, he did, en tied 'im to de rack, en den sot out in de peazzer wid de gals a smokin' er his seegyar wid mo' proudness dan wa't you mos' ever see. Dey talk, en dey sing, en dey play on de peanner, de gals did, twel bimeby hit come time fer Brer Rabbit fer to be gwine, en he tell um all good-by, en strut out to de hoss-rack same's ef he was de king er de patter-rollers,[1] en den he mount Brer Fox en ride off.

"Brer Fox ain't sayin' nuthin 'tall. He des rack off, he did, en keep his mouf shet, en Brer Rabbit know'd der wuz buzness cookin' up fer him, en he feel monstus skittish. Brer Fox amble on twel he git in de long lane, outer sight er Miss Meadows's

---

[1] Patrols. In the country districts, order was kept on the plantations at night by the knowledge that they were liable to be visited at any moment by the patrols. Hence a song current among the negroes, the chorus of which was:

> "Run, nigger, run; patter-roller ketch you—
> Run, nigger, run; hit's almos' day."

house, en den he tu'n loose, he did. He rip en he r'ar, en he cuss, en he swar ; he snort en he cavort."

"What was he doing that for, Uncle Remus ? " the little boy inquired.

"He wuz tryin' fer ter fling Brer Rabbit off'n his back, bless yo' soul ! But he des might ez well er rastle wid his own shadder. Every time he hump hisse'f Brer Rabbit slap the spurrers in 'im, en dar dey had it, up en down. Brer Fox fa'rly to' up de groun', he did, en he jump so high en he jump so quick dat he mighty nigh snatch his own tail off. Dey kep' on gwine on dis way twel bimeby Brer Fox lay down en roll over, he did, en dis sorter onsettle Brer Rabbit, but by the time Brer Fox got back on his footses agin, Brer Rabbit was gwine thoo de underbresh mo' samer dan a race-hoss. Brer Fox he lit out atter 'im, he did, en he push Brer Rabbit so close dat it wuz 'bout all he could do fer to git in a holler tree. Hole too little fer Brer Fox fer ter git in, en he hatter lay down en res' en gedder his mine tergedder.

"While he wuz layin' dar, Mr. Buzzard come floppin' long, en seein' Brer Fox stretch out on de groun', he lit en view de premusses. Den Mr. Buzzard sorter shake his wing, en put his head on one side, en say to hisse'f like, sezee :

" ' Brer Fox dead, en I so sorry,' sezee.

" ' No I ain't dead, nudder,' sez Brer Fox, sezee. ' I got ole man Rabbit pent up in yer,' sezee, ' en I'm a gwineter git 'im dis time ef it take twel Chris'mus,' sezee.

"Den, atter some mo' palaver, Brer Fox make a bargain dat Mr. Buzzard wuz ter watch de hole, en keep Brer Rabbit dar wiles Brer Fox went atter his axe. Den Brer Fox, he lope off, he did, en Mr. Buzzard, he tuck up his stan' at de hole. Bimeby,

w'en all git still, Brer Rabbit sorter scramble down
close ter de hole, he did, en holler out:

"'Brer Fox! Oh! Brer Fox!'"

"Brer Fox done gone, en nobody say nuthin'.
Den Brer Rabbit squall out like he wuz mad;
sezee:

"'You needn't talk less you wanter,' sezee;
'I knows youer dar, an I ain't keerin',' sezee; 'I
des wanter tell you dat I wish mighty bad Brer
Tukkey Buzzard was here,' sezee.

"Den Mr. Buzzard try ter talk like Brer Fox:

"'W'at you want wid Mr. Buzzard?' sezee.

"'Oh, nuthin' in 'tickler, 'cep' dere's de fattes'
gray squir'l in yer dat ever I see,' sezee, 'en ef
Brer Tukkey Buzzard was 'roun' he'd be mighty
glad fer ter git 'im,' sezee.

"'How Mr. Buzzard gwine ter git 'im?' sez de
Buzzard, sezee.

"Well, dars a little hole roun' on de udder side er
de tree,' sez Brer Rabbit, sezee, 'en ef Brer Tukkey
Buzzard was here so he could take up his stan'
dar,' sezee, 'I'd drive dat squir'l out,' sezee.

"'Drive 'im out, den,' sez Mr. Buzzard, sezee,
'en I'll see dat Brer Tukkey Buzzard gits 'im,'
sezee.

"Den Brer Rabbit kick up a racket, like he wer'
drivin' sumpin' out, en Mr. Buzzard he rush 'roun'
fer ter ketch de squir'l, en Brer Rabbit, he dash out,
he did, en he des fly fer home."

At this point Uncle Remus took one of the tea-
cakes, held his head back, opened his mouth,
dropped the cake in with a sudden motion, looked
at the little boy with an expression of astonish-
ment, and then closed his eyes, and began to chew,
mumbling as an accompaniment the plaintive tune
of "Don't you Grieve atter Me."

The *séance* was over; but, before the little boy went into the "big house," Uncle Remus laid his rough hand tenderly on the child's shoulder, and remarked, in a confidential tone:

"Honey, you mus' git up soon Chris'mus mawnin' en open de do'; kaze I'm gwineter bounce in on Mars John en Miss Sally, en holler Chris'mus gif' des like I useter endurin' de fahmin' days 'fo' de war, w'en ole Miss wuz 'live. I boun' dey don't fergit de ole nigger, nudder. W'en you hear me callin' de pigs, honey, you des hop up en onfassen de do'. I lay I'll give Mars John wunner deze yer 'sprize parties."

VIII

MR. FOX IS "OUTDONE" BY MR. BUZZARD

"Ef I don't run inter no mistakes," remarked Uncle Remus, as the little boy came tripping in to see him after supper, "Mr. Tukkey Buzzard was gyardin' de holler whar Brer Rabbit went in at, en w'ich he come out un."

The silence of the little boy verified the old man's recollection.

"Well, Mr. Buzzard, he feel mighty lonesome, he did, but he done prommust Brer Fox dat he'd stay, en he 'termin' fer ter sorter hang 'roun' en jine in de joke. En he ain't hatter wait long, nudder, kaze bimeby yer come Brer Fox gallopin' thoo de woods wid his axe on his shoulder.

"'How you speck Brer Rabbit gittin' on, Brer Buzzard?' sez Brer Fox, sezee.

"'Oh, he in dar,' sez Brer Buzzard, sezee. 'He mighty still, dough. I speck he takin' a nap,' sezee.

"'Den I'm des in time fer ter wake 'im up,' sez Brer Fox, sezee. En wid dat he fling off his coat, en spit in his han's, en grab de axe. Den he draw back en come down on de tree—pow! En eve'y time he come down wid he axe—pow!—Mr. Buzzard, he step high, he did, en holler out:

"'Oh, he in dar, Brer Fox. He in dar, sho.'

33

"En eve'y time a chip ud fly off, Mr. Buzzard, he'd jump, en dodge, en hole his head sideways, he would, en holler:

"'He in dar, Brer Fox. I done heerd 'im. He in dar, sho.'

"En Brer Fox, he lammed away at dat holler tree, he did, like a man maulin' rails, twel bimeby, atter he done got de tree mos' cut thoo, he stop fer ter ketch his bref, en he seed Mr. Buzzard laffin' behime his back, he did, en right den en dar, widout gwine enny fudder, Brer Fox, he smelt a rat. But Mr. Buzzard, he keep on holler'n:

"'He in dar, Brer Fox. He in dar, sho. I done seed 'im.''

"Den Brer Fox, he make like he peepin' up de holler, en he say, sezee:

"'Run yer, Brer Buzzard, en look ef dis ain't Brer Rabbit's foot hanging down yer.'

"En Mr. Buzzard, he come steppin' up, he did, same ez ef he wer treddin' on kurkle-burrs, en he stick his head in de hole; en no sooner did he done dat dan Brer Fox grab 'im. Mr. Buzzard flap his wings, en scramble 'roun' right smartually, he did, but 'twant no use. Brer Fox had de 'vantage er de grip, he did, en he hilt 'im right down ter de groun'. Den Mr. Buzzard squall out, sezee:

"'Lemme 'lone, Brer Fox. Tu'n me loose,' sezee; 'Brer Rabbit'll git out. Youer gittin' close at 'im,' sezee, 'en leb'm mo' licks'll fetch 'im,' sezee.

"'I'm nigher ter you, Brer Buzzard,' sez Brer Fox, sezee, 'dan I'll be ter Brer Rabbit dis day,' sezee. 'W'at yer fool me fer?' sezee.

"'Lemme 'lone, Brer Fox,' sez Mr. Buzzard, sezee; 'my ole 'oman waitin' fer me. Brer Rabbit in dar,' sezee.

" ' Dar's a bunch er his fur on dat black-be'y bush, 'sez Brer Fox, sezee, ' en dat ain't de way he come,' sezee.

" Den Mr. Buzzard up'n tell Brer Fox how 'twuz, en he low'd, Mr. Buzzard did, dat Brer Rabbit, wuz de low-downest w'atsizname w'at he ever run up wid. Den Brer Fox say, sezee :

" ' Dat's needer here ner dar, Brer Buzzard,' sezee. ' I lef' you yer fer ter watch dish yer hole, en I lef' Brer Rabbit in dar. I comes back en I fines you at de hole en Brer Rabbit ain't in dar,' sezee. ' I'm gwineter make you pay fer't. I done bin tampered wid twel plum' down ter de sap sucker'll set on a log en sassy me. I'm gwineter fling you in a bresh-heap en burn you up,' sezee.

" ' Ef you fling me on der fier, Brer Fox, I'll fly 'way,' sez Mr. Buzzard, sezee.

" ' Well, den, I'll settle yo' hash right now,' sez Brer Fox, sezee, en wid dat he grab Mr. Buzzard by de tail, he did, en make fer ter dash 'im 'gin de groun', but des 'bout dat time de tail fedders come out, en Mr. Buzzard sail off like wunner dese yer berloons ; en ez he riz, he holler back :

" ' You gimme good start, Brer Fox,' sezee, en Brer Fox sot dar en watch 'im fly outer sight."

" But what became of the Rabbit, Uncle Remus ? " asked the little boy.

" Don't you pester 'longer Brer Rabbit, honey, en don't you fret 'bout 'im. You'll year whar he went en how he come out. Dish yer cole snap rastles wid my bones, now," continued the old man, putting on his hat and picking up his walking-stick. " Hit rastles wid me monstus, en I gotter rack 'roun' en see if I kin run up agin some Chris'mus leavin's."

IX

MISS COW FALLS A VICTIM TO MR. RABBIT

"UNCLE REMUS," said the little boy, "what became of the Rabbit after he fooled the Buzzard, and got out of the hollow tree ?"

"Who ? Brer Rabbit ? Bless yo' soul, honey, Brer Rabbit went skippin' 'long home, he did, des ez sassy ez a jay-bird at a sparrer's nes'. He went gallopin' 'long, he did, but he feel mighty tired out, en stiff en his jints, en he wuz mighty nigh dead for sumpin fer ter drink, en bimeby, w'en he got mos' home, he spied ole Miss Cow feedin' roun' in a fiel', he did, en he 'termin' fer ter try his han' wid 'er. Brer Rabbit know mighty well dat Miss Cow won't give 'im no milk, kaze she done 'fuse 'im mo'n once, en w'en his ole 'oman wuz sick, at dat. But never mind dat. Brer Rabbit sorter dance up 'long side er de fence, he did, en holler out :

"'Howdy, Sis Cow,' sez Brer Rabbit, sezee.

"'W'y, howdy, Brer Rabbit,' sez Miss Cow, sez she.

"'How you fine yo'se'f deze days, Sis Cow ?' sez Brer Rabbit, sezee.

"'I'm sorter toler'ble, Brer Rabbit; how you come on ?' sez Miss Cow, sez she.

27

" ' Oh, I'm des. toler'ble myse'f, Sis Cow; sorter linger'n' twix' a bauk en a break-down,' sez Brer Rabbit, sezee.

" ' How yo' fokes, Brer Rabbit ? ' sez Miss Cow, sez she.

" ' Dey er des middlin', Sis Cow; how Brer Bull gittin' on ? ' sez Brer Rabbit, sezee.

" ' Sorter so-so,' sez Miss Cow, sez she.

" ' Dey er some mighty nice 'simmons up dis tree, Sis Cow,' sez Brer Rabbit, sezee, ' en I'd like mighty well fer ter have some un um,' sezee.

" ' How you gwineter git um, Brer Rabbit ? ' sez she.

" ' I 'low'd maybe dat I might ax you fer ter butt 'gin de tree, en shake some down, Sis Cow,' sez Brer Rabbit, sezee.

" Co'se Miss Cow don't wanter diskommerdate Brer Rabbit, en she march up ter de 'simmon tree, she did, en hit it a rap wid'er hawns—blam ! Now, den," continued Uncle Remus, tearing off the corner of a plug of tobacco, and cramming it into his mouth—" now, den, dem 'simmons wuz green ez grass, en na'er one never drap. Den Miss Cow butt de tree—blim ! Na'er 'simmon drap. Den Miss Cow sorter back off little, en run agin de tree—blip ! No 'simmons never drap. Den Miss Cow back off little fudder, she did, en hi'st her tail on 'er back, en come agin de tree, kerblam ! en she come so fas', en she come so hard, twel wunner her hawns went spang thoo de tree, en dar she wuz. She can't go forreds, en she can't go backerds. Dis zackly w'at Brer Rabbit waitin' fer, en he no sooner seed ole Miss Cow all fas'en'd up dan he jump up, he did, en cut de pidjin-wing.

" ' Come he'p me out, Brer Rabbit,' sez Miss Cow, sez she.

" ' I can't clime, Sis Cow,' sez Brer Rabbit, sezee,
' but I'll run 'n tell Brer Bull,' sezee ; en wid dat
Brer Rabbit put out fer home, en 'twan't long
'fo' here he come wid his ole 'oman en all his
chilluns, en de las' wunner de fambly wuz totin'
a pail. De big uns had big pails, en de little uns
had little pails. En dey all s'rounded ole Miss
Cow, dey did, en you hear me, honey, dey milk't 'er
dry. De ole uns milk't en de young uns milk't,
en den w'en dey done got nuff, Brer Rabbit, he
up'n say, sezee :

" ' I wish you mighty well, Sis Cow. I 'low'd
bein's how dat you'd hatter sorter camp out all
night dat I'd better come en swaje yo' bag,' sezee."

" Do which, Uncle Remus ? " asked the little
boy.

" Go 'long, honey ! Swaje 'er bag. W'en cows
don't git milk't, der bag swells, en youk'n hear em
a moanin' en a beller'n des like dey wuz gittin'
hurtid. Dat's w'at Brer Rabbit done. He 'sem-
bled his fambly, he did, en he swaje ole Miss Cow's
bag.

" Miss Cow, she stood dar, she did, en she study
en study, en strive fer ter break loose, but de hawn
done bin jam in de tree so tight dat twuz way
'fo' day in de mornin' 'fo' she loose it. Ennyhow
hit wuz endurin' er de night, en atter she git loose
she sorter graze 'roun', she did, for ter jestify 'er
stummuck. She 'low'd ole Miss Cow did, dat Brer
Rabbit be hoppin' 'long dat way fer ter see how
she gittin' on, en she tuck'n lay er trap fer 'im ;
en des 'bout sunrise wat'd ole Miss Cow do but
march up ter de 'simmon tree en stick er hawn
back in de hole ? But, bless yo' soul, honey, w'ile
she wuz croppin' de grass, she tuck one mouful too
menny, kaze w'en she hitch on ter de 'simmon

tree agin, Brer Rabbit wuz settin' in de fence cornder awatchin' un 'er. Den Brer Rabbit he say ter hisse'f:

"'Heyo,' sezee, 'wa't dis yer gwine on now? Hole yo' hosses, Sis Cow, twel you hear me comin',' sezee.

"En den he crope off down de fence, Brer Rabbit did, en bimeby here he come—lippity-clippity, clippity-lippity—des a sailin' down de big road.

"'Mawnin', Sis Cow,' sez Brer Rabbit, sezee, 'how you come on dis mawnin'?' sezee.

"'Po'ly, Brer Rabbit, po'ly,' sez Miss Cow, sez she. 'I ain't had no res' all night,' sez she. 'I can't pull loose,' sez she, 'but ef you'll come en ketch holt er my tale, Brer Rabbit,' sez she, 'I reckin maybe I kin fetch my hawn out,' sez she. Den Brer Rabbit, he come up little closer, but he ain't gittin' too close.

"'I speck I'm nigh nuff, Sis Cow,' sez Brer Rabbit, sezee. 'I'm a mighty puny man, en I might git trompled,' sezee. 'You do de pullin', Sis Cow,' sezee, 'en I'll do de gruntin',' sezee.

"Den Miss Cow, she pull out 'er hawn, she did, en tuck atter Brer Rabbit, en down de big road dey had it, Brer Rabbit wid his years laid back, en Miss Cow wid 'er head down en 'er tail curl. Brer Rabbit kep' on gainin', en bimeby he dart in a brier-patch, en by de time Miss Cow come 'long he had his head stickin' out, en his eyes look big as Miss Sally's chany sassers.

"'Heyo, Sis Cow! Whare you gwine?' sez Brer Rabbit, sezee.

"'Howdy, Brer Big-Eyes,' sez Miss Cow, sez she. 'Is you seed Brer Rabbit go by?'"

"'He des dis minit pass,' sez Brer Rabbit, sezee, 'en he look mighty sick,' sezee.

" En wid dat, Miss Cow tuck down de road like de dogs wuz atter 'er, en Brer Rabbit, he des lay down dar in de brier-patch, en roll en laff twel his sides hurtid 'im. He bleedzd ter laff. Fox atter 'im, Buzzard atter 'im, en Cow atter 'im, en dey ain't kotch 'im yit."

X

MR. TARRYPIN APPEARS UPON THE SCENE

"Miss Sally's" little boy again occupying the anxious position of auditor, Uncle Remus took the shovel and "put de noses er de chunks tergedder," as he expressed it, and then began :

"One day, atter Sis Cow done run pas' 'er own shadder tryin' fer ter ketch 'im, Brer Rabbit tuck'n 'low dat he wuz gwineter drap in en see Miss Meadows en de gals, en he got out his piece er lookin'-glass en primp up, he did, en sot out. Gwine canterin' 'long de road, who should Brer Rabbit run up wid but ole Brer Tarrypin—de same ole one-en-sixpunce. Brer Rabbit stop, he did, en rap on de roof er Brer Tarrypin house."

"On the roof of his house, Uncle Remus ?" interrupted the little boy.

"Co'se, honey, Brer Tarrypin kare his house wid 'im. Rain er shine, hot er cole, strike up wid ole Brer Tarrypin w'en you will en w'ilst you may, en whar you fine im', dar you'll fine his shanty. Hit's des like I tell you. So den ! Brer Rabbit he rap on de roof er Brer Tarrypin's house, he did, en ax wuz he in, en Brer Tarrypin 'low dat he wuz, en den Brer Rabbit, he ax 'im howdy, en den Brer Tarrypin he likewise 'spon' howdy, en den Brer Rabbit he say whar wuz Brer Tarrypin gwine, en Brer Tarrypin, he say w'ich he wern't gwine nowhar

skasely. Den Brer Rabbit 'low he wuz on his way
fer ter see Miss Meadows en de gals, en he ax Brer
Tarrypin ef he won't jine in en go long, en Brer
Tarrypin 'spon' he don't keer ef he do, en den dey
sot out. Dey had plenty er time fer confabbin'
'long de way, but bimeby dey got dar, en Miss
Meadows en de gals dey come ter de do', dey din,
en ax um in, en in dey went.

"W'en dey got in, Brer Tarrypin wuz so flat-
footed dat he wuz too low on de flo', en he weren't
high nuff in a cheer, but while they wuz all scramblin' 'roun' tryin' fer ter git Brer Tarrypin a cheer,
Brer Rabbit, he pick 'im up en put 'im on de shelf
whar de water-bucket sot, en ole Brer Tarrypin,
he lay back up dar, he did, des es proud ez a nigger
widder cook 'possum.

"Co'se de talk fell on Brer Fox, en Miss Meadows
en de gals make a great 'miration 'bout w'at a
gaily ridin'-hoss Brer Fox wuz, en dey make lots er
fun, en laff en giggle same like gals duz deze days.
Brer Rabbit, he sot dar in de cheer smokin' his
seegyar, en he sorter kler up his th'oat, en say,
sezee :

"'I'd er rid 'im over dis mawnin', ladies,' sezee,
' but I rid 'im so hard yistiddy dat he went lame in
de off fo' leg, en I speck I'll hatter swop 'im off yit,'
sezee.

"Den Brer Tarrypin, he up'n say, sezee :

"'Well, ef you gwineter sell 'im, Brer Rabbit,'
sezee, ' sell him some'rs outen dis naberhood, kaze
he done bin yer too long now,' sezee. ' No longer'n
day 'fo' yistiddy,' sezee, ' Brer Fox pass me on de
road, en whatter you reckin he say ?' sezee :

"'Law, Brer Tarrypin,' sez Miss Meadows, sez
she, ' you don't mean ter say he cust ?' sez she,
en den de gals hilt der fans up 'fo' der faces.

" ' Oh, no, ma'am,' sez Brer Tarrypin, sezee,
' he didn't cust, but he holler out—" Heyo, Stinkin'
Jim ! " ' " sezee.

" ' Oh, my !   You hear dat, gals ? ' sez Miss
Meadows, sez she ; ' Brer Fox call Brer Tarrypin
Stinkin' Jim,' sez she, en den Miss Meadows en de
gals make great wonderment how Brer Fox kin
talk dat a way 'bout nice man like Brer Tarrypin.

" But bless grashus, honey ! w'ilst all dis gwine
on, Brer Fox wuz stannin' at de back do' wid one
year at de cat-hole lissenin'.   Eave-drappers
don't hear no good er deyse'f, en de way Brer Fox
wuz 'bused dat day wuz a caution.

" Bimeby Brer Fox stick his head in de do', en
holler out :

" ' Good evenin', fokes, I wish you mighty well,'
sezee, en wid dat he make a dash fer Brer Rabbit,
but Miss Meadows en de gals dey holler en squall,
dey did, en Brer Tarrypin he got ter scramblin'
roun' up dar on de shelf, en off he come, en blip
he tuck Brer Fox on de back er de head. Dis
sorter stunted Brer Fox, en w'en he gedder his
'membunce de mos' he seed wuz a pot er greens
turnt over in de fireplace, en a broke cheer. Brer
Rabbit wuz gone, en Brer Tarrypin wuz gone, en
Miss Meadows en de gals wuz gone."

" Where did the Rabbit go, Uncle Remus ? "
the little boy asked, after a pause.

" Bless yo' soul, honey ! Brer Rabbit he skint
up de chimney—dats w'at turnt de pot er greens
over. Brer Tarrypin, he crope under de bed, he
did, en got behime de cloze-chist, en Miss Meadows
en de gals, they run out in de yard.

" Brer Fox, he sorter look roun' en feel er de
back er his head, whar Brer Tarrypin lit, but he
don't see no sine er Brer Rabbit. But de smoke en

de ashes gwine up de chimbly got de best er Brer
Rabbit, en bimeby he sneeze—*huckychow!*

"'Aha!' sez Brer Fox, sezee: 'youer dar, is
you?' sezee. 'Well, I'm gwineter smoke you out,
ef it takes a mont'. Youer mine dis time,' sezee.
Brer Rabbit ain't sayin' nuthin'.

"'Ain't you comin' down?' sez Brer Fox, sezee.
Brer Rabbit ain't sayin' nuthin'. Den Brer Fox,
he went out atter some wood, he did, en w'en he
come back he hear Brer Rabbit laffin'.

"'W'at you laffin' at, Brer Rabbit?' sez Brer
Fox, sezee.

"'Can't tell you, Brer Fox,' sez Brer Rabbit,
sezee.

"'Better tell, Brer Rabbit,' sez Brer Fox, sezee.

"''Taint nuthin but a box er money somebody
done gone en lef' up yer in de chink er de chimbly,'
sez Brer Rabbit, sezee.

"'Don't b'lieve you,' sez Brer Fox, sezee.

"'Look up en see,' sez Brer Rabbit, sezee, en
w'en Brer Fox look up, Brer Rabbit spit his eyes
full er terbarker joose, he did, en Brer Fox, he
make a break fer de branch, en Brer Rabbit he
come down en tole de ladies good-by.

"'How you git 'im off, Brer Rabbit?' sez
Miss Meadows, sez she.

"'Who? me?' sez Brer Rabbit, sezee; 'w'y
I des tuck en tole 'im dat ef he didn't go 'long home
en stop playin' his pranks on spectubble fokes, dat
I'd take 'im out and th'ash 'im,' sezee."

"And what became of the Terrapin?" asked
the little boy.

"Oh, well den!" exclaimed the old man, "chilluns can't speck ter know all 'bout eve'ything 'fo'
dey git some res'. Dem eyeleds er yone wanter be
propped wid straws dis minnit."

XI

MR. WOLF MAKES A FAILURE

"I LAY yo' ma got comp'ny," said Uncle Remus, as
the little boy entered the old man's door with a
huge piece of mince-pie in his hand, "en ef she
ain't got comp'ny, den she done gone en drap de
cubberd key som'ers whar you done run up wid
it."

"Well, I saw the pie lying there, Uncle Remus,
and I just thought I'd fetch it out to you."

"'Tooby sho, honey," replied the old man,
regarding the child with admiration. "Tooby sho,
honey ; dat changes marters. Chris'mus doin's is
outer date, en dey ain't got no bizness layin' roun'
loose. Dish yer pie," Uncle Remus continued,
holding it up and measuring it with an experienced
eye, "will gimme strenk fer ter persoo on atter Brer
Fox en Brer Rabbit en de udder beastesses w'at dey
roped in 'long wid um."

Here the old man paused, and proceeded to de-
molish the pie—a feat accomplished in a very
short time. Then he wiped the crumbs from his
beard and began :

"Brer Fox feel so bad, en he git so mad 'bout Brer
Rabbit, dat he dunno wa't ter do, en he look mighty
down-hearted. Bimeby, one day wiles he wuz
gwine 'long de road, ole Brer Wolf come up wid 'im.

W'en dey done howdyin' en axin' atter one nudder's fambly kunnexshun, Brer Wolf, he 'low, he did, dat der wuz sump'n wrong wid Brer Fox, en Brer Fox, he 'low'd der wern't, en he went on en laff en make great ter-do, kase Brer Wolf look like he spishun sump'n. But Brer Wolf, he got mighty long head, en he sorter broach 'bout Brer Rabbit's kyar'ns on, kaze de way dat Brer Rabbit 'ceive Brer Fox done got ter be de talk er de naberhood. Den Brer Fox and Brer Wolf dey sorter palavered on, dey did, twel bimeby, Brer Wolf he up'n say dat he done got plan fix fer ter trap Brer Rabbit Den Brer Fox say how. Den Brer Wolf up'n tell 'im dat de way fer ter git de drap on Brer Rabbit wuz ter git 'im in Brer Fox house. Brer Fox dun know Brer Rabbit uv ole, en he know dat sorter game done wo' ter a frazzle, but Brer Wolf, he talk mighty 'swadin'.

"'How you gwine git 'im dar?' sez Brer Fox, sezee.

"'Fool 'im dar,' sez Brer Wolf, sezee.

"'Who gwine do de foolin'?' sez Brer Fox, sezee.

"'I'll do de foolin',' sez Brer Wolf, sezee, 'ef you'll do de gamin',' sezee.

"'How you gwine do it?' sez Brer Fox, sezee.

"'You run 'long home, en git on de bed, en make like you dead, en don't you say nuthin' twel Brer Rabbit come en put his han's onter you,' sez Brer Wolf, sezee, 'en ef we don't git 'im fer supper, Joe's dead en Sal's a widder,' sezee.

"Dis look like mighty nice game, en Brer Fox 'greed. So den he amble off home, en Brer Wolf, he march off ter Brer Rabbit house. W'en he got dar, hit look like nobody at home, but Brer Wolf he walk up en knock on de do'—blam! blam! No-

body come. Den he lam aloose en knock 'gin—
blim ! blim !

"'Who dar ?' sez Brer Rabbit, sezee.

"'Fr'en',' sez Brer Wolf.

"'Too menny fr'en's spiles de dinner,' sez Brer
Rabbit, sezee ; 'w'ich un's dis ?' sezee.

"'I fetch bad news, Brer Rabbit,' sez Brer
Wolf, sezee.

"'Bad news is soon tole,' sez Brer Rabbit,
sezee.

"By dis time Brer Rabbit done come ter de do',
wid his head tied up in a red hankcher.

"'Brer Fox died dis mawnin',' sez Brer Wolf,
sezee.

"'Whar yo' mo'nin' gown, Brer Wolf ?' sez
Brer Rabbit, sezee.

"'Gwine atter it now,' sez Brer Wolf, sezee. 'I
des call by fer ter bring de news. I went down ter
Brer Fox house little bit 'go, en dar I foun' 'im
stiff,' sezee.

"Den Brer Wolf lope off. Brer Rabbit sot
down en scratch his head, he did, en bimeby he
say ter hisse'f dat he b'leeve he sorter drap 'roun'
by Brer Fox house fer ter see how de lan' lay.
No sooner said'n done. Up he jump, en out he
went. W'en Brer Rabbit got close to Brer Fox
house, all look lonesome. Den he went up nigher.
Nobody stirrin'. Den he look in, en der lay Brer
Fox stretch out on de bed des ez big ez life. Den
Brer Rabbit make like he talkin' to hisse'f.

"'Nobody 'roun' fer ter look atter Brer Fox—
not even Brer Tukkey Buzzard ain't come ter de
funer'l,' sezee. 'I hope Brer Fox ain't dead, but
I speck he is,' sezee. 'Even down ter Brer Wolf
done gone en lef' 'im. Hit's de busy season wid
me, but I'll set up wid 'im. He seem like he dead,

yet he mayn't be,' sez Brer Rabbit, sezee.   'W'en
a man go ter see dead fokes, dead fokes allers raises
up der behime leg en hollers, *wahoo!*' sezee.

"Brer Fox he stay still.   Den Brer Rabbit he
talk little louder :

"'Mighty funny.   Brer Fox look like he dead,
yit he don't do like he dead.   Dead fokes hists der
behime leg en hollers *wahoo!* w'en a man come ter
see um,' sez Brer Rabbit, sezee.

"Sho' nuff, Brer Fox lif' up his foot en holler
wahoo! en Brer Rabbit he tear out de house like
de dogs wuz atter 'im.   Brer Wolf mighty smart,
but nex' time you hear fum 'im, honey, he'll be in
trouble.   You des hole yo' breff'n wait."

XII

MR. FOX TACKLES OLD MAN TARRYPIN

"One day," said Uncle Remus, sharpening his knife on the palm of his hand—"one day Brer Fox strike up wid Brer Tarrypin right in de middle er de big road. Brer Tarrypin done heerd 'im comin', en he 'low ter hisse'f dat he'd sorter keep one eye open; but Brer Fox wuz monstus perlite, en he open up de confab, he did, like he ain't see Brer Tarrypin sence de las' freshit.

"'Heyo, Brer Tarrypin, whar you bin dis long-come-short?' sez Brer Fox, sezee.

"'Lounjun 'roun', Brer Fox, lounjun 'roun',' sez Brer Tarrypin.

"'You don't look sprucy like you did, Brer Tarrypin,' sez Brer Fox, sezee.

"'Lounjun 'roun' en suffer'n',' sez Brer Tarrypin, sezee.

"Den de talk sorter run on like dis:

"'W'at ail you, Brer Tarrypin? Yo' eye look mighty red,' sez Brer Fox, sezee.

"'Lor', Brer Fox, you dunner w'at trubble is. You ain't bin lounjun 'roun' en suffer'n',' sez Brer Tarrypin, sezee.

"'Bofe eyes red, en you look like you mighty weak, Brer Tarrypin,' sez Brer Fox, sezee.

" ' Lor', Brer Fox, you dunner w'at trubble is,' sez Brer Tarrypin, sezee.

" ' W'at ail you now, Brer Tarrypin ? ' sez Brer Fox, sezee.

" ' Tuck a walk de udder day, en man come 'long en sot de fiel' a-fier. Lor', Brer Fox, you dunner w'at trubble is,' sez Brer Tarrypin, sezee.

" ' How you git out de fier, Brer Tarrypin ? ' sez Brer Fox, sezee.

" ' Sot en tuck it, Brer Fox,' sez Brer Tarrypin, sezee. ' Sot en tuck it, en de smoke sif' in my eye, en de fier scorch my back,' sez Brer Tarrypin, sezee.

" ' Likewise hit bu'n yo' tail off,' sez Brer Fox, sezee.

" ' Oh, no, dar's de tail, Brer Fox,' sez Brer Tarrypin, sezee, en wid dat he oncurl his tail fum under de shell, en no sooner did he do dat dan Brer Fox grab it, en holler out :

" ' Oh, yes, Brer Tarrypin ! Oh, yes ! En so youer de man w'at lam me on de head at Miss Meadows's, is you ? Youer in wid Brer Rabbit, is you ? Well, I'm gwineter out you.'

" Brer Tarrypin beg en beg, but 'twan't no use. Brer Fox done bin fool so much dat he look like he 'termin fer ter have Brer Tarrypin haslett. Den Brer Tarrypin beg Brer Fox not fer ter drown 'im, but Brer Fox ain't makin' no prommus, en den he beg Brer Fox fer ter bu'n 'im, kaze he done useter fier, but Brer Fox don't say nuthin'. Bimeby Brer Fox drag Brer Tarrypin off little ways b'low de spring-'ouse, en souze 'im under de water. Den Brer Tarrypin begin fer ter holler :

" ' Tu'n loose dat stump root en ketch holt er me—tu'n loose dat stump root en ketch holt er me.'

"Brer Fox he holler back:

"'I ain't got holt er no stump root, en I is got holt er you.'

"Brer Tarrypin he kept on holler'n:

"'Ketch holt er me—I'm a drownin'—I'm a drownin'—tu'n loose de stump root en ketch holt er me.'

"Sho nuff, Brer Fox tu'n loose de tail, en Brer Tarrypin, he went down ter de bottom—kerblunkity-blink!"

No typographical combination or description could do justice to the guttural sonorousness—the peculiar intonation—which Uncle Remus imparted to this combination. It was so peculiar, indeed, that the little boy asked:

"How did he go to the bottom, Uncle Remus?"

"Kerblunkity-blink!"

"Was he drowned, Uncle Remus?"

"Who? Ole man Tarrypin? Is you drowndid w'en yo' ma tucks you in de bed?"

"Well, no," replied the little boy dubiously.

"Ole man Tarrypin wuz at home, I tell you, honey. Kerblinkity-blunk!"

XIII

THE AWFUL FATE OF MR. WOLF

UNCLE REMUS was half-soling one of his shoes,
and his Miss Sally's little boy had been handling
his awls, his hammers, and his knives to such an
extent that the old man was compelled to assume
a threatening attitude; but peace reigned again,
and the little boy perched himself on a chair, watching Uncle Remus driving in pegs.

"Folks w'at's allers pesterin' people, en bod-
derin' 'longer dat w'at ain't dern don't never come
ter no good end. Dar wuz Brer Wolf; stidder mindin'
un his own bizness, he hatter take en go in pardner-
ships wid Brer Fox, en dey want skacely a minnit
in de day dat he went atter Brer Rabbit, en he kep'
on en kep' on twel fus' news you knowed he got
kotch up wid—en he got kotch up with monstus
bad."

"Goodness, Uncle Remus! I thought the
Wolf let the Rabbit alone, after he tried to fool
him about the Fox being dead."

"Better lemme tell dish yer my way. Bimeby
hit'll be yo' bed time, en Miss Sally'll be a hollerin'
atter you, en you'll be a whimplin' 'roun', en den
Mars John'll fetch up de re'r wid dat ar strop
w'at I made fer 'im."

The child laughed, and playfully shook his fist
in the simple, serious face of the venerable old
darkey, but said no more. Uncle Remus waited
awhile to be sure there was to be no other
demonstration, and then proceeded:

"Brer Rabbit ain't see no peace w'atsumever.
He can't leave home 'cep Brer Wolf 'ud made a raid
en tote off some er de fambly. Brer Rabbit b'ilt 'im
a straw house, en hit wuz tored down; den he made a
house outen pine-tops, en dat went de same way; den
he made 'im a bark house en dat wuz raided on, en
eve'y time he los' a house he los' wunner his chilluns.
Las' Brer Rabbit got mad, he did, en cust, en
den he went off, he did, en got some kyarpinters, en
dey b'ilt 'im a plank house wid rock foundashuns.
Atter dat he could have some peace en quietness.
He could go out en pass de time er day wid his
nabers, en come back en set by de fier, en smoke his
pipe, en read de newspapers same like enny man
w'at got a fambly. He made a hole, he did, in
de cellar whar de little Rabbits could hide out
w'en dar wuz much uv a racket in de naberhood,
en de latch er de front do' kotch on de inside.
Brer Wolf, he see how de lan' lay, he did, en he
lay low. De little Rabbits wuz mighty skittish,
but hit got so dat cole chills ain't run up Brer
Rabbit's back no mo' w'en he heerd Brer Wolf
go gallopin' by.

"Bimeby, one day w'en Brer Rabbit wuz fixin'
fer ter call on Miss Coon, he heerd a monstus fuss
en clatter up de big road, en 'mos 'fo' he could fix
his years fer ter lissen, Brer Wolf run in de do'.
De little Rabbits dey went inter dere hole in
de cellar, dey did, like blowin' out a cannle. Brer
Wolf wuz ar'ly kivver'd wid mud, en mighty
nigh outer win'.

" 'Oh, do pray save me, Brer Rabbit!' sez Brer
Wolf, sezee. 'Do please, Brer Rabbit! de dogs
is atter me, en dey'll t'ar me up. Don't you
year um comin' ? Oh, do please save me, Brer
Rabbit! Hide me some'rs whar de dogs won't
git me.'

" No quicker sed dan done.

" 'Jump in dat big chist dar, Brer Wolf,' sez
Brer Rabbit, sezee ; 'jump in dar en make yo'se'f
at home.'

" In jump Brer Wolf, down come de lid, en
inter de hasp went de hook, en dar Mr. Wolf wuz.
Den Brer Rabbit went ter de lookin'-glass, he did,
en wink at hisse'f, en den he drawd de rockin'-cheer
in front er de fier, he did, en tuck a big chaw terbarker."

" Tobacco, Uncle Remus ? " asked the little boy,
incredulously.

" Rabbit terbarker, honey. You know dis
yer life ev'lustin' w'at Miss Sally puts 'mong de
cloze in de trunk ; well, dat's rabbit terbarker.
Den Brer Rabbit sot dar long time, he did, turnin'
his mine over en wukken his thinkin' masheen.
Bimeby he got up, en sorter stiz 'roun'. Den
Brer Wolf open up :

" 'Is de dogs all gone, Brer Rabbit ?'

" 'Seem like I hear one un um smellin' roun'
de chimbly-cornder des now.'

" Den Brer Rabbit git de kittle en fill it full er
water, en put it on de fier.

" 'W'at you doin' now, Brer Rabbit ?'

" 'I'm fixin' fer ter make you a nice cup er
tea, Brer Wolf.'

" Den Brer Rabbit went ter de cubberd en git de
gimlet, en commence for ter bo' little holes in de
chist-led.

" ' W'at you doin' now, Brer Rabbit ? ' "

" ' I'm a bo'in' little holes so you kin git bref, Brer Wolf.'

" Den Brer Rabbit went out en git some mo' wood, en fling it on de fier.

" ' W'at you doin' now, Brer Rabbit ? '

" ' I'm a chunkin up der fier so you won't git cole, Brer Wolf.'

" Den Brer Rabbit went down inter de cellar en fotch out all his chilluns.

" ' W'at you doin' now, Brer Rabbit ? '

" ' I'm a tellin' my chilluns w'at a nice man you is, Brer Wolf.'

" En de chilluns, dey had ter put der han's on der moufs fer ter keep fum laffin'.   Den Brer Rabbit he got de kittle en commenced fer to po' de hot water on de chist-led.

" ' W'at dat I hear, Brer Rabbit ? '

" ' You hear de wind a blowin', Brer Wolf.'

" Den de water began fer ter sif' thoo.

" ' W'at dat I feel, Brer Rabbit ? '

" ' You feels de fleas a bitin', Brer Wolf.'

" ' Dey er bitin' mighty hard, Brer Rabbit.'

" ' Tu'n over on de udder side, Brer Wolf.'

" ' W'at dat I feel now, Brer Rabbit ? '

" ' Still you feels de fleas, Brer Wolf.'

" ' Dey er eatin' me up, Brer Rabbit,' en dem wuz de las' words er Brer Wolf, kaze the scaldin' water done de bizness.

" Den Brer Rabbit call in his nabers, he did, en dey hilt a reg'lar juberlee ; en ef yer go ter Brer Rabbit's house right now, I dunno but w'at you'll find Brer Wolf's hide hangin' in de back-po'ch, en all bekase he wuz so bizzy wid udder fo'kses doin's."

XIV

MR. FOX AND THE DECEITFUL FROGS

WHEN the little boy ran in to see Uncle Remus the night after he had told him of the awful fate of Brer Wolf, the only response to his greeting was :

" I-doom-er-ker-kum-mer-ker ! "

No explanation could convey an adequate idea of the intonation and pronunciation which Uncle Remus brought to bear upon this wonderful word. Those who can recall to mind the peculiar gurgling, jerking, liquid sound made by pouring water from a large jug, or the sound produced by throwing several stones in rapid succession into a pond of deep water, may be able to form a very faint idea of the sound, but it cannot be reproduced in print. The little boy was astonished.

" What did you say, Uncle Remus ? "

" I-doom-er-ker-kum-mer-ker ? I doom-er-ker-kum-mer-ker ! "

" What is that ? "

" Dat's Tarrypin talk, dat is. Bless yo' soul, honey," continued the old man, brightening up, " w'en you git ole ez me—w'en you see w'at I sees, en year w'at I years, de creeturs dat you

can't talk wid 'll be mighty skase—dey will
dat. W'y, ders er old gray rat w'at uses 'bout
yer, en time atter time he comes out w'en you
all done gone ter bed en sets up dar in de cornder
en dozes, en me en him talks by de 'our; en w'at
dat ole rat dunno ain't down in de spellin' book.
Des now, w'en you run in and broke me up, I
wuz fetchin inter my mind w'at Brer Tarrypin
say ter Brer Fox w'en he turn 'im loose in de
branch."

"What did he say, Uncle Remus ?"

"Dat w'at he said—I-doom-er-ker-kum-mer-
ker ! Brer Tarrypin wuz at de bottom er de
pon', en he talk back, he did, in bubbles—I-doom-
er-ker-kum-mer-ker ! Brer Fox, he ain't sayin'
nuthin', but Brer Bull-Frog, settin' on de bank,
he hear Brer Tarrypin, he did, en he holler back:

"'Jug-er-rum-kum-dum !   Jug-er-rum-kum-
dum !'

"Den n'er Frog holler out:

"'Knee-deep ! Knee-deep !'

"Den ole Brer Bull-Frog, he holler back:

"'Don't-you-berlieve-'im ! Don't-you-berlieve-
'im !'

"Den de bubbles come up fum Brer Tarrypin:

"'I-doom-er-ker-kum-mer-ker !'

"Den n'er Frog sing out:

"'Wade in ! Wade in !'

"Den ole Brer Bull-Frog talk thoo his ho'seness:

"'Dar-you'll-fine-yo'-brudder ? Dar-you'll-fine-
yo'-brudder !'

"Sho nuff, Brer Fox look over de bank, he did,
en dar wuz n'er Fox lookin' at 'im outer de water.
Den he retch out fer ter shake han's en in he went,
heels over head, en Brer Tarrypin bubble out:

"'I-doom-er-ker-kum-mer-ker !'"

"Was the Fox drowned, Uncle Remus?" asked the little boy.

"He wern't zackly drowndid, honey," replied the old man, with an air of cautious reserve. "He did manage fer ter scramble out, but a little mo' en de Mud Turkle would er got 'im, en den he'd er bin made hash un worril widout een'."

XV

MR. FOX GOES A-HUNTING, BUT MR. RABBIT BAGS THE GAME

" ATTER Brer Fox hear 'bout how Brer Rabbit done Brer Wolf," said Uncle Remus, scratching his head with the point of his awl, " he 'low, he did, dat he better not be so brash, en he sorter let Brer Rabbit 'lone. Dey wuz all time seein' one nudder, en 'bunnunce er times Brer Fox could er nab Brer Rabbit, but eve'y time he got de chance, his mind 'ud sorter rezume 'bout Brer Wolf en he let Brer Rabbit 'lone. Bimeby dey 'gun ter git kinder familious wid wunner nudder like dey useter, en it got so Brer Fox'd call on Brer Rabbit, en dey's set up en smoke der pipes, dey would, like no ha'sh feelin's'd ever rested 'twixt um.

" Las', one day Brer Fox 'long all rig out, en ax Brer Rabbit fer ter go nuntin' wid 'im, but Brer Rabbit, he sorter feel lazy, en he tell Brer Fox dat he got some udder fish fer ter fry. Brer Fox feel mighty sorry, he did, but he say he b'leeve he'd try his han' enny how, en off he put. He wuz gone all day, en he had a monstus streak er luck, Brer Fox did, en he bagged a sight er game. Bimbey, to'rds de shank er de evenin', Brer Rabbit sorter stretch hisse'f, he did, en 'low hit's mos' time fer

63

Brer Fox fer ter git 'long home. Den Brer Rabbit,
he went'n mounted a stump fer ter see ef he could
year Brer Fox comin'. He ain't bin dar long,
twel sho' nuff, yer come Brer Fox thoo de woods,
singing like a nigger at a frolic. Brer Rabbit,
he lipt down off'n de stump, he did, en lay down
in de road en make like he dead. Brer Fox he
come 'long, he did, en see Brer Rabbit layin'
dar. He tu'n 'im over, he did, en 'zamine 'im, en
say, sezee.

"'Dis yer rabbit dead. He look like he bin
dead long time. He dead, but he mighty fat.
He de fattes' rabbit w'at I ever see, but he bin
dead too long. I fear'd ter take 'im home,' sezee.

"Brer Rabbit ain't sayin' nuthin'. Brer Fox, he
sorter lick his chops, but he went on en lef'
Brer Rabbit layin' in de road. Dreckly he wuz outer
sight, Brer Rabbit, he jump up, he did, en run roun'
thoo de woods en git befo' Brer Fox agin. Brer
Fox, he come up, en dar lay Brer Rabbit, periently
cole en stiff. Brer Fox, he look at Brer Rabbit, en he
sorter study. Atter while he onslung his game-bag,
en say ter hisse'f sezee :

"'Deze yer rabbit's gwine ter was'e. I'll des
'bout leave my game yer, en I'll go back'n git dat
udder rabbit, en I'll make fokes b'leeve that I'm
ole man Hunter fum Huntsville,' sezee.

"En wid dat he drapt his game en loped
back up de road atter de udder rabbit, en w'en he
got outer sight, ole Brer Rabbit, he snatch up Brer
Fox game en put out fer home. Nex' time he
see Brer Fox, he holler out :

"'What you kill de udder day, Brer Fox ?'
sezee.

"Den Brer Fox, he sorter koam his flank wid
his tongue, en holler back :

"'I kotch a han'ful er hard sense, Brer Rabbit,' sezee.

"Den ole Brer Rabbit, he laff, he did, en up en 'spon', sezee:

"'Ef I'd a know'd you wuz atter dat, Brer Fox, I'd a loant you some er mine,' sezee."

XVI

OLD MR. RABBIT HE'S A GOOD FISHERMAN

"BRER RABBIT en Brer Fox wuz like some chilluns w'at I knows un," said Uncle Remus, regarding the little boy, who had come to hear another story, with an affectation of great solemnity. "Bofe un um wuz allers atter wunner nudder, a prankin' en a pester'n 'roun', but Brer Rabbit did had some peace, kaze Brer Fox done got skittish' bout puttin' de clamps on Brer Rabbit.

"One day, w'en Brer Rabbit, en Brer Fox, en Brer Coon, en Brer B'ar, en a whole lot un um wuz clearin' up a new groun' fer ter plant a roas'n'-year patch, de sun 'gun ter git sorter hot, en Brer Rabbit he got tired; but he didn't let on, kaze he 'fear'd de balance un um'd call 'im lazy, en he keep on totin' off trash en pilin' up bresh, twel bimeby he holler out dat he gotter brier in his han' en den he tak'n slip off, en hunt fer cool place· fer ter res'. Atter w'ile he came 'crosst a well wid a bucket hangin' in it.

"'Dat look cool,' sez Brer Rabbit, sezee, 'en cool I speck she is. I des 'bout git in dar en take a nap,' en wid dat in he jump, he did, en he ain't no sooner fix hisse'f dan de bucket 'gun ter go down.'"

67

"Wasn't the Rabbit scared, Uncle Remus?" asked the little boy.

"Honey, dey ain't bin no wusser skeer'd beas' since de worril begin dan dis yer same Brer Rabbit. He fa'rly had a ager. He know whar he cum fum, but he dunner whar he gwine. Dreckly he feel de bucket hit de water, en dar she sot, but Brer Rabbit he keep mighty still, kaze he dunner w'at minnit gwineter be de nex'. He des lay dar en shuck en shiver.

"Brer Fox allers got one eye on Brer Rabbit, en w'en he slip off fum de new groun', Brer Fox he sneak atter 'im. He know Brer Rabbit wuz atter some projick er nudder, en he tuck'n crope off, he did, en watch 'im. Brer Fox see Brer Rabbit come to de well en stop, en den he see 'im jump in de bucket, en den, lo, en beholes, he see 'im go down outer sight. Brer Fox wuz de mos' 'stonish Fox dat you ever laid eyes on. He sot off dar in de bushes en study en study, but he don't make no head ner tails ter dis kinder bizness. Den he say ter hisse'f, sezee:

"'Well, ef dis don't bang my times,' sezee, 'den Joe's dead en Sal's a widder. Right down dar in dat well Brer Rabbit keep his money hid, en ef 'tain't dat den he done gone en 'skiver'd a gole-mine, en ef 'tain't dat, den I'm a gwineter see w'at's in dar,' sezee.

"Brer Fox crope up little nigher, he did, en lissen, but he don't year no fuss, en he keep on gitting nigher, en yit he don't year nuthin'. Bimeby he git up close en peep down, but he don't see nuthin' en he don't year nuthin'. All dis time Brer Rabbit mighty nigh skeer'd outen his skin, en he fear'd fer ter move kaze de bucket might keel over en spill him out in de water. W'ile he sayin'

his pra'rs over like a train er kyars runnin', ole Brer
Fox holler out:

"Heyo, Brer Rabbit! Who you wizzitin'
down dar?' sezee.

"'Who? Me? Oh, I'm des a fishin', Brer Fox,'
sez Brer Rabbit, sezee. "I des say ter myse'f
dat I'd sorter 'sprize you all wid a mess er fishes
fer dinner, en so here I is, en dar's de fishes. I'm
afishin' fer suckers, Brer Fox,' sez Brer Rabbit, sezee.

"'Is dey many un um down dar, Brer Rabbit?'
sez Brer Fox, sezee.

"'Lots un um, Brer Fox; scoze en scoze un um.
De water is natally live wid um. Come down en
he'p me haul um in, Brer Fox,' sez Brer Rabbit,
sezee.

"'How I gwineter git down, Brer Rabbit?'

"'Jump inter de bucket, Brer Fox. Hit'll
fetch you down all safe en soun'.'

"Brer Rabbit talk so happy en talk so sweet dat
Brer Fox he jump in de bucket, he did, en, ez
he went down, co'se his weight pull Brer Rabbit
up. W'en dey pass one nudder on de half-way
groun', Brer Rabbit he sing out:

"'Good-bye, Brer Fox, take keer yo' cloze,
    Fer dis is de way de worril goes;
  Some goes up en some goes down,
    You'll git ter de bottom all safe en soun'. [1]

"W'en Brer Rabbit got out, he gallop off en
tole de fokes w'at de well b'long ter dat Brer Fox wuz
down in dar muddyin' up de drinkin' w..ter, en den

---

[1] As a Northern friend suggests that this story may
be somewhat obscure, it may be as well to state that
the well is supposed to be supplied with a rope over a
wheel, or pulley, with a bucket at each end.

he gallop back ter de well, en holler down ter Brer Fox :

> " ' Yer come a man wid a great big gun—
> W'en he haul you up, you jump en run.' "

"What then, Uncle Remus ? " asked the little boy, as the old man paused.

"In des 'bout half n'our, honey, bofe un um wuz back in de new groun' wukkin' des like dey never heer'd er no well, ceppin' dat eve'y now'n den Brer Rabbit 'd burst out in er laff, en ole Brer Fox, he'd git a spell er de dry grins.''

XVII

MR. RABBIT NIBBLES UP THE BUTTER

" DE animils en de beastesses," said Uncle Remus,
shaking his coffee around in the bottom of his
tin-cup, in order to gather up all the sugar, " dey
kep' on gittin' mo' en mo' familious wid wunner
nudder, twel bimeby, 'twan't long 'fo' Brer Rabbit,
en Brer Fox, en Brer Possum got ter sorter bunchin'
der perwishuns tergedder in de same shanty.
Atter w'ile de roof sorter 'gun ter leak, en one day
Brer Rabbit, en Brer Fox, en Brer Possum, 'semble
fer ter see ef dey can't kinder patch her up. Dey
had a big day's work in front un um, en dey fotch
der dinner wid um. Dey lump de vittles up in
one pile, en de butter w'at Brer Fox brung, dey
goes en puts in de spring-'ouse fer ter keep cool,
en den dey went ter wuk, en 'twan't long 'fo' Brer
Rabbit stummuck 'gun ter sorter growl en pester
'im. Dat butter er Brer Fox sot heavy on his
mine, en his mouf water eve'y time he 'member
'bout it. Present'y he say ter hisse'f dat he bleedzd
ter have a nip at dat butter, en den he lay his
plans, he did. Fus' news, you know, w'ile dey wuz
all wukkin' 'long, Brer Rabbit raise his head quick
en fling his years forrerd en holler out :

" ' Here I is. W'at you want wid me ?' en
off he put like sump'n wuz atter 'im.

" He sallied 'roun', ole Brer Rabbit did, en atter

he make sho dat nobody ain't foller'n un 'im, inter de spring-'ouse he bounces, en der he stays twel he git a bait er butter.   Den he santer on back en go to wuk.

"'Whar you bin?' sez Brer Fox, sezee.

"'I hear my chilluns callin' me,' sez Brer Rabbit, sezee, 'en I hatter go see w'at dey want. My ole 'oman done gone en tuck mighty sick,' sezee.

"Dey wuk on, twel bimeby de butter tas'e so good dat ole Brer Rabbit want some mo'. Den he raise up his head, he did, en holler out:

"'Heyo! Hole on! I'm a-comin'!' en off he put.

"Dis time he stay right smart w'ile, en w'en he git back Brer Fox ax him whar he bin.

"'I bin ter see my ole 'oman, en she's a sinkin',' sezee.

"Dreckly Brer Rabbit hear um callin' 'im ag'in en off he goes, en dis time, bless yo' soul, he gits de butter out so clean dat he kin see hisse'f in de bottom er de bucket. He scrape it clean en lick it dry, en den he go back ter wuk lookin' mo' samer dan a nigger w'at de patter-rollers bin had holt un.

"'How's yo' ole 'oman dis time?' sez Brer Fox, sezee.

"'I'm oblije ter you, Brer Fox,' sez Brer Rabbit, sezee, 'but I'm fear'd she's done gone by now,' en dat sorter make Brer Fox en Brer Possum feel in moanin' wid Brer Rabbit.

"Bimeby, w'en dinner-time come, dey all got out der vittles, but Brer Rabbit keep on lookin' lonesome, en Brer Fox en Brer Possum dey sorter rustle roun' fer ter see ef dey can't make Brer Rabbit feel sorter splimmy."

"What is that, uncle Remus?" asked the little boy.

"Sorter splimmy-splammy, honey—sorter like he in a crowd—sorter like his ole 'oman ain't dead ez she mout be.   You know how fokes duz w'en dey gits whar people's a-moanin'."

The little boy didn't know, fortunately for him, and Uncle Remus went on:

"Brer Fox en Brer Possum rustle roun', dey did, gittin' out de vittles, en bimeby Brer Fox, he say, sezee:

"'Brer Possum, you run down ter de spring en fetch de butter, en I'll sail 'roun' yer en set de table,' sezee.

"Brer Possum, he lope off atter de butter, en dreckly here he come lopin' back wid his years a trimblin' en his tongue a hangin' out.   Brer Fox, he holler out:

"'W'at de matter now, Brer Possum?' sezee.

"'You all better run yer, fokes,' sez Brer Possum, sezee.   'De las' drap er dat butter done gone!'

"'Whar she gone?' sez Brer Fox, sezee.

"'Look like she dry up,' sez Brer Possum, sezee.

"Den Brer Rabbit, he look sorter sollum, he did, en he up'n say, sezee:

"'I speck dat butter melt in somebody mouf,' sezee.

"Den dey went down ter der spring wid Brer Possum, en sho nuff de butter done gone.   W'iles dey wuz sputin' over der wunderment, Brer Rabbit say he see tracks all 'roun' dar, en he p'int out dat ef dey'll all go ter sleep, he kin ketch de chap w'at stole de butter.   Den dey all lie down en Brer Fox en Brer Possum dey soon drapt off ter sleep, but Brer Rabbit he stay 'wake, en w'en de time come he raise up easy en smear Brer Possum mouf wid de butter on his paws, en den he run off en nibble up de bes' er de dinner w'at dey lef' layin'

out, en den he come back en wake up Brer Fox,
en show 'im de butter on Brer Possum mouf. Den
dey wake up Brer Possum, en tell 'im 'bout it, but
co'se Brer Possum 'ny it ter de las'. Brer Fox,
dough, he's a kinder lawyer, en he argafy dis way—
Dat Brer Possum wuz de fus' one at de butter, en
de fus' one fer ter miss it, en mo'n dat, dar hang de
signs on his mouf. Brer Possum see dat dey got
'im jamed up in a cornder, en den he up en say dat
de way fer ter ketch de man w'at stole de butter is
ter b'il' a big bresh-heap en set her afier, en all
han's try ter jump over, en de one w'at fall in, den
he de chap what stole de butter. Brer Rabbit en
Brer Fox dey bofe 'gree, dey did, en dey whirl in
en b'il' de bresh-heap, en dey b'il' her high, en dey
b'il' her wide, en den dey totch her off. W'en she
got ter blazin' up good, Brer Rabbit, he tuck de fus'
turn. He sorter step back, en look 'roun' en giggle,
en over he went mo' samer dan a bird flyin'. Den
come Brer Fox. He got back little fudder, en spit
on his han's, en lit out en made de jump, en he come
so nigh gittin' in dat de een' er his tail kotch afier.
Ain't you never see no fox, honey?" inquired Uncle
Remus, in a tone that implied both conciliation
and information

The little boy thought probably he had, but he
wouldn't commit himself.

"Well, den," continued the old man, "nex'
time you see one un um, you look right close en see
ef de een' er his tail ain't w'ite. Hit's des like I
tell you. Dey b'ars de skyar er dat bresh-heap down
ter dis day. Dey er marked—dat's w'at dey is—
dey er marked."

"And what about Brother Possum?" asked
the little boy.

"Ole Brer Possum, he tuck a runnin' start, he

did, en he come lumberin' 'long, en he lit—kerblam !
—right in de middle er de fier, en dat wuz de las'
er ole Brer Possum."

"But, Uncle Remus, Brother Possum didn't
steal the butter after all," said the little boy, who
was not at all satisfied with such summary injustice.

"Dat w'at make I say w'at I duz, honey In
dis worril, lots er fokes is gotter suffer fer udder
fokes' sins. Look like hit's mighty onwrong ; but
hit's des dat away. Tribbalashun seem like she's
a waitin' 'roun' de cornder fer ter ketch one en all
un us, honey."

XVIII

MR. RABBIT FINDS HIS MATCH AT LAST

" HIT look like ter me dat I let on de udder night dat in dem days w'en de beastesses wuz santer'n 'roun' same like fokes, none un um wuz brash nuff fer ter ketch up wid Brer Rabbit," remarked Uncle Remus, reflectively.

" Yes," replied the little boy, " that's what you said."

" Well, den," continued the old man with unc- tion, " dar's whar my 'membunce gin out, kaze Brer Rabbit did git kotched up wid, en hit cool 'im off like po'in' spring water on one er deze yer biggity fices."

" How was that, Uncle Remus ? " asked the little boy.

" One day w'en Brer Rabbit wuz gwine lippity- clippitin' down de road, he meet up wid ole Brer Tarrypin, en atter dey pass de time er day wid wunner nudder, Brer Rabbit, he 'low dat he wuz much 'blije ter Brer Tarrypin fer de han' he tuck in de rumpus dat day down at Miss Meadows's."

" When he dropped off the water-shelf on the Fox's head," suggested the little boy.

" Dat's de same time, honey. Den Brer Tarrypin 'low dat Brer Fox run mighty fas' dat day, but dat ef he'd er been atter 'im stidder Brer Rabbit, he'd

er kotch 'im. Brer Rabbit say he could er kotch
'im hisse'f but he didn't keer 'bout leavin' de ladies.
Dey keep on talkin', they did, twel bimeby dey
gotter 'sputin' 'bout w'ich wuz de swif'es'. Brer
Rabbit, he say he kin outrun Brer Tarrypin, en
Brer Tarrypin, he des vow dat he kin outrun Brer
Rabbit. Up en down dey had it, twel fus' news you
know Brer Tarrypin say he got a fifty dollar bill
in de chink er de chimbly at home, en dat bill done
tole 'im dat he could beat Brer Rabbit in a fa'r race.
Den Brer Rabbit say he got a fifty-dollar bill w'at
say dat he kin leave Brer Tarrypin so fur behime,
dat he could sow barley ez he went 'long en hit 'ud
be ripe nuff fer ter cut by de time Brer Tarrypin
pass dat way.

"Enny how dey make de bet en put up de money,
en ole Brer Tukkey Buzzard, he wuz summonzd fer
ter be de jedge, en de stakeholder; en 'twan't long
'fo' all de 'rangements wuz made. De race wuz a
five-mile heat, en de groun' wuz medjud off, en
at de een' er eve'y mile a pos' wuz stuck up. Brer
Rabbit wuz ter run down de big road, en Brer Tarrypin, he say he'd gallup thoo de woods. Fokes tole
'im he could git long faster in de road, but ole Brer
Tarrypin, he know w'at he doin'. Miss Meadows
en de gals en mos' all de nabers got win' er de fun,
en w'en de day wuz sot dey 'termin' fer ter be on
han'. Brer Rabbit he train hisse'f eve'y day en
he skip over de groun' des ez gayly ez a June cricket.
Ole Brer Tarrypin, he lay low in de swamp. He had
a wife en th'ee chilluns, ole Brer Tarrypin did, en
dey wuz all de ve'y spit en image er de ole man.
Ennybody w'at know one fum de udder gotter take
a spy-glass, en den dey er li'ble fer ter git fooled.

"Dat's de way marters stan' twel de day er de
race, en on dat day, ole Brer Tarrypin, en his ole

'oman, en his th'ee chilluns, dey got up 'fo' sun-up,
en went ter de place. De ole 'oman, she tuck 'er
stan' nigh de fus' mile-pos', she did, en de chilluns
nigh de udders, up ter de las', en dar ole Brer Tarrypin, he tuck his stan'. Bimeby, here come de
fokes : Jedge Buzzard, he come, en Miss Meadows
en de gals, dey come, en den yer come Brer Rabbit
wid ribbons tied 'roun' his neck en streamin' fum
his years. De fokes all went ter de udder een'
er de track fer ter see how dey come out. W'en de
time come Jedge Buzzard strut 'roun' en pull out
his watch, en holler out :

" ' Gents, is you ready ? '

" Brer Rabbit, he say ' yes,' en ole Miss Tarrypin
holler ' go ' fum de aidge er de woods. Brer Rabbit,
he lit out on de race, en ole Miss Tarrypin, she put
out for home. Jedge Buzzard, he riz en skimmed
'long fer ter see dat de race wuz runned fa'r. W'en
Brer Rabbit got ter de fus' mile-pos' wunner de
Tarrypin chilluns crawl out de woods, he did, en
make fer de place. Brer Rabbit, he holler out :

" ' Whar is you, Brer Tarrypin ? '

" ' Yer I come a-bulgin',' sez de Tarrypin, sezee.

" Brer Rabbit so glad he's ahead dat he put out
harder dan ever, en de Tarrypin, he make fer home.
W'en he come ter de nex' pos', nudder Tarrypin
crawl out er de woods.

" ' Whar is you, Brer Tarrypin ? ' sez Brer
Rabbit, sezee.

" ' Yer I come a-bilin',' sez de Tarrypin, sezee.

" Brer Rabbit, he lit out, he did, en come ter
nex' pos', en dar wuz de Tarrypin. Den he come
ter nex', en dar wuz de Tarrypin. Den he had one
mo' mile fer ter run, en he feel like he gittin' bellust.
Bimeby, ole Brer Tarrypin look way off down de
road en he see Jedge Buzzard sailin' 'long en he

know hit's time fer 'im fer ter be up. So he scramble
outen de woods, en roll 'cross de ditch, en shuffle
thoo de crowd er folks en git ter de mile-pos' en
crawl behime it. Bimeby, fus' news you know, yer
come Brer Rabbit. He look 'roun' en he don't see
Brer Tarrypin, en den he squall out :

" ' Gimme de money, Brer Buzzard ! Gimme de
money ! '

" Den Miss Meadows en de gals, dey holler and
laff fit ter kill deyse'f, en ole Brer Tarrypin, he
raise up fum behime de pos' en sez, sezee :

" ' Ef you'll gimme time fer ter ketch my breff,
gents en ladies, one en all, I speck I'll finger dat
money myse'f,' sezee, en sho nuff, Brer Tarrypin
tie de pu's 'roun' his neck en skaddle[1] off home."

" But, Uncle Remus," said the little boy, dole-
fully, " that was cheating."

" Co'se, honey. De beastesses 'gun ter cheat,
en den fokes tuck it up, en hit keep on spreadin'.
Hit mighty ketchin', en you mine yo' eye, honey,
dat somebody don't cheat you 'fo' yo' ha'r git gray
ez de ole nigger's."

---

[1] It may be interesting to note here that in all pro-
bability the word " skedaddle," about which there was
some controversy during the war, came from the Vir-
ginia negro's use of " skaddle," which is a corruption
of " scatter." The matter, however, is hardly worth
referring to.

XIX

THE FATE OF MR. JACK SPARROW

"You'll tromple on dat bark twel hit won't be
fitten fer ter fling 'way, let 'lone make hoss-collars
out'n," said Uncle Remus, as the little boy came
running into his cabin out of the rain. All over
the floor long strips of "wahoo" bark were spread,
and these the old man was weaving into horse-
collars.

"I'll sit down, Uncle Remus," said the little
boy.

"Well, den, you better, honey," responded the
old man, "kaze I 'spizes fer ter have my wahoo
trompled on. Ef 'twuz shucks, now, hit mout
be diffunt, but I'm a gettin' too ole fer ter be
projickin' longer shuck collars."

For a few minutes the old man went on with his
work, but with a solemn air altogether unusual.
Once or twice he sighed deeply, and the sighs ended
in a prolonged groan, that seemed to the little boy
to be the result of the most unspeakable mental
agony. He knew by experience that he had done
something which failed to meet the approval of
Uncle Remus, and he tried to remember what it
was, so as to frame an excuse; but his memory
failed him. He could think of nothing he had done

calculated to stir Uncle Remus's grief. He was
not exactly seized with remorse, but he was very
uneasy. Presently Uncle Remus looked at him in
a sad and hopeless way, and asked :

"W'at dat long rigmarole you bin tellin' Miss
Sally 'bout yo' little brer dis mawnin' ? "

"Which, Uncle Remus ? " asked the little boy,
blushing guiltily.

"Dat des w'at I'm a-axin' un you now. I hear
Miss Sally say she's a-gwineter stripe his jacket,
en den I knowed you bin tellin' on 'im."

"Well, Uncle Remus, he was pulling up your
onions, and then he went and flung a rock at me,"
said the child, plaintively.

"Lemme tell you dis," said the old man, laying
down the section of horse-collar he had been plaiting,
and looking hard at the little boy, "lemme tell you
dis—der ain't no way fer ter make tattlers en tail-
b'arers turn out good. No, dey ain't. I bin
mixin' up wid fokes now gwine on eighty year, en
I ain't seed no tattler come ter no good een'. Dat
I ain't. En ef ole man M'thoozlum wuz livin' clean
twel yit, he'd up'n tell you de same. Sho ez
youer settin' dar. You 'member w'at 'come er de
bird w'at went tattlin' 'roun' 'bout Brer Rabbit ? "

The little boy didn't remember, but he was very
anxious to know, and he also wanted to know what
kind of a bird it was that so disgraced itself.

"Hit wuz wunner deze yer uppity little Jack
Sparrers, I speck," said the old man ; "dey wuz
allers bodder'n' longer udder fokes's bizness, en
dey keeps at it down ter dis day, peckin' yer, and
pickin' dar, en scratchin' out yander. One day,
atter he bin fool by ole Brer Tarrypin, Brer Rabbit
wuz settin' down in de woods studdyin' how he wuz
gwineter git even. He feel mighty lonesome, en

he feel mighty mad, Brer Rabbit did. Tain't put down in de tale, but I speck he cusst en r'ar'ed 'roun' considerbul. Leas'ways, he wuz settin' out by hisse'f, en dar he sot, en study en study, twel bimeby he jump up en holler out:

"'Well, doggone my cats ef I can't gallop 'roun' ole Brer Fox, en I'm gwineter do it. I'll show Miss Meadows en de gals dat I'm de boss er Brer Fox,' sezee.

"Jack Sparrer up in de tree, he hear Brer Rabbit, he did, en he sing out:

"'I'm gwine tell Brer Fox! I'm gwine tell Brer Fox! Chick-a-biddy-win'-a-blowin'-acuns-fal-lin'! I'm gwine tell Brer Fox!'"

Uncle Remus accompanied the speech of the bird with a peculiar whistling sound in his throat, that was a marvellous imitation of a sparrow's chirp, and the little boy clapped his hands with delight, and insisted on a repetition.

"Dis kinder tarrify Brer Rabbit, en he skasely know w'at he gwine do; but bimeby he study ter hisse'f dat de man w'at see Brer Fox fus' was boun' ter have de inturn, en den he go hoppin' off to'rds home. He didn't got fur w'en who should he meet but Brer Fox, en den Brer Rabbit, he open up:

"'W'at dis twix' you en me, Brer Fox?' said Brer Rabbit, sezee. 'I hear tell you gwineter sen' me ter 'struckshun, en nab my fambly, en 'stroy my shanty,' sezee.

"Den Brer Fox he git mighty mad.

"'Who bin tellin' you all dis?' sezee.

"Brer Rabbit make like he didn't want ter tell, but Brer Fox he 'sist en 'sist, twel at las' Brer Rabbit he up en tell Brer Fox dat he hear Jack Sparrer say all dis.

"'Co'se,' sez Brer Rabbit, sezee, 'w'en Brer Jack Sparrer tell me dat I flew up, I did, en I use some langwidge w'ich I'm mighty glad dey wern't no ladies 'roun' nowhars so dey could hear me go on,' sezee.

"Brer Fox he sorter gap, he did, en say he speck he better be sa'nter'n on. But, bless yo' soul, honey, Brer Fox ain't sa'nter fur, 'fo' Jack Sparrer flipp down on a 'simmon-bush by de side er de road, en holler out:

"'Brer Fox! Oh, Brer Fox!—Brer Fox!'

"Brer Fox he des sorter canter 'long, he did, en make like he don't hear 'im. Den Jack Sparrer up'n sing out ag'in:

"'Brer Fox! Oh, Brer Fox! Hole on, Brer Fox! I got some news fer you. Wait, Brer Fox! Hit'll 'stonish you.'

"Brer Fox he make like he don't see Jack Sparrer, ner needer do he hear 'im, but bimeby he lay down by de road, en sorter stretch hisse'f like he fixin' fer ter nap. De tattlin' Jack Sparrer he flew'd 'long, en keep on callin' Brer Fox, but Brer Fox, he ain't sayin' nuthin'. Den little Jack Sparrer, he hop down on de groun' en flutter 'roun' 'mongst de trash. Dis sorter 'track Brer Fox 'tenshun, en he look at de tattlin' bird, en de bird he keep on callin':

"'I got sump'n fer ter tell you, Brer Fox.'

"'Git on my tail, little Jack Sparrer,' sez Brer Fox, sezee, 'kaze I'm de'f in one year, en I can't hear out'n de udder. Git on my tail,' sezee.

"Den de little bird he up'n hop on Brer Fox's tail.

"'Git on my back, little Jack Sparrer, kaze I'm de'f in one year en I can't hear out'n de udder.'

"Den de little bird hop on his back.

"'Hop on my head, little Jack Sparrer, kaze I'm de'f in bofe years.'

"Up hop de little bird.

"'Hop on my toof, little Jack Sparrer, kaze I'm de'f in one year en I can't hear out'n de udder.'

"De tattlin' little bird hop on Brer Fox's toof, en den——"

Here Uncle Remus paused, opened wide his mouth and closed it again in a way that told the whole story.[1]

"Did the Fox eat the bird all—all—up?" asked the little boy.

"Jedge B'ar come 'long nex' day," replied Uncle Remus, "en he fine some fedders, en fum dat word went roun' dat ole man Squinch Owl done kotch nudder watzizname."

[1] An Atlanta friend heard this story in Florida, but an aligator was substituted for the fox, and a little boy for the rabbit. There is another version in which the impertinent gosling goes to tell the fox something her mother has said, and is caught ; and there may be other versions. I have adhered to the middle Georgia version, which is characteristic enough. It may be well to state that there are different versions of all the stories —the shrewd narrators of the mythology of the old plantation adapting themselves with ready tact to the years, tastes, and expectations of their juvenile audiences.

XX

HOW MR. RABBIT SAVED HIS MEAT

"ONE time," said Uncle Remus, whetting his knife slowly and thoughtfully on the palm of his hand, and gazing reflectively in the fire—" one time Brer Wolf——"

"Why, Uncle Remus!" the little boy broke in, "I thought you said the Rabbit scalded the Wolf to death a long time ago."

The old man was fairly caught, and he knew it; but this made little difference to him. A frown gathered on his usually serene brow as he turned his gaze upon the child—a frown in which both scorn and indignation were visible. Then all at once he seemed to regain control of himself. The frown was chased away by a look of Christian resignation.

"Dar now! W'at I tell you?" he exclaimed as if addressing a witness concealed under the bed. "Ain't I done tole you so? Bless grashus! ef chilluns ain't gittin' so dey knows mo'n ole folkes, en dey'll 'spute longer you en 'spute longer you, 'ceppin der ma call um w,'ich I speck twon't be long 'fo' she will, en den I'll set yere by de chimbly-cornder en git some peace er mine. W'en ole Miss wuz livin'," continued the old man, still addressing some imaginary person, "hit 'uz mo'n enny her chilluns 'ud dast ter do ter come 'sputin' longer me, en Mars John'll tell you de same enny day you ax 'im."

"Well, Uncle Remus, you know you said the Rabbit poured hot water on the Wolf and killed him," said the little boy.

The old man pretended not to hear. He was engaged in searching among some scraps of leather under his chair, and kept on talking to the imaginary person. Finally, he found and drew forth a nicely plaited whipthong with a red snapper all waxed and knotted.

"I wuz fixin' up a w'ip fer a little chap," he continued, with a sigh, "but, bless grashus! 'fo' I kin git 'er done, de little chap done grow'd up twel he know mon'n I duz."

The child's eyes filled with tears and his lips began to quiver, but he said nothing; whereupon Uncle Remus immediately melted.

"I 'clar' to goodness," he said, reaching out and taking the little boy tenderly by the hand, "ef you ain't de ve'y spit en image er ole Miss w'en I brung 'er de las' news er de war. Hit's des like skeerin' up a ghos' w'at you ain't fear'd un."

Then there was a pause, the old man patting the little child's hand caressingly.

"You ain't mad, is you, honey?" Uncle Remus asked finally, "kaze ef you is, I'm gwine out yere en butt my head 'gin de do' jam'."

But the little boy wasn't mad. Uncle Remus had conquered him and he had conquered Uncle Remus in pretty much the same way before. But it was some time before Uncle Remus would go on with the story. He had to be coaxed. At last, however, he settled himself back in the chair and began:

"Co'se, honey, hit mout er bin ole Brer Wolf, er hit mout er bin er n'er Brer Wolf; it mout er bin 'fo' he got kotch up wid, er it mout er bin atterwards. Ez de tale wer gun to me des dat away I gin it unter you. One time Brer Wolf wuz comin' 'long home fum a fishin' frolic. He sa'nter 'long de road, he did, wid his string er fish 'cross his shoulder, wen fus' news you know ole Miss Pa'tridge, she hop outer de bushes en flutter 'long right at Brer Wolf nose. Brer Wolf he say ter hisse'f dat ole Miss Pa'tridge tryin' fer ter tcll 'im 'way fum her nes', en wid dat he lay his fish down en put out inter de bushes whar old Miss Pa'tridge come fum, en 'bout dat time Brer Rabbit, he happen 'long. Dar wuz de fishes, en dar wuz Brer Rabbit, en w'en dat de case w'at you speck a sorter innerpen'ent man like Brer Rabbit gwine do? I kin tell you dis, dat dem fishes ain't stay whar Brer Wolf put um at, en w'en Brer Wolf come back dey wuz gone.

"Brer Wolf, he sot down en scratch his head, he did, en study en study, en den hit sorter rush inter his mine dat Brer Rabbit bin 'long dar, en den Brer Wolf, he put out fer Brer Rabbit house, en w'en he git dar he hail 'im. Brer Rabbit, he dunno nuthin' tall 'bout no fishes. Brer Wolf he up'n say he bleedzd ter b'leeve Brer Rabbit got dem fishes. Brer Rabbit 'ny it up en down, but Brer Wolf stan' to it dat Brer Rabbit got dem fishes. Brer Rabbit, he say dat if Brer Wolf b'leeve he got de fishes, den he give Brer Wolf lief fer ter kill de bes' cow he got. Brer Wolf he tuck Brer Rabbit at his word, en go off ter de pastur' en drive up de cattle en kill Brer Rabbit bes' cow.

"Brer Rabbit, he hate mighty bad fer ter lose his cow, but he lay his plans, en he tell his chilluns

dat he gwineter have dat beef yit. Brer Wolf,
he been tuck up by de patter rollers 'fo' now, en he
mighty skeer'd un um, en fus' news you know, yer
come Brer Rabbit hollerin' en tellin' Brer Wolf
dat de patter-rollers comin'.

"'You run en hide, Brer Wolf,' sez Brer Rabbit,
sezee, 'en I'll stay yer en take keer er de cow twel
you gits back,' sezee.

"Soon's Brer Wolf hear talk er de patter-rollers,
he scramble off inter de underbresh like he bin
shot out'n a gun. En he want mo'n gone 'fo' Brer
Rabbit, he whirl in en skunt de cow en salt de hide
down, and den he tuck'n cut up de kyarkiss en stow
it 'way in de smoke-'ouse, en den he tuck'n stick
de een' er de cowtail in de groun'. Atter he gone
en done all dis, den Brer Rabbit he squall out for
Brer Wolf:

"'Run yer, Brer Wolf! Run yer! Yo' cow
gwine in de groun'! Run yer!'

"W'en ole Brer Wolf got dar, w'ich he come er
scootin', dar wuz Brer Rabbit hol'in' on ter de
cowtail, fer ter keep it fum gwine in de groun'.
Brer Wolf, he kotch holt, en dey 'gin a pull er two
en up come de tail. Den Brer Rabbit, he wink his
off eye en say, sezee:

"'Dar! de tail done pull out en de cow gone,'
sezee.

"But Brer Wolf he wern't de man fer ter give
it up dat away, en de got 'im a spade, en a pick-axe,
en a shovel, en he dig en dig fer dat cow twel diggin'
wuz pas' all endu'unce, en ole Brer Rabbit he sot
up dar in his front po'ch en smoke his seegyar.
Eve'y time ole Brer Wolf stuck de pick-axe in de
clay, Brer Rabbit, he giggle ter his chilluns:

"'He diggy, diggy, diggy, but no meat dar!
He diggy, diggy, diggy, but no meat dar!'

"Kaze all de time de cow wuz layin' pile up in his smoke-'ouse, en him en his chilluns wuz eatin' fried beef en inguns eve'y time dey mouf water.

"Now den, honey, you take dis yer w'ip," continued the old man, twining the leather thong around the little boy's neck, "en scamper up ter de big 'ouse en tell Miss Sally fer ter gin you some un it de nex' time she fine yo' tracks in de sugar-bairl."

XXI

MR. RABBIT MEETS HIS MATCH AGAIN

" DERE wuz nudder man dat sorter play it sharp
on Brer Rabbit," said Uncle Remus, as, by some
mysterious process, he twisted a hog's bristle into
the end of a piece of thread—an operation which
the little boy watched with great interest. " In
dem days," continued the old man, " de beastesses
kyar'd on marters same ez fokes. Dey went inter
fahmin', en I speck ef de troof wuz ter come out,
dey kep' sto', en had der camp-meetin' times en
der bobycues w'en de wedder wuz 'greeble."

Uncle Remus evidently thought that the little
boy wouldn't like to hear of any further discom-
fiture of Brer Rabbit, who had come to be a sort of a
hero, and he was not mistaken.

" I thought the Terrapin was the only one that
fooled the Rabbit," said the little boy, dismally.

" Hit's des like I tell you, honey. Dey ain't no
smart man, 'cep' w'at dey's a smarter. Ef ole
Brer Rabbit hadn't er got kotch ud wid, de nabers
'ud er tuck 'im for a h'ant, en in dem times dey
bu'nt witches 'fo' you could squinch yo' eyeballs.
Dey did dat."

" Who fooled the Rabbit this time ? " the little

boy asked. When Uncle Remus had the bristle
"sot" in the thread, he proceeded with the story:

"One time Brer Rabbit en ole Brer Buzzard
'cluded dey'd sorter go snacks, en crap tergedder.
Hit wuz a mighty good year, en de truck t'un out
monstus well; but bimeby, w'en de time come fer
dividjun, hit come ter light dat ole Brer Buzzard
ain't got nuthin'. De crap wuz all gone, en dey
want nuthin' dar fer ter show fer it. Brer Rabbit,
he make like he in a wuss fix'n Brer Buzzard, en
he mope 'roun', he did, like he fear'd dey gwineter
sell 'im out.

"Brer Buzzard, he ain't sayin' nuthin', but he
keep up a monstus thinkin', en one day he come
'long en holler en tell Brer Rabbit dat he done fine
rich gole-mine des 'cross de river.

"'You come en go 'longer me, Brer Rabbit,'
sez Brer Tukkey Buzzard, sezee. 'I'll scratch en
you kin grabble, en 'tween de two un us we'll make
short wuk er dat gole-mine,' sezee.

"Brer Rabbit, he wuz high up fer de job, but
he study en study, he did, how he gwineter git
'cross de water, kaze evr'y time he git his foot wet
all the fambly kotch cole. Den he up'n ax Brer
Buzzard how he gwine do, en Brer Buzzard he up'n
say dat he kyar Brer Rabbit 'cross, en wid dat ole
Brer Buzzard, he squot down, he did, en spread
his wings, en Brer Rabbit, he mounted, en up dey
riz." There was a pause.

"What did the Buzzard do then?" asked the
little boy.

"Dey riz," continued Uncle Remus, "en w'en
dey lit, dey lit in de top er de highest sorter pine,
en de pine w'at dey lit in wuz growin' on er ilun,
en de ilun wuz in de middle er de river, wid de deep
water runnun' all 'roun'. Dey ain't mo'n lit 'fo'

Brer Rabbit, he know w'ich way de win' 'uz blowin',
en by de time ole Brer Buzzard got hisse'f ballunce
on a lim', Brer Rabbit, he up'n say, sezee:

"'W'iles we er res'n here, Brer Buzzard, en
bein's you bin so good, I got sump'n fer ter tell
you,' sezee. 'I got a gole-mine er my own, one
w'at I make myse'f, en I speck we better go back
ter mine 'fo' we bodder 'longer yone,' sezee.

"Den ole Brer Buzzard, he laff, he did, twel he
shake, en Brer Rabbit, he sing out:

"'Hole on, Brer Buzzard! Don't flop yo' wings
w'en you laff, kaze den ef you duz, sump'n'ill drap
fum up yer, en my gole-mine won't do you no good,
en needer will yone do me no good.'

"But 'fo' dey got down fum dar, Brer Rabbit
done tole all 'bout de crap, en he hatter promus
fer ter 'vide fa'r en squar'. So Brer Buzzard,
he kyar 'im back, en Brer Rabbit he walk weak
in de knees a mont' atterwuds."

XXII

A STORY ABOUT THE LITTLE RABBITS

"Fine um whar you will en w'en you may," remarked Uncle Remus with emphasis, "good chilluns allers gits tuck keer on. Dar wuz Brer Rabbit's chilluns; dey minded der daddy en mammy fum day's een' ter day's een'. W'en ole man Rabbit say ' scoot,' dey scooted, en w'en ole Miss Rabbit say ' scat,' dey scatted. Dey did dat. En dey kep der cloze clean, en dey ain't had no smut on der nose nudder."

Involuntarily the hand of the little boy went up to his face, and he scrubbed the end of his nose with his coat-sleeve.

"Dey wuz good chilluns," continued the old man, heartily, "en ef dey hadn't er bin, der wuz one time w'en dey wouldn't er bin no little rabbits— na'er one. Dat's w'at."

"What time was that, Uncle Remus?" the little boy asked.

"De time w'en Brer Fox drapt in at Brer Rabbit house, en didn't foun' nobody dar 'ceppin' de little Rabbits. Ole Brer Rabbit, he wuz off some'rs raiding on a collard patch, en ole Miss Rabbit she wuz tendin' on a quiltin' in de naberhood, en wiles de little Rabbits wuz playin' hidin'-switch, in drapt

Brer Fox. De little Rabbits wuz so fat dat dey
fa'rly make his mouf water, but he 'member 'bout
Brer Wolf, en he skeered fer ter gobble um up
'ceppin' he got some skuse. De little Rabbits,
dey mighty skittish, en dey sorter huddle deyse'f up tergedder en watch Brer Fox motions.
Brer Fox, he sot dar en study w'at sorter skuse he
gwineter make up. Bimeby he see a great big stalk
er sugar-cane stan'in' up in de cornder, en he cle'r
up his th'oat en talk biggity:

"'Yer! you young Rabs dar, sail 'roun' yer en
broke me a piece er dat sweetnin'-tree,' sezee, en
den he koff.

"De little Rabbits, dey got out de sugar-cane,
dey did, en dey rastle wid it, en sweat over it,
but twan't no use. Dey couldn't broke it. Brer
Fox, he make like he ain't watchin', but he keeps on
holler'n:

"'Hurry up dar, Rabs! I'm a waitin' on you.'

"En de little Rabbits, dey hustle 'roun' en
rastle wid it, but dey couldn't broke it. Bimeby
dey hear little bird singin' on top er de house, en
de song wa't de little bird sing wuz dis yer:

"'Take yo' toofies en gnyaw it,
Take yo' toofies en saw it,
Saw it en yoke it,
En den you kin broke it.'

"Den de little Rabbits, dey git mighty glad, en
dey gnyawed de cane mos' 'fo' ole Brer Fox could
git his legs oncrosst, en w'en dey kyard 'im de
cane, Brer Fox, he sot dar en study how he gwineter
make some mo' skuse fer nabbin' un um, en bimeby
he git up en git down de sifter w'at wuz hangin' on
de wall, en holler out:

"'Come yer, Rabs! Take dis yer sifter, en

run down't de spring en fetch me some fresh water.'

"De little Rabbits, dey run down't de spring, en try ter dip up de water wid de sifter, but co'se hit all run out, en hit keep on runnin' out, twel bimeby de little Rabbits sot down en 'gun ter cry. Den de little bird settin' up in de tree he begin for ter sing, en dis yer's de song wa't he sing :

"'Sifter hole water same ez a tray,
    Ef you fill it wid moss en dob it wid clay ;
De Fox git madder de longer you stay—
    Fill it wid moss en dob it wid clay.'

"Up dey jump, de little Rabbits did, en dey fix de sifter so 'twon't leak, en den dey kyar de water ter ole Brer Fox. Den Brer Fox he git mighty mad, en p'int out a great big stick er wood, en tell de little Rabbits fer ter put dat on de fier. De little chaps dey got 'roun' de wood, dey did, en dey lif' at it so hard twel dey could see der own sins, but de wood ain't budge. Den dey hear de little bird singin', en dis yer's de song wa't he sing :

"'Spit in yo' han's en tug it en toll it,
    En git behine it, en push it, en pole it ;
Spit in yo' han's en r'ar back and roll it.'

"En dos 'bout de time dey got de wood on de fier, der daddy, he come skippin' in, en de little bird, he flew'd away. Brer Fox, he seed his game wuz up, en 'twan't long 'fo' he make his skuse en start fer ter go.

"'You better stay en take a snack wid me, Brer Fox,' sez Brer Rabbit, sezee. 'Sence Brer Wolf done quit comin' en settin' up wid me, I gittin' so I feels right lonesome dese long nights,' sezee.

"But Brer Fox, he button up his coat-collar tight en des put out fer home. En dat w'at you better do, honey, kaze I see Miss Sally's shadder sailin' backerds en for'ds 'fo' de winder, en de fus' news you know she'll be spectin' un you."

XXIII

MR. RABBIT AND MR. BEAR

"Dar wuz one season," said Uncle Remus, pulling thoughtfully at his whiskers, "w'en Brer Fox say to hisse'f dat he speck he better whirl in en plant a goober-patch, en in dem days, mon, hit wuz tech en go. De wud wern't mo'n out'n his mouf 'fo' de groun' 'uz brok'd up en de goobers 'uz planted. Ole Brer Rabbit, he sot off en watch de motions, he did, en he sorter shet one eye en sing to his chilluns:

"'Ti-yi! Tungalee!
I eat um pea, I pick um pea.
Hit grow in de groun', hit grow so free;
Ti-yi! dem goober pea.'

"Sho' 'nuff w'en de goobers 'gun ter ripen up, eve'y time Brer Fox go down ter his patch, he fine whar somebody bin grabblin' 'mongst de vines, en he git mighty mad. He sorter speck who de somebody is, but ole Brer Rabbit he cover his tracks so cute dat Brer Fox dunner how ter ketch 'im. Bimeby, one day Brer Fox take a walk all roun' de groun'-pea patch, en 'twant long 'fo' he fine crack in de fence whar de rail done bin rub right smoove, en right dar he sot 'im a trap. He tuck'n ben' down a hick'ry saplin', growin' in de fence-cornder, en tie one een' un a plow-line on de

101

top, en in de udder een' he fix a loop-knot, en dat he fasten wid a trigger right in de crack. Nex' mawnin' w'en ole Brer Rabbit come slippin' 'long en crope thoo de crack, de loop-knot kotch 'im behime de fo' legs, en de saplin' flew'd up, en dar he wuz 'twix' de heavens en de yeth. Dar he swung, en he fear'd he gwineter fall, en he fear'd he wer'n't gwineter fall. W'ile he wuz a fixin' up a tale fer Brer Fox, he hear a lumberin' down de road, en present'y yer cum ole Brer B'ar amblin' 'long fum whar he bin takin' a bee-tree. Brer Rabbit, he hail 'im:

" ' Howdy, Brer B'ar ! '

" Brer B'ar, he look 'roun', en bimeby he see Brer Rabbit swingin' fum de saplin', en he holler out :

" ' Heyo, Brer Rabbit ! How you come on dis mawnin' ? '

" ' Much oblije, I'm middlin', Brer B'ar,' sez Brer Rabbit, sezee.

" Den Brer B'ar, he ax Brer Rabbit w'at he doin' up dar in de elements, en Brer Rabbit, he up'n say he makin' dollar minnit. Brer B'ar, he say how. Brer Rabbit say he keepin' crows out'n Brer Fox's groun'-pea patch, en den he ax Brer B'ar ef he do'n't wanter make dollar minnit, kaze he got big fambly er chilluns fer ter take keer un, en den he make sech nice skeer-crow. Brer B'ar 'low dat he take de job, en den Brer Rabbit show 'im how ter ben' down de saplin', en twan't long 'fo' Brer B'ar wuz swingin' up dar in Brer Rabbit place. Den Brer Rabbit, he put out fer Brer Fox house, en w'en he got dar he sing out :

" ' Brer Fox ! Oh, Brer Fox ! Come out yer, Brer Fox, en I'll show you de man w'at been stealin' yo' goobers.'

" Brer Fox, he grab up his walkin'-stick, en bofe un um went runnin' back down ter der goober-patch, en w'en dey got dar, sho 'nuff, dar wuz ole Brer B'ar.

" ' Oh, yes ! youer kotch, is you ? ' sez Brer Fox, en 'fo' Brer B'ar could 'splain, Brer Rabbit he jump up en down, en holler out :

" ' Hit 'im in de mouf, Brer Fox ; hit 'im in de mouf ; ' en Brer Fox, he draw back wid de walkin'-cane, en blip he tuck 'im, en eve'y time Brer B'ar'd try ter 'splain, Brer Fox'd shower down on him.

" W'iles all dis 'uz gwine on, Brer Rabbit, he slip off en git in a mud-hole en des lef' his eyes stickin' out, kaze he know'd dat Brer B'ar'd be a comin' atter 'im. Sho 'nuff, bimeby here come Brer B'ar down de road, en w'en he git ter de mud-hole, he say :

" ' Howdy, Brer Frog ; is you seed Brer Rabbit go by yer ? '

" ' He des gone by,' sez Brer Rabbit, en ole man B'ar tuck off down de road like a skeer'd mule, en Brer Rabbit, he come out en dry hisse'f in de sun, en go home ter his fambly same ez enny udder man."

" The Bear didn't catch the Rabbit, then ? " inquired the little boy, sleepily.

" Jump up fum dar, honey ! " exclaimed Uncle Remus, by way of reply. " I ain't got no time fer ter be settin' yer proppin' yo' eyeleds open."

XXIV

MR. BEAR CATCHES OLD MR. BULL-FROG

" WELL, Uncle Remus," said the little boy, count-
ing to see if he hadn't lost a marble somewhere,
" the Bear didn't catch the Rabbit after all, did
he ? "

" Now you talkin', honey," replied the old man,
his earnest face breaking up into little eddies of
smiles—" now you talkin' sho. 'Tain't bin proned
inter no Brer B'ar fer ter kotch Brer Rabbit. Hit
sorter like settin' a mule fer ter trap a hummin'-
bird. But Brer B'ar, he tuck'n got hisse'f inter
some mo' trubble, w'ich it look like it mighty easy.
Ef folks could make der livin' longer gittin' inter
trubble," continued the old man, looking curiously
at the little boy, " ole Miss Favers wouldn't be
bodder'n yo' ma fer ter borry a cup full er sugar
eve'y now en den ; en it look like ter me dat I
knows a nigger dat wouldn't be squattin' 'roun'
yer makin' dese yer fish-baskits."

" How did the Bear get into more trouble, Uncle
Remus ? " asked the little boy.

" Natchul, honey. Brer B'ar, he tuck a notion
dat ole Brer Bull-frog wuz de man wa't fool 'im,
en he say dat he'd come up wid 'im ef 'twuz a

105

year atterwuds. But 'twan't no year, an 'twan't
no mont', en mo'n dat, hit wan't skasely a week,
w'en bimeby one day Brer B'ar wuz gwine home
fum de takin' un a bee-tree, en lo en beholes,
who should he see but ole Brer Bull-frog settin'
out on de aidge er de mud-puddle fas' 'sleep!
Brer B'ar drap his axe, he did, en crope up, en
retch out wid his paw, en scoop old Brer Bull-frog
in des dis away." Here the old man used his
hand ladle-fashion, by way of illustration. "He
scoop 'im in, en dar he wuz. W'en Brer B'ar got
his clampers on 'im good, he sot down en talk at
'im."

"'Howdy, Brer Bull-frog, howdy! En how
yo' fambly? I hope deyer well, Brer Bull-frog,
kaze dis day you got some bizness wid me w'at'll
las' you a mighty long time.'

"Brer Bull-frog, he dunner w'at ter say. He
dunner wat's up, en he don't say nuthin'. Ole
Brer B'ar he keep runnin' on:

"'Youer de man w'at tuck en fool me 'bout
Brer Rabbit t'er day. You had yo' fun, Brer
Bull-frog, en now I'll git mine.'

"Den Brer Bull-frog, he gin ter git skeer'd, he
did, en he up'n say:

"'W'at I bin doin', Brer B'ar? How I bin
foolin' you?'

"Den Brer B'ar laff, en make like he dunno, but
he keep on talkin':

"'Oh, no, Brer Bull-frog! You ain't de man
w'at stick yo' head up out'n de water en tell me
Brer Rabbit done gone on by. Oh, no! you
ain't de man. I boun' you ain't. 'Bout dat
time, you wuz at home wid yo' fambly, whar you
allers is. I dunner whar you wuz, but I knows
whar you is, Brer Bull-frog, en hit's you en me

fer it. Atter de sun goes down dis day you don't
fool no mo' folks gwine 'long dis road.'

"Co'se, Brer Bull-frog dunner w'at Brer B'ar
drivin' at, but he knows sump'n hatter be done,
en dat mighty soon, kaze Brer B'ar 'gun to snap
his jaws tergedder en foam at de mouf, en Brer Bull-
frog holler out:

"'Oh, pray, Brer B'ar! Lemme off dis time,
en I won't never do so no mo'. Oh, pray, Brer
B'ar! do lemme off dis time, en I'll show you de
fattes' bee-tree in de woods.'

"Ole Brer B'ar, he chomp his toofies en foam at
de mouf. Brer Bull-frog he des up'n squall:

"'Oh, pray, Brer B'ar! I won't never do so
no mo'! Oh, pray, Brer B'ar! lemme off dis
time!'

"But ole Brer B'ar say he gwineter make way
wid 'im, en den he sot en study, ole Brer B'ar did,
how he gwineter squench Brer Bull-frog. He
know he can't drown 'im, en he ain't got no fier fer
ter bu'n 'im, en he git mighty pestered. Bimeby
ole Brer Bull-frog he sorter stop his cryin' en his
boo-hooin', en he up'n say:

"'Ef you gwineter kill me, Brer B'ar, kyar me
ter dat big flat rock out dar on de aidge er de mill-
pon', whar I kin see my fambly, en atter I see um,
den you kin take you axe en squash me.'

"Dis look so fa'r and squar' dat Brer B'ar he
'gree, en he take ole Brer Bull-frog by wunner
his behime legs, en sling his axe on his shoulder, en
off he put fer de big flat rock. When he git dar he
lay Brer Bull-frog down on de rock, en Brer Bull-
frog make like he lookin' 'roun' fer his folks. Den
Brer B'ar, he draw long breff en pick up his axe.
Den he spit in his han's en draw back en come
down on de rock—pow!"

"Did he kill the frog, Uncle Remus?" asked the little boy, as the old man paused to scoop up a thimbleful of glowing embers in his pipe.

"'Deed, en dat he didn't, honey. 'Twix' de time w'en Brer B'ar raise up wid his axe en w'en he come down wid it, ole Brer Bull-frog he lipt up en dove down in de mill-pon', kerblink-kerblunk! En w'en he riz way out in de pon' he riz a singin', en dis yer's de song w'at he sing:

"'Ingle-go-jang, my joy, my joy—
    Ingle-go-jang, my joy!
I'm right at home, my joy, my joy—
    Ingle-go-jang, my joy!'"

"That's a mighty funny song," said the little boy.

"Funny now, I speck," said the old man, "but 'twern't funny in dem days, en 'twouldn't be funny now ef folks know'd much 'bout de Bull-frog langwidge ez dey useter. Dat's w'at."

XXV

HOW MR. RABBIT LOST HIS FINE BUSHY TAIL

"ONE time," said Uncle Remus, sighing heavily and settling himself back in his seat with an air of melancholy resignation—"one time Brer Rabbit wuz gwine 'long down de road shakin' his big bushy tail, en feelin' des ez scrumpshus ez a bee-martin wid a fresh bug." Here the old man paused and glanced at the little boy, but it was evident that the youngster had become so accustomed to the marvellous developments of Uncle Remus's stories, that the extraordinary statement made no unusual impression upon him. Therefore the old man began again, and this time in a louder and more insinuating tone:

"One time ole man Rabbit, he wuz gwine 'long down de road shakin' his long, bushy tail, en feelin' mighty biggity."

This was effective.

"Great goodness, Uncle Remus!" exclaimed the little boy in open-eyed wonder, "everybody knows that rabbits haven't got long, bushy tails."

The old man shifted his position in his chair and allowed his venerable head to drop forward until his whole appearance was suggestive of the deepest dejection; and this was intensified by a groan that seemed to be the result of great mental agony.

Finally he spoke, but not as addressing himself to the little boy.

"I notices dat dem fokes w'at makes a great 'miration 'bout w'at dey knows is des de folks w'ich you can't put no 'pennunce in w'en de 'cashun come up. Yer one un um now, en he done come en excuse me er 'lowin' dat rabbits is got long, bushy tails, w'ich goodness knows ef I'd a dremp' it, I'd a whirl in en ondremp it."

"Well, but Uncle Remus, you said rabbits had long bushy tails," replied the little boy. "Now you know you did."

"Ef I ain't fergit it off'n my mine, I say dat ole Brer Rabbit wuz gwine down de big road shakin' his long, bushy tail. Dat w'at I say, en dat I stan's by."

The little boy looked puzzled, but he didn't say anything. After a while the old man continued:

"Now, den, ef dat's 'greed ter, I'm gwine on, en ef tain't 'greed ter, den I'm gwineter pick up my cane en look atter my own intrust. I git wuk lyin' roun' yer dat's des natally gittin' moldy."

The little boy remained quiet, and Uncle Remus proceeded:

"One day Brer Rabbit wuz gwine down de road shakin' his long, bushy tail, w'en who should he strike up wid but ole Brer Fox gwine amblin' long wid a big string er fish ! W'en dey pass de time er day wid wunner nudder, Brer Rabbit, he open up de confab, he did, en he ax Brer Fox whar he git dat nice string er fish, en Brer Fox, he up'n 'spon' dat he kotch um, en Brer Rabbit, he say whar'bouts, en Brer Fox, he say down at de babtizin' creek, en Brer Rabbit he ax how, kaze in dem days dey wuz monstus fon' er minners, en Brer Fox, he sot down on a log, he did, en he up'n.

tell Brer Rabbit dat all he gotter do fer ter git er big mess er minners is ter go ter de creek atter sun down, en drap his tail in de water en set dar twel daylight, en den draw up a whole armful er fishes, en dem w'at he don't want, he kin fling back.   Right dar's whar Brer Rabbit drap his watermillion, kaze he tuck'n sot out dat night en went a fishin'.   De wedder wuz sorter cole, en Brer Rabbit, he got 'im a bottle er dram en put out fer de creek, en w'en he git dar he pick out a good place, en he sorter squot down, he did, en let his tail hang in de water.   He sot dar, en he sot dar, en he drunk his dram, en he think he gwineter freeze, but bimeby day come, en dar de wuz.   He make a pull, en he feel like he comin' in two, en he fetch nudder jerk, en lo en beholes, whar wuz his tail ? "

There was a long pause.

" Did it come off, Uncle Remus ? " asked the little boy, presently.

" She did dat ! " replied the old man with unction.   " She did dat, and dat w'at make all deze yer bob-tail rabbits w'at you see hoppin' en skaddlin thoo de woods."

" Are they all that way just because the old Rabbit lost his tail in the creek ? " asked the little boy.

" Dat's it, honey," replied the old man.   " Dat's w'at dey tells me.   Look like dey er bleedzd ter take atter der pa."

XXVI

MR. TARRYPIN SHOWS HIS STRENGTH

"BRER TARRYPIN wuz de out'nes' man," said Uncle Remus, rubbing his hands together contemplatively, and chuckling to himself in a very significant manner; "he wuz de out'nes' man er de whole gang. He wuz dat."

The little boy sat perfectly quiet, betraying no impatience when Uncle Remus paused to hunt, first in one pocket and then in another, for enough crumbs of tobacco to replenish his pipe. Presently the old man proceeded:

"One night Miss Meadows en de gals dey gun a candy-pullin', en so many er de nabers come in 'sponse ter de invite dat dey hatter put de 'lasses in de wash pot en b'il' de fier in de yard. Brer B'ar, he hope[1] Miss Meadows bring de wood, Brer Fox, he men' de fier, Brer Wolf, he kep' de dogs off, Brer Rabbit, he grease de bottom er de plates fer ter keep de candy fum stickin', en Brer Tarrypin, he klum up in a cheer, en say he'd watch en see dat de 'lasses didn't bile over. Dey wuz all dere, en dey wern't cuttin' up no didos, nudder, kaze Miss Meadows, she done put her foot down, she did, en say dat w'en dey come ter her

---

[1] Holp; helped.

place dey hatter hang up a flag er truce at de front
gate en 'bide by it.

"Well, den, w'iles dey wuz all a-settin' dar en
de 'lasses wuz a-bilin' en a-blubberin', dey got ter
runnin' on talkin' mighty biggity. Brer Rabbit,
he say he de swiffes'; but Brer Tarrypin, he rock
'long in de cheer en watch de 'lasses. Brer Fox,
he say he de sharpes', but Brer Tarrypin he rock
'long. Brer Wolf, he say he de mos' suvvigus,
but Brer Tarrypin, he rock en he rock 'long. Brer
B'ar, he say he de mos' stronges', but Brer Tarrypin he rock, en he keep on rockin'. Bimeby, he
sorter shet one eye, en say, sezee:

"'Hit look like 'periently dat de old hardshell
ain't nowhars 'longside er dis crowd, yit yer I is,
en I'm de same man w'at show Brer Rabbit dat he
ain't de swiffes'; en I'm de same man w'at kin
show Brer B'ar dat he ain't de stronges',' sezee.

"Den dey all laff en holler, kaze it look like
Brer B'ar mo' stronger dan a steer. Bimeby, Miss
Meadows, she up'n ax, she did, how he gwine do it.

"'Gimme a good strong rope,' sez Brer Tarrypin, sezee, 'en lemme git in er puddle er water, en
den let Brer B'ar see ef he kin pull me out,' sezee.

"Den dey all laff g'in, en Brer B'ar, he ups en
sez, sezee: 'We ain't got no rope,' sezee.

"'No,' sez Brer Tarrypin, sezee, 'en needer is
you got de strenk,' sezee, en den Brer Tarrypin, he
rock en rock 'long, en watch de 'lasses a-bilin' en a-
blubberin'.

"Atter w'ile Miss Meadows, she up en say, she
did, dat she'd take'n loan de young men her bed-
cord, en w'iles de candy wuz a coolin' in de plates,
dey could all go ter de branch en see Brer Tarrypin kyar out his projick. Brer Tarrypin," continued Uncle Remus, in a tone at once confidential

and argumentative, "wern't much bigger'n de pa'm er my han', en it look mighty funny fer ter year 'im braggin' 'bout how he kin outpull Brer B'ar. But dey got de bed-cord atter w'ile, en den dey all put out ter de branch. W'en Brer Tarrypin fine de place he wanter, he tuck one een' er de bed-cord, en gun de yuther een' ter Brer B'ar.

" 'Now den, ladies en gents', sez Brer Tarrypin, sezee, 'you all go wid Brer B'ar up dar in de woods en I'll stay yer, en w'en you year me holler, den's de time fer Brer B'ar fer ter see ef he kin haul in de slack er de rope. You all take keer er dat ar een',' sezee, 'en I'll take keer er dis yer een',' sezee.

"Den dey all put out en lef' Brer Tarrypin at de branch, en w'en dey got good en gone, he dove down inter de water, he did, en tie de bed-cord hard en fas' ter wunner deze yer big clay-roots, en den he riz up en gin a woop.

"Brer B'ar he wrop de bed-cord roun' his han', en wink at de gals, en wid dat he gin a big juk, but Brer Tarrypin ain't budge. Den he take bofe han's en gin a big pull, but, all de same, Brer Tarrypin ain't budge. Den he tu'n 'roun', he did, en put de rope cross his shoulders en try ter walk off wid Brer Tarrypin, but Brer Tarrypin look like he don't feel like walkin'. Den Brer Wolf, he put in en hope Brer B'ar pull, but dez like he didn't, en den dey all hope 'im, en, bless grashus ! wiles dey wuz all a-pullin', Brer Tarrypin, he holler, en ax um w'y dey don't take up de slack. Den w'en Brer Tarrypin feel um quit pullin', he dove down, he did, en ontie de rope, en by de time dey got ter branch, Brer Tarrypin, he wuz settin' in de aidge er de water des ez natchul ez de nex' un, en he up'n say, sezee :

"'Dat las' pull er yone wuz a mighty stiff un, en a leetle mo'n you'd er had me,' sezee. 'Youer monstus stout, Brer B'ar,' sezee, 'en you pulls like a yoke er steers, but I sorter had de purchis on you,' sezee.

"Den Brer B'ar, bein's his mouf 'gun ter water atter de sweetnin', he up'n say he speck de candy's ripe, en off dey put atter it!"

"It's a wonder," said the little boy, after awhile, "that the rope didn't break."

"Break who?" exclaimed Uncle Remus, with a touch of indignation in his tone—"break who? In dem days, Miss Meadows's bed-cord would a-hilt a mule."

This put an end to whatever doubts the child might have entertained.

XXVII

WHY MR. POSSUM HAS NO HAIR ON HIS TAIL

"HIT look like ter me," said Uncle Remus, frowning, as the little boy came hopping and skipping into the old man's cabin, "dat I see a young un 'bout yo' size playin' en makin' free wid dem ar chilluns er ole Miss Favers's yistiddy, en w'en I seed dat, I drap my axe, en I come in yer en sot flat down right whar youer settin' now, en I say ter myse'f dat it's 'bout time fer ole Remus fer ter hang up en quit. Dat's des zackly w'at I say."

"Well, Uncle Remus, they called me," said the little boy, in a penitent tone. "They come and called me, and said they had a pistol and some powder over there."

"Dar now!" exclaimed the old man, indignantly. "Dar now! w'at I bin sayin'? Hit's des a born blessin' dat you wa'n't brung home on a litter wid bofe eyeballs hangin' out en one year clean gone; dat's w'at 't is! Hit's des a born blessin'. Hit hope me up might'ly de udder day w'en I hear Miss Sally layin' down de law 'bout you en dem Favers chillun, yit, lo en beholes, de fus news I knows yer you is han'-in-glove wid um. Hit's nuff fer ter fetch ole Miss right up out'n dat berryin'-groun' fum down dar in Putmon County, en w'at yo' gran'ma wouldn't er stood me en yo' ma ain't

117

gwineter stan' nudder, en de nex' time I hear
'bout sech a come off az dis, right den en dar I'm
boun' ter lay de case 'fo' Miss Sally. Dem Favers's
wa'n't no 'count 'fo' de war, en dey wa'n't
'count endurin' er de war, en dey ain't no 'count
atterwards, en w'iles my head's hot you ain't
gwineter go mixin' up yo'se'f wid de riff-raff er
creashun."

The little boy made no further attempt to justify
his conduct. He was a very wise little boy, and
he knew that, in Uncle Remus's eyes, he had been
guilty of a flagrant violation of the family code.
Therefore, instead of attempting to justify himself,
he pleaded guilty, and promised that he would
never do so any more. After this there was a long
period of silence, broken only by the vigorous
style in which Uncle Remus puffed away at his
pipe. This was the invariable result. Whenever
the old man had occasion to reprimand the little
boy—and the occasions were frequent—he would
relapse into a dignified but stubborn silence.
Presently the youngster drew forth from his pocket
a long piece of candle. The sharp eyes of the old
man saw it at once.

"Don't you come a-tellin' me dat Miss Sally
gun you dat," he exclaimed, "kaze she didn't.
En I lay you hatterbe monstus sly 'fo' you gotter
chance fer ter snatch up dat piece er cannle."

"Well, Uncle Remus," the little boy explained,
"it was lying there all by itself, and I just thought
I'd fetch it out to you."

"Dat's so, honey," said Uncle Remus, greatly
mollified; "dat's so kaze by now some er dem
yuther niggers 'ud er done had her light up. Dey
er mighty biggity, dem house niggers is, but I
notices dat dey don't let nuthin' pass. Dey goes

'long wid der han's en der mouf open, en w'at one don't ketch de tother one do."

There was another pause, and finally the little boy said:

"Uncle Remus, you know you promised to-day to tell me why the 'Possum has no hair on his tail."

"Law, honey! ain't you done gone en fergot dat off'n yo' mine yit? Hit look like ter me," continued the old man, leisurely refilling his pipe, "dat she sorter run like dis: One time ole Brer Possum, he git so hongry, he did, dat he bleedzed fer ter have a mess er 'simmons. He monstus lazy man, ole Brer Possum wuz, but bimeby his stummuck 'gun ter growl en holler at 'im so dat he des hatter rack 'roun' en hunt up sump'n; en w'iles he wuz rackin' 'roun', who sh'd he run up wid but Brer Rabbit, en dey wuz hail-fellers, kaze Brer Possum, he ain't bin bodder'n Brer Rabbit like dem yuther beas's. Dey sot down by de side er de big road, en dar dey jabber en confab 'mong wunner nudder, twel bimeby old Brer Possum, he take 'n tell Brer Rabbit dat he mos pe'sh out, en Brer Rabbit, he lip up in de a'r, he did, en smack his han's tergedder, en say dat he know right whar Brer Possum kin git a bait er 'simmons. Den Brer Possum, he say whar, en Brer Rabbit, he say w'ich 'twuz over at Brer B'ar's 'simmon orchard."

"Did the Bear have a 'simmon orchard, Uncle Remus?" the little boy asked.

"Co'se, honey, kaze in dem days Brer B'ar wuz a bee-hunter. He make his livin' findin' bee trees, en de way he fine um he plant 'im some 'simmon-trees, w'ich de bees dey'd come ter suck de 'simmons, en den ole Brer B'ar he'd watch um whar dey'd go, en den he'd be mighty ap' fer ter come up

wid um. No matter 'bout dat, de 'simmon patch
'uz dar des like I tell you, en ole Brer Possum mouf
'gun ter water soon's he year talk un um, en mos'
'fo' Brer Rabbit done tellin' 'im de news, Brer
Possum, he put out, he did, en 'twa'n't long 'fo'
he wuz perch up in de highes' tree in Brer B'ar
'simmon patch. But Brer Rabbit, he done 'termin'
fer ter see some fun, en w'iles all dis 'uz gwine on,
he run 'roun' ter Brer B'ar house, en holler en tell
'im w'ich dey wuz somebody 'stroyin' un his 'simmons, en Brer B'ar, he hustle off fer ter ketch 'im.

"Eve'y now en den Brer Possum think he year
Brer B'ar comin', but he keep on sayin', sezee:

"'I'll des git one mo' 'simmon en den I'll go;
one 'simmon 'mo en den I'll go.'

"Las' he year Brer B'ar comin' sho nuff, but
'twuz de same ole chune—' One 'simmon mo' en den
I'll go'—en des 'bout dat time Brer B'ar busted inter
de patch, en gin de tree a shake, en Brer Possum,
he drapt out longer de yuther ripe 'simmons, but
time he totch de groun' he got his foots tergedder,
en he lit out fer de fence same ez a race-hoss, en
'cross dat patch him en Brer B'ar had it, en Brer
B'ar gain' eve'y jump, twel time Brer Possum make
de fence Brer B'ar grab 'im by de tail, en Brer
Possum, he went out 'tween de rails en gin a power-
ful juk en pull his tail out 'twixt Brer B'ar tuskes;
en, lo en beholes, Brer B'ar hole so tight, en Brer
Possum pull so hard dat all de ha'r come off in Brer
B'ar's mouf, w'ich, ef Brer Rabbit hadn't er happen
up wid a go'd er water, Brer B'ar'd er got strankle.

"Fum dat day ter dis," said Uncle Remus,
knocking the ashes carefully out of his pipe, "Brer
Possum ain't had no ha'r on his tail, en needer do
his chilluns."

XXVIII

THE END OF MR. BEAR

THE next time the little boy sought Uncle Remus
out, he found the old man unusually cheerful and
good-humoured. His rheumatism had ceased to
trouble him, and he was even disposed to be bois-
terous. He was singing when the little boy got
near the cabin, and the child paused on the outside
to listen to the vigorous but mellow voice of the
old man, as it rose and fell with the burden of the
curiously plaintive song—a senseless affair so far
as the words were concerned, but sung to a melody
almost thrilling in its sweetness :

> " Han' me down my walkin'-cane
>   (Hey my Lily ! go down de road !)
> Yo' true lover gone down de lane
>   (Hey my Lily ! go down de road !) "

The quick ear of Uncle Remus, however, had
detected the presence of the little boy, and he
allowed his song to run into a recitation of nonsense,
of which the following if it be rapidly spoken,
will give a faint idea :

" Ole M'er Jackson, fines' confraction, fell down-
sta'rs fer to git satisfaction ; big Bill Fray, he rule
de day, eve'ything he call fer come one. two by
three. Gwine 'long one day, met Johnny Huby,
ax him grine nine yards er steel fer me, tole me
w'ich he couldn't ; den I hist 'im over Hickerson

Dickerson's barn-doors; knock 'im ninety-nine miles under water, w'en he rise, he rise in Pike straddle un a hanspike, en I lef' 'im dar smokin' er de hornpipe, Juba reda seda breda. Aunt Kate at de gate; I want to eat, she fry de meat en gimme skin, w'ich I fling it back ag'in. Juba!"

All this, rattled off at a rapid rate and with apparent seriousness, was calculated to puzzle the little boy, and he slipped into his accustomed seat with an expression of awed bewilderment upon his face.

"Hit's all des dat away, honey," continued the old man, with the air of one who had just given an important piece of information. "En w'en you bin cas'n shadders long ez de ole nigger, den you'll fine out who's w'ich, en w'ich's who."

The little boy made no response. He was in thorough sympathy with all the whims and humours of the old man, and his capacity for enjoying them was large enough to include even those he could not understand. Uncle Remus was finishing an axe-handle, and upon these occasions it was his custom to allow the child to hold one end while he applied sand-paper to the other. These relations were pretty soon established, to the mutual satisfaction of the parties most interested, and the old man continued his remarks, but this time not at random:

"W'en I see deze yer swell-head folks like dat 'oman w'at come en tell yo' ma 'bout you chunkin' at her chilluns, w'ich yo' ma make Mars John strop you, hit make my mine run back to old Brer B'ar. Ole Brer B'ar, he got de swell-headedness hisse'f, en ef der wuz enny swinkin', hit swunk too late fer to he'p ole Brer B'ar. Leas'ways da'ts w'at dey tells me, en I ain't never yearn it 'sputed."

"Was the Bear's head sure enough swelled, Uncle Remus?"

"Now you talkin', honey!" exclaimed the old man.

"Goodness! what made it swell?"

This was Uncle Remus's cue. Applying the sand-paper to the axe-helve with gentle vigour, he began:

"One time when Brer Rabbit wus gwine lopin' home fum a frolic w'at dey bin havin' up at Miss Meadows's, who should he happin up wid but ole Brer B'ar. Co'se, atter w'at done pass 'twix um dey wa'n't no good feelin's 'tween Brer Rabbit en ole Brer B'ar, but Brer Rabbit he wanter save his manners, en so he holler out:

"'Heyo, Brer B'ar! how you come on? I ain't seed you in a coon's age. How all down at yo' house? How Miss Brune en Miss Brindle?'"

"Who was that, Uncle Remus?" the little boy interrupted.

"Miss Brune en Miss Brindle? Miss Brune wuz Brer B'ar's ole 'oman, en Miss Brindle wuz his gal. Dat w'at dey call um in dem days. So den Brer Rabbit, he ax him howdy, he did, en Brer B'ar, he 'spon' dat he wuz mighty po'ly, en dey amble 'long, dey did, sorter familious like, but Brer Rabbit, he keep one eye on Brer B'ar, he study how he gwine nab Brer Rabbit. Las' Brer Rabbit, he up'n say, sezee:

"'Brer B'ar, I speck I got some bizness cut out fer you,' sezee.

"'W'at dat, Brer Rabbit?' sez Brer B'ar, sezee.

"'W'iles I wuz cleanin' up my new-groun' day 'fo' yistiddy', sez Brer Rabbit, sezee, 'I come 'cross wunner deze yer ole time bee trees. Hit start holler at de bottom, en stay holler plum ter de top, en de honey's des natally oozin' out, en ef you'll drap yo' 'gagements en go 'longer me,' sez Brer Rabbit, sezee, ' you'll git a bait dat'll las' you en yo' family twel de middle er nex' mont',' sezee.

" Brer B'ar say he much oblije en he b'leeve he'll go 'long, en wid dat dey put out fer Brer Rabbit's new-groun', w'ich twa'n't so mighty fur. Leas'-ways, dey got dar atter w'ile. Ole Brer B'ar, he 'low dat he kin smell de honey. Brer Rabbit, he 'low dat he kin see de honey-koam. Brer B'ar, he 'low dat he kin hear de bees a-zoonin'. Dey stan' 'roun' en talk biggity, dey did, twel bimeby Brer Rabbit, he up'n say, sezee :

" ' You do de clim'in', Brer B'ar, en I'll do de rushin' 'roun' ; you clime up ter de hole, en I'll take dis yer pine pole en shove de honey up whar you kin git 'er,' sezee.

" Ole Brer B'ar, he spit on his han's en skint up de tree, en jam his head in de hole, en sho nuff, Brer Rabbit, he grab de pine pole, en de way he stir up dem bees wuz sinful—dat's w'at it wuz. Hit wuz sinful. En de bees dey swawm'd on Brer B'ar's head, twel 'fo' he could take it out'n de hole hit wuz done swell up bigger dan dat dinner-pot, en dar he swung, en ole Brer Rabbit, he dance 'roun' en sing :

" ' Tree stan' high, but honey mighty sweet—
    Watch dem bees wid stingers on der feet.'

" But dar ole Brer B'ar hung, en ef his head ain't swunk, I speck he hangin' dar yit—dat w'at I speck.''

XXIX

MR. FOX GETS INTO SERIOUS BUSINESS

" Hit turn out one time," said Uncle Remus, grinding some crumbs of tobacco between the palms of his hands, preparatory to enjoying his usual smoke after supper—" hit turn out one time dat Brer Rabbit make so free wid de man's collard-patch dat de man he tuck'n sot a trap fer ole Brer Rabbit."

" Which man was that, Uncle Remus ? " asked the little boy.

" Des a man, honey. Dat's all. Dat's all I knows —des wunner deze yer man's w'at you see trollopin 'roun' eve'y day. Nobody ain't never year w'at his name is, en ef dey did dey kep' de news mighty close fum me. Ef dis yer man is bleedzd fer ter have a name, den I'm done, kaze you'll hatter go fudder dan me. Ef you bleedzd ter know mo' dan w'at I duz, den you'll hatter hunt up some er deze yer niggers w'at's sprung up sence I commence fer ter shed my ha'r."

" Well, I just thought, Uncle Remus," said the little boy, in a tone remarkable for self-deprecation, " that the man had a name."

" Tooby sho," replied the old man, with unction, puffing away at his pipe. " Co'se. Dat w'at make I say w'at I duz. Dis yer man mout a-had a name, en den ag'in he moutn't. He mout er bin

125

name Slipshot Sam, en he mouter bin name ole
One-eye Riley, w'ich ef 'twuz hit ain't bin handed
roun' ter me. But dis yer man, he in de tale, en
w'at we gwine do wid 'im ? Dat's de p'int, kaze
w'en I git ter huntin' 'roun' 'mong my 'membunce
atter dish yer Mister W'atyoumaycollum's name,
she ain't dar. Now den, less des call 'im Mr. Man
en let 'im go at dat."

The silence of the little boy gave consent.

"One time," said Uncle Remus, carefully taking
up the thread of the story where it had been dropped,
"hit turn out dat Brer Rabbit bin makin' so free
wid Mr. Man's greens en truck dat Mr. Man, he
tuck'n sot a trap fer Brer Rabbit, en Brer Rabbit
he so greedy dat he tuck'n walk right spang in it
'fo' he know hisse'f. Well, 'twa'n't long 'fo' yer come
Mr. Man, broozin' 'roun', en he ain't no sooner see
ole Brer Rabbit dan he smack his han's tergedder
en holler out :

"'Youer nice feller, you is ! Yer you bin gobblin'
up my green truck, en now you tryin' ter tote off
my trap. You er mighty nice chap—dat's w'at
you is ! But now dat I got you, I'll des 'bout
settle wid you fer de ole en de new.'

"En wid dat, Mr. Man, he go off, he did, down in
de bushes atter han'ful er switches. Ole Brer
Rabbit he ain't sayin' nuthin', but he feelin' mighty
lonesome, en he sot dar lookin' like eve'y minnit
wuz gwineter be de nex'. En w'iles Mr. Man wuz
prepa'r'n his bresh-broom, who should come p'radin'
'long but Brer Fox ? Brer Fox made a great
'miration, he did, 'bout de fix w'at he fine Brer
Rabbit in, but Brer Rabbit he make like he fit
ter kill hisse'f laffin', en he up'n tell Brer Fox, he
did, dat Miss Meadows's fokes want 'im ter go down
ter der house in 'tennunce on a weddin', en he 'low

w'ich he couldn't, en dey 'low how he could, en den
bimeby dey take'n tie 'im dar w'iles dey go atter
de preacher, so he be dar w'en dey come back. En
mo'n dat, Brer Rabbit up'n tell Brer Fox dat his
chillun's mighty low wid de fever, en he bleedzd
ter go atter some pill's fer'm, en he ax Brer Fox
fer ter take his place en go down ter Miss Meadows's
en have nice time wid de gals. Brer Fox, he in fer
dem kinder pranks, en 'twa'n't no time 'fo' Brer
Rabbit had ole Brer Fox harness up dar in his
place, en den he make like he got ter make 'as'e
en git de pills for dem sick chilluns. Brer Rabbit
wa'n't mo'n out er sight 'fo' yer come Mr. Man
wid a han'ful er hick'ries, but w'en he see Brer
Fox tied up dar, he look like he 'stonished.

" ' Heyo ! ' sez Mr. Man, sezee, ' you done change
colour, en you done got bigger, en yo' tail done grow
out. W'at kin'er w'atzyname is you, ennyhow ? '
sezee.

" Brer Fox, he stay still, en Mr. Man, he talk on :

" ' Hit's mighty big luck,' sezee, ' ef w'en I catch
the chap w'at nibble my greens, likewise I ketch
de feller w'at gnyaw my goose,' sezee, en wid dat
he let inter Brer Fox wid de hick'ries, en de way he
play rap-jacket was a caution ter de naberhood.
Brer Fox, he juk en he jump, en he squeal en he
squall, but Mr. Man, he shower down on 'im, he
did, like fightin' a red was'-nes'."

The little boy laughed, and Uncle Remus supple-
mented this endorsement of his descriptive powers
with a most infectious chuckle.

"Bimeby," continued the old man, " de switches,
dey got frazzle out, en Mr. Man he put out atter
mo', en w'en he done got fa'rly outer yearin', Brer
Rabbit, he show'd up, he did, kaze he des bin hidin'
out in de bushes lis'nin' at de racket, en he 'low hit

mighty funny dat Miss Meadows ain't come 'long, kaze he done bin down ter de doctor house, en dat's fudder dan de preacher, yit. Brer Rabbit make like he hurr'in' on home, but Brer Fox, he open up, he did, en he say:

"'I thank you fer ter tu'n me loose, Brer Rabbit, en I'll be 'blije,' sezee, 'kaze you done tie me up so tight dat it make my head swim, en I don't speck I'd las' fer ter git ter Miss Meadows's,' sezee.

"Brer Rabbit, he sot down sorter keerless like, en begin fer ter scratch one year like a man studyin' 'bout sump'n.

"'Dat's so, Brer Fox,' sezee, 'you duz look sorter stove up. Look like sump'n bin onkoamin' yo' ha'rs,' sezee.

"Brer Fox ain't sayin' nothin', but Brer Rabbit he keep on talkin':

"'Dey ain't no bad feelin's 'twixt us, is dey, Brer Fox? Kaze ef dey is, I ain't got no time fer ter be tarryin' 'roun' yer.'

"Brer Fox say w'ich he don't have no onfrennelness, en wid dat Brer Rabbit cut Brer Fox loose des in time fer ter hear Mr. Man w'isserlin up his dogs, en one went one way en de udder went nudder."

XXX

HOW MR. RABBIT SUCCEEDED IN RAISING A DUST

" In dem times," said Uncle Remus, gazing admir-
ingly at himself in a fragment of looking-glass,
" Brer Rabbit, en Brer Fox, en Brer Coon, en dem
yuther beas's go co'tin en sparklin' 'roun' de naberhood mo' samer dan folks. 'Twan't no ' Lemme
a hoss,' ner ' Fetch me my buggy,' but dey des
up'n lit out en tote deyse'f. Dar's ole Brer Fox,
he des wheel 'roun' en fetch his flank one swipe
wid 'is tongue, en he'd be koam up; en Brer
Rabbit, he des spit on his han' en twis' it 'roun'
'mongst de roots un his years en his ha'r'd be roach.
Dey wuz dat flirtashus," continued the ole man,
closing one eye at his image in the glass, " dat Miss
Meadows en de gals don't see no peace fum one week
een' ter de udder. Chuseday wuz same as Sunday,
en Friday wuz same as Chuseday, en it come down
ter dat pass w'en Miss Meadows 'ud have chicken-
fixins fer dinner, in 'ud drap Brer Fox en Brer Possum, en w'en she'd have fried greens in 'ud pop ole
Brer Rabbit, twel 'las' Miss Meadows, she tuck'n tell
de gals dat she be dad-blame ef she gwineter keep
no tavvun. So dey fix it up 'mong deyse'f, Miss
Meadows en de gals did, dat de nex' time de gents
call dey'd gin um a game. De gents, dey wuz
a co'tin, but Miss Meadows, she don't wanter marry
none un um, en needer duz de gals, en likewise dey

don't wanter have um pester'n 'roun'. Las',
one Chuseday, Miss Meadows, she tole um dat ef
dey come down ter her house de nex' Sat'day evenin',
de whole caboodle un um 'ud go down de road a
piece, whar der wuz a big flint rock, en de man w'at
could take a sludge - hammer en knock de
dus' out'n dat rock, he wuz de man w'at 'ud get
de pick er de gals. Dey all say dey gwine do it,
but ole Brer Rabbit, he crope off whar der wuz a
cool place under some jimson weeds, en dar he sot
wukking his mind how he gwineter git dus' out'n
dat rock. Bimeby, w'ile he wuz a-settin' dar, up
he jump and crack his heels tergedder en sing out:

" ' Make a bow ter de Buzzard en den ter de Crow,
    Takes a limber-toe gemmun fer ter jump Jim Crow,'

en wid dat he put out for Brer Coon house en borrer
his slippers. W'en Sat'day evenin' come, dey wuz
all dere. Miss Meadows, en de gals, dey wuz dere ;
en Brer Coon, en Brer Fox, en Brer Possum, en
Brer Tarrypin, dey wuz dere."

"Where was the Rabbit ?" the little boy asked.

"Youk'n put yo' 'pennunce in ole Brer Rabbit,"
the old man replied with a chuckle. "He wuz dere,
but he shuffle up kinder late, kase w'en Miss Meadows ·en de ballunce un um done gone down ter de
place, Brer Rabbit, he crope roun' ter de ash-hopper,
en fill Brer Coon slippers full er ashes, en den he
tuck'n put um on en march off. He got dar atter
'w'ile, en soon's Miss Meadows en de gals seed im,
dey up'n giggle, en make a great 'miration kaze
Brer Rabbit got on slippers. Brer Fox, he so
smart, he holler out, he did, en say he lay Brer
Rabbit got de groun'-eatch, but Brer Rabbit, he
sorter shet one eye, he did, en say, sezee :

" ' I bin so useter ridin' hoss-back, ez des ladies

knows, dat I'm gittin' sorter tender-footed ; ' en dey don't hear much mo' fum Brer Fox dat day, kaze he 'member how Brer Rabbit done bin en rid him ; en hit 'uz des 'bout much ez Miss Meadows en de gals could do fer ter keep der snickers fum gitting up a 'sturbance 'mong de congergashun. But, never mine dat, old Brer Rabbit he wuz dar, en he so brash dat leetle mo' en he'd er grab up de sludge-hammer en er open up de racket 'fo' ennybody gun de word ; but Brer Fox, he shove Brer Rabbit out'n de way en pick up de sludge hisse'f. Now den," continued the old man, with pretty much the air of one who had been the master of similar ceremonies, " de progance wuz dis yer : Eve'y gent wer ter have th'ee licks at de rock, en de gent w'at fetch de dus' he wer de one w'at gwineter take de pick er de gals.   Old Brer Fox, he grab de sludge-hammer, he did, en he come down on de rock—*blim !* No dus' ain't come. Den he draw back en down he come ag'in—*blam !* No dus' ain't come.   Den he spit in his han's, en he give 'er a big swing en down she come—*ker-blap !* En yit no dus' ain't flew'd. Den Brer Possum he make triul, en Brer Coon, en all de ballunce un um 'cep' Brer Tarrypin, en he 'low dat he got a crick in his neck.   Den Brer Rabbit, he grab holt er de sludge, en he lift up in de a'r en come down on de rock all at de same time—*pow !*—en de ashes, dey flew'd up so, dey did, dat Brer Fox, he tuck'n had a sneezin' spell, en Miss Meadows en de gals dey up'n koff. Th'ee times Brer Rabbit jump up en crack his heels tergedder en come down wid de sludge-hammer— *ker-blam !*—en eve'y time he jump up, he holler out :

" ' Stan' fudder, ladies !   Yer come de dus' ! ' " en sho nuff, de dus' come.

"Leas'ways," continued Uncle Remus, "Brer Rabbit got one er de gals, en dey had a weddin' en a big infa'r."

"Which of the girls did the Rabbit marry?" asked the little boy, dubiously.

"I did year tell un 'er name," replied the old man with a great affectation of interest, "but look like I done gone en fergit it off'n my mine. Ef I don't disremember," he continued, "hit wuz Miss Molly Cottontail, en I speck we better let it go at dat."

XXXI

A PLANTATION WITCH

THE next time the little boy got permission to call upon Uncle Remus, the old man was sitting in his door, with his elbows on his knees and his face buried in his hands, and he appeared to be in great trouble.

"What's the matter, Uncle Remus?" the youngster asked.

"Nuff de matter, honey—mo' dan dey's enny kyo fer. Ef dey ain't some quare gwines on 'roun' dis place I ain't name Remus."

The serious tone of the old man caused the little boy to open his eyes. The moon, just at its full, cast long, vague, wavering shadows in front of the cabin. A colony of tree-frogs somewhere in the distance were treating their neighbours to a serenade, but to the little boy it sounded like a chorus of lost and long-forgotten whistlers. The sound was wherever the imagination chose to locate it— to the right, to the left, in the air, on the ground, far away or near at hand, but always dim and always indistinct. Something in Uncle Remus's tone exactly fitted all these surroundings, and the child nestled closer to the old man.

"Yasser," continued Uncle Remus, with an ominous sign and a mysterious shake of the head, "ef dey ain't some quare gwines on in dis yer naberhood, den I'm de ball-headest creetur 'twix' dis en nex' Jinawerry wuz a year 'go, w'ich I knows I ain't. Dat's what."

"What is it, Uncle Remus?"

"I know Mars John bin drivin' Cholly sorter hard ter-day, en I say ter myse'f dat I'd drap 'roun' 'bout dus' en fling nudder year er corn in de troff en kinder gin 'im a techin' up wid de kurrier-koam; en bless grashus! I ain't bin in de lot mo'n a minnit 'fo' I seed sump'n wuz wrong wid de hoss, and sho' nuff dar wuz his mane full er witch-stirrups."

"Full of what, Uncle Remus?"

"Full er witch-stirrups, honey. Ain't you seed no witch-stirrups? Well, w'en you see two stran' er ha'r tied tergedder in a hoss' mane, dar you see a witch-stirrup, en, mo'n dat, dat hoss done bin rid by um."

"Do you reckon they have been riding Charley?" inquired the little boy.

"Co'se, honey. Tooby sho dey is. W'at else dey bin doin'?"

"Did you ever see a witch, Uncle Remus?"

"Dat ain't needer yer ner dar. W'en I see coon track in de branch, I know de coon bin 'long dar."

The argument seemed unanswerable, and the little boy asked, in a confidential tone:

"Uncle Remus, what are witches like?"

"Dey comes diffunt," responded the cautious old darkey. "Dey comes en dey conjus fokes. Squinch-owl holler eve'y time he see a witch, en w'en you hear de dog howlin' in de middle er de night, one nn um's mighty ap' ter be prowlin' 'roun'. Conjun fokes kin tell a witch de minnit dey lays der eyes on it, but dem w'at ain't conjun, hit's mighty hard ter tell w'en dey see one, kaze dey might come in de 'pearunce un a cow en all kinder beas's. I ain't bin useter no conjun myse'f, but I bin livin' long nuff fer ter know w'en you meets up wid a big black cat in de middle er de road, wid yaller eyeballs, dars yo' witch fresh fum de Ole Boy. En, fuddermo', I know dat 'tain't proned inter no dogs fer ter ketch de rabbit w'at use in a berryin'-groun'. Dey er de mos' ongodlies' creeturs w'at you ever laid eyes on," continued Uncle Remus, with unction. " Down dar in Putmon County yo' Unk Jeems, he make like he gwineter ketch wunner dem dar graveyard rabbits. Sho nuff, out he goes, en de dogs ain't no mo'n got ter de place 'fo' up jump de ole rabbit right 'mong um, en atter runnin' 'roun' a time or two, she skip right up ter Mars Jeems, en Mars Jeems, he des put de gun-bairl right on 'er en lammed aloose. Hit tored up de groun' all 'roun', en de dogs, dey rush up, but dey wan't no rabbit dar ; but bimeby Mars Jeems, he seed de dogs tuckin' der tails 'tween der legs, en he look up, en dar wuz de rabbit caperin' 'roun' on a toomstone, en wid dat Mars Jeems say he sorter feel like de time done come w'en yo' gran'ma was 'specktin' un him home, en he call off de dogs en put out. But dem wuz ha'nts. Witches is deze yer kinder fokes wat kin drap der body en change inter a cat en a wolf en all kinder creeturs."

" Papa says there ain't any witches," the little boy interrupted.

" Mars John ain't live long ez I is," said Uncle Remus, by way of comment. " He ain't bin

broozin' 'roun' all hours er de night en day. I
know'd a nigger w'ich his brer wuz a witch, kaze
he up'n tole me how he tuck'n kyo'd 'im ; en he
kyo'd 'im good, mon."

"How was that ? " inquired the little boy.

"Hit seem like," continued Uncle Remus,
"dat witch fokes is got a slit in de back er de
neck, en w'en dey wanter change derse'f, dey des
pull de hide over der head same ez if 'twuz a shut,
en dar dey is "

"Do they get out of their skins ? " asked the
little boy, in an awed tone.

"Tooby sho, honey. You see yo' pa pull his
shut off ? Well, dat des 'zackly de way dey duz.
But dish yere nigger w'at I'm tellin' you 'bout,
he kyo'd his brer de ve'y fuss pass he made
at him. Hit got so dat fokes in de settlement didn't have no peace. De chilluns 'ud
wake up in de mawnins wid her ha'r tangled
up, en wid scratches on um like dey bin thoo a
brier patch, twel bimeby one day de nigger he
'low dat he'd set up dat night en keep one eye on
his brer ; en sho' nuff dat night, des ez de chickens
wuz crowing for twelve, up jump de brer an' pull
off his skin en sail out'n de house in de shape un a
bat, en w'at duz de nigger do but grab up de hide,
en turn it wrongsud-out'ards en sprinkle it wid salt.
Den he lay down en watch fer ter see w'at de news
wuz gwineter be. Des 'fo' day yer come a big black
cat in de do', en de nigger git up, he did, en druv
her away. Bimeby, yer come a big black dog
snuffin' roun', en de nigger up wid a chunk en
lammed 'im side er de head. Den a squinch-
owl lit on de koam er de house, en de nigger
jam de shovel in de fier en make 'im flew
away. Las', yer come a great big black wolf

wid his eyes shinin' like fier coals, en he
grab de hide and rush out. 'Twa'n't long 'fo'
de nigger year his brer holler'n en squallin',
en he tuck a light, he did, en went out, en dar wuz
his brer des a waller'n on de groun' en squirmin'
'roun', kaze de salt on de skin wuz stingin' wuss'n
ef he had his britches lineded wid yaller-jackets.
By nex' mawnin' he got so he could sorter
shuffle 'long, but he gun up conjun, en ef dere wuz
enny mo' witches in dat settlement dey kep'
mighty close, en dat nigger he ain't skunt hisse'f
no mo' not endurin' er my 'membunce."

The result of this was that Uncle Remus had
to take the little boy by the hand and go with him
to the " big house," which the old man was not
loth to do ; and, when the child went to bed, he
lay awake a long time expecting an unseemly
visitation from some mysterious source. It soothed
him, however, to hear the strong musical voice of his
sable patron, not very far away, tenderly contend-
ing with a lusty tune ; and to this accompaniment
the little boy dropped asleep :

" Hit's eighteen hunder'd, forty-en-eight,
    Christ done made dat crooked way straight—
      En I don't wanter stay here no longer ;
  Hit's eighteen hunder'd, forty-en-nine,
    Christ done turn dat water inter wine—
      En I don't wanter stay here no longer."

XXXII

"JACKY-MY-LANTERN" [1]

Upon his next visit to Uncle Remus, the little boy was exceedingly anxious to know more about witches, but the old man prudently refrained from exciting the youngster's imagination any further in that direction. Uncle Remus had a board across his lap, and, armed with a mallet and a shoe-knife, was engaged in making shoe-pegs.

"W'iles I wus crossin' de branch des now," he said, endeavouring to change the subject, "I come up wid a Jacky-my-lantern, en she wuz bu'nin' wuss'n a bunch er lightnin'-buys, mon. I know'd she was a-fixin' fer ter lead me inter dat quogmire down in de swamp, en I steer'd cle'r un 'er. Yasser. I did dat. You ain't never seed no Jacky-my-lanterns, is you, honey ?"

The little boy never had, but he had heard of them, and he wanted to know what they were, and thereupon Uncle Remus proceeded to tell him.

[1] This story is popular on the coast and among the rice-plantations, and, since the publication of some of the animal-myths in the newspapers, I have received a version of it from a planter in south-west Georgia ; but it seems to me to be an intruder among the genuine myth stories of the negroes. It is a trifle too elaborate. Nevertheless, it is told upon the plantations with great gusto, and there are several versions in circulation.

"One time," said the old darkey, transferring
his spectacles from his nose to the top of his head
and leaning his elbows upon his peg-board, "dere
wuz a blacksmif man, en dish yer blacksmif man,
he tuck'n stuck closer by his dram dan he did
by his bellus. Monday mawnin' he'd git on a
spree, en all dat week he'd be on a spree, en de
nex' Monday mawnin' he'd take a fresh start.
Bimeby, one day, atter de blacksmif bin spreein'
roun' en cussin' might'ly, he hear a sorter rustlin'
fuss at de do', en in walk de Bad Man."

"Who, Uncle Remus?" the little boy asked.

"De Bad Man, honey; de Ole Boy hisse'f
right fresh from de ridjun w'at you hear Miss Sally
readin' 'bout. He done hide his hawns, en his
tail, en his hoof, en he come dress up like w'ite
fokes. He tuck off his hat en he bow, en den he
tell de blacksmif who he is, en dat he done come
atter 'im. Den de blacksmif, he 'gun ter cry
en beg, en he beg so hard en he cry so loud
dat de Bad Man say he make a trade wid 'im.
At de een' er one year de sperit er de blacksmif
wuz to be his'n, en endurin' er dat time de blacksmif
mus' put in his hottes' licks in de intruss er de Bad
Man, en den he put a spell on de cheer de blacksmif was settin' in, en on his sludge-hammer.
De man w'at sot in de cheer couldn't git up less'n
de blacksmif let 'im, en de man w'at pick up de
sludge 'ud hatter keep on knockin' wid it twel
de blacksmif say quit; en den he gun 'im money
plenty, en off he put.

"De blacksmif, he sail in fer ter have his fun,
en he have so much dat he done clean forgot 'bout
his contrack, but bimeby, one day he look down
de road, en dar he see de Bad Man comin', en den
he know'd de year wuz out. W'en de Bad Man got

in de do', de blacksmif wuz poundin' 'way at a
hoss-shoe, but he wa'n't so bizzy dat he didn't
ax 'im in. De Bad Man sorter do like he ain't
got no time fer ter tarry, but de blacksmif say he
got some little jobs dat he bleedzd ter finish up, en
den he ax de Bad Man fer ter set down a
minnit, en de Bad Man, he tuck'n sot down,
en he sot in dat cheer w'at he done conju'd, en,
co'se, dar he wuz. Den de blacksmif, he 'gun
ter poke fun at de Bad Man, en he ax him don't
he want a dram, en won't he hitch his cheer up
little nigher de fier ; en de Bad Man, he beg en
he beg, but 'twan't doin' no good, kase de blacksmif
'low dat he gwineter keep 'im dar twel he promus dat
he let 'im off one year mo', en, sho nuff, de Bad Man
promus dat ef de blacksmif let 'im up he give 'im
an' er showin'. So den de blacksmif 'gun de
wud, en de Bad Man sa'nter off down de big road,
settin' traps en layin' his progance fer ter catch
mo' sinners.

" De nex' year hit pass some like t'er one. At de
p'inted time yer come de Ole Boy atter de blacksmif,
but still de blacksmif had some jobs dat he
bleedzd ter finish up, en he ax de Bad Man fer ter
take holt er de sludge en he'p 'im out ; en de Bad
Man, he 'low dat r'er'n be disperlite, he don't keer
of he do hit 'er a biff er two ; en wid dat he grab up
de sludge, en dar he wuz 'g'in, kase he done conju'd
de sludge so dat whosomedever tuck 'er up can't
put 'er down less'n de blacksmif say de wud. Dey
perlaver'd dar, dey did, twel bimeby de Bad Man
he up'n let 'im off n'er year.

" Well, den, dat year pass same ez t'er one.
Mont' in en mont' out dat man wuz rollin' in dram,
en bimeby yer come de bad Man. De blacksmif cry en he holler, en he rip 'roun' en t'ar his

ha'r, but hit des like he didn't, kase de Bad Man grab
'im up en cram 'im in a bag en tote 'im off.   W'iles
dey wuz gwine 'long dey come up wid a passel er
fokes w'at wuz havin' wunner deze yer fote er July
bobbycues, en de Ole Boy, he 'low dat maybe he
kin git some mo' game, en w'at do he do but jine
in wid um.   He jines in en he talk politics same like
t'er fokes, twel bimeby dinner-time come 'roun', en
dey ax 'im up, w'ich 'greed wid his stummuck, en
he pozzit his bag underneed de table 'longside de
udder bags w'at de hongry fokes'd brung.

"No sooner did de blacksmif git back on de groun'
dan he 'gun ter wuk his way outer de bag. He
crope out, he did, en den he tuck'n change de bag.
He tuck'n tuck a n'er bag en lay it down whar dis
yer bag wuz, en den he crope outer de crowd en
lay low in de underbresh.

"Las', w'en de time come fer ter go, de Ole
Boy up wid his bag en slung her on his shoulder,
en off he put fer de Bad Place.   W'en he got dar he
tuck'n drap de bag off'n his back en call up de imps,
en dey des come a-squallin' en a-caperin', w'ich
I speck dey mus' a-bin hongry.   Leas'ways dey
des swawm'd 'roun', hollerin' out:

"'Daddy, w'at you brung—daddy, w'at you
brung ?'

"So den dey open de bag, en lo en beholes, out
jump a big bull-dog, en de way he shuck dem
little imps wuz a caution, en kep' on gnyawin' un
um twel de Ole Boy open de gate en tu'n 'im out."

"And what became of the blacksmif ?" the
little boy asked, as Uncle Remus paused to snuff
the candle with his fingers.

"I'm drivin' on 'roun', honey.   Atter 'long
time, de blacksmif he tuck'n die, en w'en he go ter
de Good Place de man at de gate dunner who he is,

en he can't squeeze in. Den he go down ter de Bad
Place, en knock. De Ole Boy, he look out, he did,
en he know'd de blacksmif de minnit he laid eyes
on 'im ; but he shake his head en say, sezee :

"'You'll hatter skuze me, Brer Blacksmif,
kase I dun had 'speunce 'longer you. You'll
hatter go some'rs else ef you wanter raise enny
racket,' sezee, en wid dat he shet de do'.'

"En dey do say," continued Uncle Remus,
with unction, "dat sence dat day de blacksmif
bin sorter huv'rin' 'roun' 'twix' de heavens en de
ye'th, en dark nights he shine out so fokes call
'im Jacky-my-lantun. Dat's w'at dey tells me.
Hit may be wrong er 't may be right, but dat's
w'at I years."

XXXIII

WHY THE NEGRO IS BLACK

ONE night, while the little boy was watching Uncle Remus twisting and waxing some shoe-thread, he made what appeared to him to be a very curious discovery. He discovered that the palms of the old man's hands were as white as his own, and the fact was such a source of wonder that he at last made it the subject of remark. The response of Uncle Remus led to the earnest recital of a piece of unwritten history that must prove interesting to ethnologists.

"Tooby sho de pa'm er my han's w'ite, honey," he quietly remarked; "en, w'en it come ter dat, dey wuz a time w'en all de w'ite folks 'uz black— blacker dan me, kaze I done bin yer so long dat I bin sorter bleach out."

The little boy laughed. He thought Uncle Remus was making him the victim of one of his jokes; but the youngster was never more mistaken. The old man was serious. Nevertheless, he failed to rebuke the ill-timed mirth of the child, appearing to be altogether engrossed in his work. After a while he resumed:

"Yasser. Fokes dunner w'at bin yit, let 'lone w'at gwineter be. Niggers is niggers now, but de time wuz w'en 'uz all niggers tergedder."

"When was that, Uncle Remus?"

"Way back yander. In dem times we 'uz all un us black; we 'uz all niggers tergedder, en cordin' ter all de 'counts w'at I years fokes 'uz gittin 'long 'bout ez well in dem days ez dey is now. But atter 'w'ile de news come dat dere wuz a pon' er water some'rs in de naberhood, w'ich ef dey'd git inter dey'd be wash off nice en w'ite, en den one un um, he fine de place en make er plunge inter de pon', en come out w'ite ez a town gal. En den, bless grashus! w'en de fokes seed it, dey make a break fer de pon', en dem w'at wuz de soopless, dey got in fus' en dey come out w'ite; en dem wa't wuz de nex' soopless, dey got in nex', en dey come out merlatters; en dey wuz sech a crowd un um dat dey mighty nigh use de water up, w'ich w'en dem yuthers come 'long, de morest dey could do wuz ter paddle about wid der foots en dabble in it wid der han's. Dem wuz de niggers, en down ter dis day dey ain't no w'ite 'bout a nigger 'ceppin' de pa'ms er der han's en de soles er der foot."

The little boy seemed to be very much interested in this new account of the origin of races, and he made some further inquiries, which elicited from Uncle Remus the following additional particulars:

"De Injun en de Chinee got ter be 'counted 'long er de merlatter. I ain't seed no Chinee dat I knows un, but dey tells me dey er sorter 'twix a brown en a brindle. Dey er all merlatters."

"But mamma says the Chinese have straight hair," the little boy suggested.

"Co'se, honey," the old man unhesitatingly responded, "dem w'at git ter de pon' time nuff fer ter git der head in de water, de water hit onkink der ha'r. Hit bleedzd ter be dat away."

XXXIV

THE SAD FATE OF MR. FOX

"Now, den," said Uncle Remus, with unusual gravity, as soon as the little boy, by taking his seat, announced that he was ready for the evening's entertainment to begin; "now, den, dis yer tale w'at I'm a-gwine ter gin you is de las' row er stumps, sho. Dis yer's whar ole Brer Fox los' his breff, en he ain't fine it no mo' down ter dis day."

"Did he kill himself, Uncle Remus?" the little boy asked, with a curious air of concern.

"Hole on dar, honey!" the old man exclaimed, with a great affectation of alarm; "hole on dar! Wait! Gimme room! I don't wanter tell you no story, en ef you keep shovin' me forrerd, I mout git some er de facks mix up 'mong deyse'f. You gotter gimme room en you gotter gimme time."

The little boy had no other premature questions to ask, and, after a pause, Uncle Remus resumed:

"Well, den, one day Brer Rabbit go to Brer Fox house, he did, en he put up mighty po' mouf. He say his ole 'oman sick, en his chilluns cole, en de fier done gone out. Brer Fox, he feel bad 'bout dis, en he tuck'n s'ply Brer Rabbit widder

147

chunk er fier. Brer Rabbit see Brer Fox cookin'
some nice beef, en his mouf gun ter water, but he
take de fier, he did, en he put out to'rds home; but
present'y yer he come back, en he say de fier gone
out. Brer Fox 'low dat he want er invite ter dinner,
but he don't say nuthin', en bimeby Brer Rabbit
he up'n say, sezee:

"'Brer Fox, whar you git so much nice beef?'
sezee, en den Brer Fox he up'n 'spon', sezee:

"'You come ter my house ter-morrow ef yo'
fokes ain't too sick, en I kin show you whar you kin
git plenty beef mo' nicer dan dis yer,' sezee:

"Well, sho nuff, de nex' day fotch Brer Rabbit,
en Brer Fox say, sezee:

"'Der's a man down yander by Miss Meadows's
w'at got heap er fine cattle, and he gotter cow name
Bookay,' sezee, 'en you des say Bookay, en she'll
open her mouf, en you kin jump in en git des as
much meat ez you kin tote,' sez Brer Fox, sezee.

"'Well, I'll go 'long,' sez Brer Rabbit, sezee,
'en you kin jump fus' en den I'll come follerin'
atter,' sezee.

"Wid dat dey put out, en dey went promerna-
din' 'roun' 'mong de cattle, dey did, twel bimeby dey
struck up wid de one dey wuz atter. Brer Fox, he up,
he did, en holler Bookay, en de cow flung 'er mouf
wide open. Sho nuff, in dey jump, en w'en dey got
dar, Brer Fox, he say, sezee:

"'You kin cut mos' ennywheres, Brer Rabbit, but
don't cut 'roun' de haslett,' sezee.

"Den Brer Rabbit, he holler back, he did:
'I'm a-gitten me out a roas'n-piece,' sezee.

"'Roas'n, 'er bakin', er fryin',' sez Brer Fox,
sezee, 'don't cut too nigh de haslett,' sezee.

"Dey cut en dey kyarved, en dey kyarved en dey
cut, en w'iles dey wuz cuttin' en kyarvin', en slashin'

'way, Brer Rabbit, he tuck'n hacked inter de haslett, en wid dat down fell de cow dead.

" ' Now, den,' sez Brer Fox, ' we er gone, sho,' sezee.

" ' W'at we gwine do ? ' sez Brer Rabbit, sezee.

" ' I'll git in de maul,' sez Brer Fox, ' en you'll jump in de gall,' sezee.

" Nex' mawnin' yer cum de man w'at de cow b'long ter, an' he ax who kill Bookay. Nobody don't say nuthin'. Den de man say he'll cut 'er open en see, en den he whirl in, en twan't no time 'fo' he had 'er intruls spread out. Brer Rabbit he crope out'n de gall, en say, sezee :

" ' Mister Man ! Oh, Mister Man ! I'll tell you who kill yo' cow. You look in de maul, en dar you'll fine 'im,' sezee.

" Wid dat de man tuck a stick and lam down on de maul so hard dat he kill Brer Fox stone-dead. W'en Brer Rabbit see Brer Fox wuz laid out fer good, he make like he mighty sorry, en he up'n ax de man fer Brer Fox head. Man say he ain't keerin', en den Brer Rabbit tuck'n brung it ter Brer Fox house. Dar he see ole Miss Fox, en he tell 'er dat he done fotch her some nice beef w'at 'er ole man sont 'er, but she ain't gotter look at it twel she go ter eat it.

" Brer Fox son wuz name Tobe, en Brer Rabbit tell Tobe fer ter keep still w'iles his mammy cook de nice beef w'at his daddy sont 'im. Tobe he wuz mighty hongry, en he look in de pot he did w'iles de cookin' wuz gwine on, en dar he see his daddy head, en wid dat he sot up a howl en tole his mammy. Miss Fox, she git mighty mad w'en she fine she cookin' her ole man head, en she call up de dogs, she did, en sickt em on Brer Rabbit ; en ole Miss Fox en Tobe en de dogs, dey push Brer

Rabbit so close dat he hatter take a holler tree. Miss
Fox, she tell Tobe fer ter stay dar en min' Brer
Rabbit, w'ile she goes en git de ax, en w'en she gone,
Brer Rabbit, he tole Tobe ef he go ter de branch
en git 'im a drink er water dat he'll gin 'im a dollar.
Tobe, he put out, he did, en bring some water in
his hat, but by de time he got back Brer Rabbit
done out and gone. Ole Miss Fox, she cut and cut
twel down come de tree, but no Brer Rabbit dar.
Den she lay de blame on Tobe, en she say she
gwineter lash 'im, en Tobe, he put out en run, de ole
'oman atter 'im. Bimeby he come up wid Brer
Rabbit, en sot down fer to tell 'im how 'twuz,
en w'iles dey wuz a-settin' dar, yer come ole
Miss Fox a slippin' up en grab um bofe. Den
she tell um w'at she gwine do. Brer Rabbit
she gwineter kill, en Tobe she gwineter lam ef its
de las' ack. Den Brer Rabbit sez, sezee :

" ' Ef you please, ma'am, Miss Fox, lay me on de
grindstone en groun' off my nose so I can't smell
no mo' w'en I'm dead.'

" Miss Fox, she tuck dis ter be a good idee, en she
fotch bofe un um ter de grindstone, en set um up
on it so dat she could groun' off Brer Rabbit nose.
Den Brer Rabbit, he up'n say, sezee :

" ' Ef you please, ma'am, Miss Fox, Tobe he kin
turn de handle w'iles you goes atter some water
fer ter wet de grindstone,' sezee.

" Co'se, soon'z Brer Rabbit see Miss Fox go atter
de water, he jump down en put out, en dis time
he git clean away."

" And was that the last of the Rabbit, too,
Uncle Remus ? " the little boy asked, with something
like a sigh.

" Don't push me too close, honey," responded the
old man ; " don't shove me up in no cornder.   I

don't wanter tell you no stories. Some say dat
Brer Rabbit's ole 'oman died fum eatin' some
pizen-weed, en dat Brer Rabbit married ole Miss
Fox, en some say not. Some tell one tale en some
tells nudder ; some say dat fum dat time forrerd de
Rabbits en de Foxes make frien's en stay so ; some
say dey kep' on quollin'. Hit look like it mixt.
Let dem tell you w'at knows. Dat w'at I years
you gits it straight like I yeard it."

There was a long pause, which was finally broken
by the old man :

"Hit's 'gin de rules fer you ter be noddin' yer,
honey. Bimeby you'll drap off en I'll hatter
tote you up ter be big 'ouse. I hear dat baby
cryin', en bimeby Miss Sally'll fly up en be a-holler'n
atter you."

"Oh, I wasn't asleep," the little boy replied. "I
was just thinking."

"Well, dat's diffunt," said the old man. "Ef you'll
clime up on my back," he continued, speaking
softly, "I speck I ain't too ole fer ter be yo' hoss fum
yer ter de house. Many en many's de time dat
I totted yo' Unk Jeems dat away, en Mars Jeems
wuz heavier sot dan w'at you is."

PLANTATION PROVERBS

Big 'possum clime little tree.

Dem w'at eats kin say grace.

Ole man Know-All died las' year.

Better de gravy dan no grease 'tall.

Dram ain't good twel you git it.

Lazy fokes' stummucks don't git tired.

Rheumatiz don't he'p at de log-rollin'.

Mole don't see w'at his naber doin'.

Save de pacin' mar' fer Sunday.

Don't rain eve'y time de pig squeal.

Crow en corn can't grow in de same fiel'.

Tattlin' 'oman can't make de bread rise.

Rails split 'fo' bre'kfus' 'll season de dinner.

Dem w'at knows too much sleeps under de ash-hopper.

Ef you wanter see yo' own sins, clean up a new groun'.

Hog dunno w'ich part un 'im'll season de turnip salad.

Hit's a blessin' de w'ite sow don't shake de plum-tree.

Winter grape sour, whedder you kin reach 'im or not.

Mighty po' bee dat don't make mo' honey dan he want.

Kwishins on mule's foots done gone out er fashun.

Pigs dunno w'at a pen's for.

Possum's tail good as a paw.

Dogs don't bite at de front gate.

Colt in de barley patch kick high.

Jay-bird don't rob his own nes'.

Pullet can't roost too high for de owl.

Meat fried 'fo' day won't las' twel night.

Stump water won't kyo de gripes.

De howlin' dog know w'at he sees.

Bline hoss don't fall w'en he follers de bit.

Hongry nigger won't w'ar his maul out.

Don't fling away de empty wallet.

Black-snake know de way ter de hin nes'.

Looks won't do ter split rails wid.

Settin' hens don't hanker arter fresh aigs.

Tater-vine growin' w'ile you sleep.

Hit take two birds fer ter make a nes'.

Ef you bleedzd ter eat dirt, eat clean dirt.

Tarrypin walk fast 'nuff fer ter go visitin'.

Empty smoke-house makes de pullet holler.

W'en coon take water he fixin' fer ter fight.

Corn makes mo' at de mill dan it does in de crib.

Good luck say : " Op'n yo' mouf en shet yo' eyes."

Nigger dat gets hurt wukkin oughter show de
skyars.

Fiddlin' nigger say hit's long ways ter de dance.

Rooster makes mo' racket dan de hin w'at lay de
aig.

Meller mush-million hollers at you fum over de
fence.

Nigger wid a pocket-han'kcher better be looked
atter.

Rain-crow don't sing no chune, but youk'n 'pen
on 'im.

One-eyed mule can't be handled on de bline side.

Moon may shine, but a lightered knot's mighty
handy.

Licker talks mighty loud w'en it git loose fum de
jug.

De proudness uns a man don't count w'en his head's cold.

Hongry rooster don't cackle w'en he fine a wum.

Some niggers mighty smart, but dey can't drive de pidgins ter roos'.

You may know de way, but better keep yo' eyes on de seven stairs.

All de buzzards in de settlement'll come to de gray mule's funer'l.

Youk'n hide de fier, but w'at you gwine do wid de smoke ?

Ter-morrow may be de carridge-driver's day for ploughin'.

Hit's a mighty deaf nigger dat don't year de dinner-ho'n.

Hit takes a bee fer ter git de sweetness out'n de hoarhoun' blossom.

Ha'nts don't bodder longer hones' folks, but you better go 'roun' de graveyard.

De pig dat runs off wid de year er corn gits little mo' dan de cob.

Sleepin' in de fence-cornder don't fetch Chris'mus in de kitchen.

De spring-house may freeze, but de niggers'll keep de shuck-pen warm.

'Twix de bug en de bee-martin 'tain't hard ter tell w'ich gwineter git cotch.

Don't 'spute wid de squinch-owl. Jam de shovel in de fier.

You'd see mo' er de mink ef he know'd whar de yard dog sleeps.

Troubles is seasonin'. 'Simmons ain't good twel dey 'er fros'-bit.

Watch out w'en you' er gittin all you want. Fat-tenin' hogs ain't in luck.

HIS SONGS

I

Oh, whar shill we go w'en de great day comes,
Wid de blowin' er de trumpits en de bangin' er de
    drums ?
How many po' sinners'll be kotched out late
En find no latch ter de golden gate ?
    No use fer ter wait twel ter-morrer !
    De sun mustn't set on yo' sorrer,
    Sin's ez sharp ez a bamboo brier—
    O Lord ! fetch de mo'ners up higher !

W'en de nashuns er de earf is a stan'in' all aroun',
Who's a-gwineter be choosen fer ter w'ar de glory-
    crown ?
Who's a-gwine fer ter stan' stiff-kneed en bol',
En answer to der name at de callin' er de roll ?
    You better come now ef you comin'—
    Ole Satun is loose en a-bummin'—
    De wheels er distruckshun is a-hummin'—
    Oh, come 'long, sinner, ef you comin' !

De song er salvashun is a mighty sweet song,
En de Pairidise win' blow fur en blow strong,
En Aberham's bosom, hit's saft en hit's wide,
En right dar's de place whar de sinners oughter
    hide !

Oh, you nee'nter be a-stoppin' en a-lookin';
Ef you fool wid ole Satun you'll git took in;
You'll hang on de aidge en get shook in,
Ef you keep on a-stoppin' en a-lookin'.

De time is right now, en dis yer's de place—
Let de sun er salvashun shine squar' in yo' face;
Fight de battles er de Lord, fight soon en fight
 late
En you'll allers fine a latch ter de golden gate.
 No use fer ter wait twel ter-morrer,
 De sun mustn't sét on yo' sorrer—
 Sin's ez sharp ez bamboo-brier,
 Ax de Lord fer ter fetch you up higher!

II

CAMP-MEETING SONG.[1]

Oh, de worril is roun' en de worril is wide—
 Lord! 'member these chillun in de mornin'—
Hit's a mighty long ways up de mountain-side,
En dey ain't no place fer dem sinners fer ter hide,
En dey ain't no place whar sin kin abide,
 W'en de Lord shill come in de mornin'!
  Look up en look aroun'
  Fling yo' burden on de groun',
 Hit's a-gittin' mighty close on ter mornin'
  Smoove away sin's frown—
  Retch up en git de crown
 W'at de Lord will fetch in de mornin'!

[1] In the days of slavery, the religious services held
by the negroes who accompanied their owners to the
camp-meetings were marvels of earnestness and devotion.

De han' er ridem'shun, hit's hilt out ter you—
    Lord ! 'member dem sinners in de mornin' !
Hit's a mighty pashent han', but de days is but
    few,
W'en Satun, he'll come a-demandin' un his due,
En de stiff-neck sinners'll be smotin' all fru—
    Oh, you better git ready fer de mornin' !
      Look up en set yo' face
      Todes de green hills er grace,
    'Fo' de sun rises up in de mornin'—
      Oh, you better change yo' base,
      Hit's yo' soul's las' race
    Fer de glory dat's a-comin' in de mornin' !

De farmer gits ready w'en de lan's all plowed
    Fer ter sow dem seeds in de mornin'—
De sperrit may be puny en de flesh may be proud,
But you better cut loose from de scoffin' crowd,
En jine dese Christuns w'at's a-cryin' out loud
    Fer de Lord fer ter come in de mornin' !
      Shout loud en shout long,
      Let de ekkoes ans'er strong,
    W'en de sun rises up in de mornin' !
      Oh, you allers will be wrong
      Twel you choose ter belong
    Ter de Marster w'at's a-comin' in de mornin' !

III

CORN-SHUCKING SONG

Oh, de fus' news you know de day'll be a-breakin'—
    (Hey O ! Hi O ! Up'n down de Bango ! [1])

[1] So far as I know, " Bango " is a meaningless term,
introduced on account of its sonorous ruggedness.

An' de fier be a-burnin' en' de ash-cake a-bakin',
   (Hey O! Hi O! Up'n down de Bango!)
An' de hen'll be a-hollerin' en de boss'll be a-
    wakin'—
   'Iey O! Hi O! Up'n down de Bango!)
   er git up, nigger, en give yo'se'f a-shakin'—
   (Hi O, Miss Sindy Ann!)

Oh, honey! w'en you see dem ripe stars a-fallin'—
   (Hey O! Hi O! Up'n down de Bango!)
Oh, honey! w'en you year de rain-crow a-callin'—
   (Hey O! Hi O! Up'n down de Bango!)
Oh, honey! w'en you year dat red calf a-bawlin'—
   (Hey O! Hi O! Up'n down de Bango!)
Den de day-time's comin', a-creepin' en a-crawlin'—
   (Hi O, Miss Sindy Ann!)

Fer de los' ell en yard [1] is a-huntin' fer de mornin',
   (Hi O! git 'long! go away!)
En she'll ketch up widdus 'fo' we ever git dis corn
    in—
   (Oh, go 'way, Sindy Ann!)

Oh, honey! w'en you year dat tin-horn a-tootin'—
   (Hey O! Hi O! Up'n down de Bango!)
Oh, honey, w'en you year de squinch-owl a-hootin'—
   (Hey O! Hi O! Up'n down de Bango!)
Oh, honey! w'en you year dem little pigs a-rootin'—
   (Hey O! Hi O! Up'n down de Bango!)
Right den she's a-comin' a-skippin' en a-scootin'—
   (Hi O, Miss Sindy Ann!)

Oh, honey, w'en you year dat roan mule whicker—
   (Hey O! Hi O! Up'n down de Bango!)

[1] The sword and belt in the constellation of Orion.

W'en you see Mister Moon turnin' pale en gittin'
    sicker—
    (Hey O! Hi O! Up'n down de Bango!)
Den hit's time fer ter handle dat corn a little
    quicker—
    (Hey O! Hi O! Up'n down de Bango!)
Ef you wanter git a smell er old Marster's jug er
    licker—
    (Hi O, Miss Sindy Ann!)

Fer de los' ell en yard is a-huntin' fer de mornin',
    (Hi O! git 'long! go 'way!)
En she'll ketch up widdus 'fo' we ever git dis corn
    in—
    (Oh, go 'way, Sindy Ann!)

You niggers 'cross dar! you better stop your
    dancin'—
    (Hey O! Hi O! Up'n down de Bango!)
No use fer ter come a-flingin' un yo' "sha'n'ts" in—
    (Hey O! Hi O! Up'n down de Bango!)
No use fer ter come a-flingin' un yo' "can'ts" in—
    (Hey O! Hi O! Up'n down de Bango!)
Kaze dey ain't no time fer yo' pattin' ner yo' pran-
    cin'!
    (Hi O, Miss Sindy Ann!)

Mr. Rabbit see de Fox, en he sass um en jaws um—
    (Hey O! Hi O! Up'n down de Bango!)
Mr. Fox ketch de Rabbit, en he scratch um and he
    claws um—
    (Hey O! Hi O! Up'n down de Bango!)
En he tar off de hide, en he chaws um en he gnyaws
    um—
    (Hey O! Hi O! Up'n down de Bango!)
Same like gal chawin' sweet gum en rozzum—
    (Hi O, Miss Sindy Ann!)

Fer de los' ell en yard is a-huntin' fer de mornin',
  (Hi O ! git 'long ! go 'way !)
En she'll ketch up widdus 'fo' we ever git dis corn
  in—
  (Oh, go 'way, Sindy Ann !)

Oh, work on, boys ! give deze shucks a mighty
    wringin'—
  (Hey O ! Hi O ! Up'n down de Bango !)
'Fo' de boss come aroun' a-dangin' en a-dingin'—
  (Hey O ! Hi O ! Up'n down de Bango !)
Git up en move aroun' ! set dem big han's ter
    swingin'—
  (Hey O ! Hi O ! Up'n down de Bango !)
Git up'n shout loud ! let de w'ite folks year you
    singin' !
  (Hi O ! Miss Sindy Ann !)

Fer de los' ell en yard is a-huntin' fer de mornin',
  (Hey O ! git 'long ! go 'way !)
En she'll ketch up widdus 'fo' we ever git dis corn
  in—
  (Oh, go 'way, Sindy Ann !)

IV

THE PLOUGH-HANDS' SONG

*Jasper County—*1860)

NIGGER mighty happy w'en he layin' by co'n—
    Dat sun's a-slantin' ;
Nigger mighty happy w'en he year de dinner-ho'n—
    Dat sun's a-slantin' ;

En he mo' happy still w'en de night draws on—
    Dat sun's a slantin';
Dat sun's a-slantin' des ez sho's you bo'n!
    En it's rise up, Primus! fetch anudder yell:
    Dat ole dun cow's des a-shakin' up 'er bell,
    En de frogs chunin' up 'fo' de jew done fell:
    Good-night, Mr. Killdee! I wish you mighty well!
      —Mr. Kildee! I wish you mighty well!
        —I wish you mighty well!

De co'n'll be ready 'g'inst dumplin day—
    Dat sun's a-slantin';
But nigger gotter watch, en stick, en stay—
    Dat sun's a-slantin';
Same ez de bee-martin watchin' un de jay—
    Dat sun's a-slantin';
Dat sun's a-slantin en a-slippen' away
    Den it's rise up, Primus! en gin it t'um strong:
    De cow's gwine home wid der ding-dang-dong—
    Sling in anudder tetch er de ole-time song:
    Good-night, Mr. Whipperwill! don't stay long!
      —Mr. Whipperwill! don't stay long!
        —Don't stay long!

V

CHRISTMAS PLAY-SONG

Myrick Place, Putnam County—1858.

Hi my rinktum! Black gal sweet,
Same like goodies w'at de w'ite folks eat;
Ho my Riley! don't you take'n tell 'er name,
En den ef sump'n' happen you won't ketch de
    blame:

Hi my rinktum ! better take'n hide yo' plum ;
Joree don't holler eve'y time he fine a wum.
   Den it's hi my rinktum !
    Don't git no udder man ;
   En it's ho my Riley !
    Fetch out Miss Dilsey Ann !

Ho my Riley !   Yaller gal fine ;
She may be yone but she oughter be mine !
Hi my rinktum !   Lemme git by,
En see w'at she mean by de cut er dat eye !
Ho my Riley ! better shet dat do'—
De w' ite folks 'll b'leeve we er t'arin' up de flo'.
   Den it's ho my Riley !
    Come a-siftin' up ter me !
   En it's hi my rinktum !
    Dis de way ter twis' yo' knee !

Hi my rinktum !   Ain't de eas' gittin' red ?
De squinch-owl shiver like he wanter go ter bed ;
Ho my Riley !   but de gals en de boys
Des now gittin' so dey kin sorter make a noise.
Hi my rinktum !   let de yaller gal 'lone ;
Niggers don't hanker arter sody in de pone.
   Den it's hi my rinktum !
    Better try anudder plan ;
   An' it's ho my Riley !
    Trot out Miss Dilsey Ann

Ho my Riley !   In de happy Chris'mus time
De niggers shake der cloze a-huntin' fer a dime.
Hi my rinktum !   En den dey shake der feet,
En greaze derse'f wid de good ham meat.
Ho my Riley ! dey eat en dey cram,
En bimeby ole Miss'll be a-sendin' out de dram.

Den it's ho my Riley!
  You hear dat, Sam!
En it's hi my rinktum!
  Be a-sendin' out de dram!

————

VI

PLANTATION PLAY-SONG

(*Putnam County—1856*)

Hit's a-gittin' mighty late, w'en de guinny-hins
    squall,
En you better dance now, ef you gwineter dance at
    all,
Fer by dis time ter-morrer night you can't hardly
    crawl,
Kaze you'll hatter take de hoe ag'in en likewise de
    maul—
Don't you hear dat bay colt a-kickin' in his stall?
        Stop yo' humpin' up yo' sho'lders—
          Dat'll never do!
        Hop light, ladies,
          Oh, Miss Loo!
        Hit takes a heap er scrougin'
          Fer ter git you thoo—
        Hop light, ladies,
          Oh, Miss Loo!

Ef you niggers don't watch, you'll sing anudder
    chune,
Fer de sun'll rise'n ketch you ef you don't be
    mighty soon;

En de stars is gittin' paler, en de ole gray coon
Is a-settin' in de grape-vine a-watchin' fer de moon.
      W'en a feller comes a knockin'
        Des holler—*Oh, shoo !*
      Hop light, ladies,
        Oh, Miss Loo !
      Oh, swing dat yaller gal !
        Do, boys do !
      Hop light, ladies,
        Oh, Miss Loo !

Oh, tu'n me loose ! Lemme 'lone ! Go 'way,
    now !
W'at you speck I come a-dancin' fer ef I dunno
    how ?
Deze de ve'y kinder footses w'at kicks up a row ;
Can't you jump inter de middle en make yo' gal a
    bow !
      Look at dat merlatter man
        A-follerin' up Sue ;
      Hop light, ladies,
        Oh, Miss Loo !
      De boys ain't a-gwine
        W'en you cry *boo hoo*—
      Hop light, ladies,
        Oh, Miss Loo !

VII

TRANSCRIPTIONS [1]

1. *A Plantation*

Hit's eighteen hunder'd forty-en-fo',
Christ done open dat He'v'mly do'—
   An' I don't wanter stay yer no longer;
Hit's eighteen hunder'd forty-en-five,
Christ done made dat dead man alive—
   An' I don't wanter stay yer no longer.
     You ax me ter run home,
      Little childun—
     Run home, dat sun done roll—
   An' I don't wanter stay yer no longer.

Hit's eighteen hunder'd forty-en-six,
Christ is got us a place done fix—
   An' I don't wanter stay yer no longer;
Hit's eighteen hunder'd forty-en-sev'm
Christ done sot a table in Hev'm—
   An' I don't wanter stay yer no longer.
     You ax me ter run home,
      Little childun—
     Run home, dat sun done roll—
   An' I don't wanter stay yer no longer.

Hit's eighteen hunder'd forty-en-eight,
Christ done make dat crooked way straight—
   An' I don't wanter stay yer no longer;
Hit's eighteen hunder'd forty-en-nine,
Christ done tu'n dat water inter wine—

[1] If these are adaptations from songs the negroes
have caught from the whites, their origin is very remote.
I have transcribed them literally, and I regard them as
in the highest degree characteristic.

An' I don't wanter stay yer no longer,
  You ax me ter run home,
    Little childun—
  Run home, dat sun done roll—
An' I don't wanter stay yer no longer.

Hit's eighteen hunder'd forty-en-ten,
Christ is de mo'ner's onliest fr'en'—
  An' I don't wanter stay yer no longer;
Hit's eighteen hunder'd forty-en-lev'm,
Christ'll be at de do' w'en we all git ter Hev'm—
  An' I don't wanter stay yer no longer.
    You ax me ter run home,
      Little childun—
    Run home, dat sun done roll—
  An' I don't wanter stay yer no longer.

2. *A Plantation Serenade*

DE ole bee make de honey-comb,
  De young bee make de honey,
De niggers make de cotton en co'n,
  En de w'ite folks gits de money.

De raccoon he's a cu'us man,
  He never walk twel dark,
En nuthin' never 'sturbs his mine,
  Twel he hear ole Bringer bark.

De raccoon totes a bushy tail,
  De 'possum totes no ha'r,
Mr. Rabbit, he come skippin' by,
  He ain't got none to spar'.

Monday mornin' break er day,
  W'ite folks got me gwine,
But Sat'dy night, w'en de sun goes down,
  Dat yaller gal's in my mine.

Fifteen poun' er meat a week,
    W'isky fer ter sell,
Oh, how can a young man stay at home,
    Dem gals dey look so well?

Met a 'possum in de road—
    Brer 'Possum, whar you gwine?
I thank my stars, I bless my life,
    I'm a-huntin' fer de muscadine.

VIII

THE BIG BETHEL CHURCH

De big Bethel chu'ch! de big Bethel chu'ch!
    Done put ole Satun behine um;
Ef a sinner git loose fum enny udder chu'ch,
    De Big Bethel chu'ch will fine um!

Hit's good ter be dere, en it's sweet ter be dere,
    Wid de sisterin' all aroun' you—
A-shakin' dem shackles er mussy en' love
    Wharwid de Lord is boun' you.

Hit's sweet ter be dere en lissen ter de hymes,
    En hear dem mo'ners a-shoutin'—
Dey done reach the place whar der ain't no room
    Fer enny mo' weepin' on doubtin'.

Hit's good ter be dere w'en de sinners all jine
    Wid be brudderin' in dere singin',
En it look like Gaberl gwine ter rack up en blow
    En set dem Heav'm bells ter ringin'!

Oh, de Big Bethel chu'ch! de Big Bethel chu'ch,
    Done put ole Satun behine um;
Ef a sinner git loose fum enny udder chu'ch
    De big Bethel chu'ch will fine um!

IX

TIME GOES BY TURNS

DAR's a pow'ful rassle 'twix de Good en de Bad,
  En de Bad's got de all-under holt ;
En w'en de wuss come, she come i'on-clad,
  En you hatter hole yo' bref fer de jolt.

But des todes de las' Good gits de knee-lock,
  En dey draps ter de groun'—*ker flop !*
Good had de inturn, en he stan' like a rock,
  En he bleedzd fer ter be on top.

De dry wedder breaks wid a big thunder-clap,
  Fer dey ain't no drout w'at kin las',
But de seasons w'at whoops up de cotton crap,
  Likewise dey freshens up de grass.

De rain fall so saf' in de long dark night,
  Twel you hatter hole yo' han' fer a sign,
But de drizzle w'at sets de tater-slips right
  Is de makin' er de May-pop vine.

In de mellerest groun' de clay root'll ketch
  En hole ter de tongue er de plow,
En a pine-pole gate at de gyardin-patch
  Never'll keep out de ole brindle cow.

One en all on us knows who's a-pullin' at de bits
  Like de lead-mule dat g'ides by de rein,
En yit, somehow er nudder, de bestest un us gits
  Mighty sick er de tuggin' at de chain.

Hump yo'se'f ter de load en fergit de distress
  En dem w'at stan's by ter scoff,
Fer de harder de pullin', de longer de res'
  En de bigger de feed in de troff.

A STORY OF THE WAR.

WHEN Miss Theodosia Huntingdon, of Burlington, Vermont, concluded to come South in 1870, she was moved by three considerations. In the first place, her brother, John Huntingdon, had become a citizen of Georgia—having astonished his acquaintances by marrying a young lady, the male members of whose family had achieved considerable distinction in the Confederate army; in the second place, she was anxious to explore a region which she almost unconsciously pictured to herself as remote and semi-barbarous; and in the third place, her friends had persuaded her that to some extent she was an invalid. It was in vain that she argued with herself as to the propriety of undertaking the journey alone and unprotected, and she finally put an end to inward and outward doubts by informing herself and her friends, including John Huntingdon, her brother, who was practising law in Atlanta, that she had decided to visit the South.

When, therefore, on the 12th of October, 1870— the date is duly recorded in one of Miss Theodosia's letters—she alighted from the cars in Atlanta, in the midst of a great crowd, she fully expected to find her brother waiting to receive her. The bells of several locomotives were ringing, a number of

trains were moving in and out, and the porters
and baggage-men were screaming and bawling
to such an extent, that for several moments Miss
Huntingdon was considerably confused; so much
so that she paused, in the hope that her brother
would suddenly appear and rescue her from the
smoke, and dust, and din.   At that moment some
one touched her on the arm, and she heard a strong,
half-confident, half-apologetic voice exclaim:

"Ain't dis yer Miss Doshy?"

Turning, Miss Theodosia saw at her side a tall,
gray-haired negro.   Elaborating the incident afterward to his friends, she was pleased to say that
the appearance of the old man was somewhat
picturesque.   He stood towering above her, his
hat in one hand, a carriage-whip in the other, and
an expectant smile lighting up his rugged face.
She remembered a name her brother had often used
in his letters, and, with a woman's tact, she held
out her hand, and said:

"Is this Uncle Remus?"

"Law, Miss Doshy! how you know de ole
nigger?   I know'd you by de faver; but how you
know me?"   And then, without waiting for a
reply: "Miss Sally, she sick in bed, en Mars John,
he bleedzd ter go in de country, en dey tuck'n sont
me.   I know'd you de minnit I laid eyes on you.
Time I seed you, I say ter myse'f, 'I lay dar's
Miss Doshy;' en' sho nuff, dar you wuz.   You ain't
gun up yo' checks, is you?   Kaze I'll get de trunk
sont up by de 'spress waggin."

The next moment Uncle Remus was elbowing
his way unceremoniously through the crowd, and
in a very short time, seated in the carriage driven
by the old man, Miss Huntingdon was whirling
through the streets of Atlanta in the direction of

her brother's home. She took advantage of the opportunity to study the old negro's face closely, her natural curiosity considerably sharpened by a knowledge of the fact that Uncle Remus had played an important part in her brother's history. The result of her observation must have been satisfactory, for presently she laughed, and said:

"Uncle Remus, you haven't told me how you knew me in that great crowd."

The old man chuckled, and gave the horses a gentle rap with the whip.

"Who? Me? I know'd you by de faver. Dat boy er Mars John's is de ve'y spit en immij un you. I'd a know'd you in New 'Leens, let 'lone down dar in de kyar-shed."

This was Miss Theodosia's introduction to Uncle Remus. One Sunday afternoon, a few weeks after her arrival, the family were assembled in the piazza enjoying the mild weather. Mr. Huntingdon was reading a newspaper; his wife was crooning softly as she rocked the baby to sleep; and the little boy was endeavouring to show his Aunt Dosia the outlines of Kennesaw Mountain through the purple haze that hung like a wonderfully fashioned curtain in the sky and almost obliterated the horizon. While they were thus engaged, Uncle Remus came around the corner of the house talking to himself.

"Dey er too lazy ter wuk," he was saying, "en dey specks hone's fokes fer ter stan' up en s'port um. I'm gwine down ter Putmon County whar Mars Jeems is—dat's w'at I'm agwine ter do."

"What's the matter now, Uncle Remus?" inquired Mr. Huntingdon, folding up his newspaper.

"Nuthin' 'tall, Mars John, 'ceppin' deze yer sunshine niggers. Dey begs my terbacker, en borrys my tools, en steals my vittles, en hit's done come ter dat pass dat I gotter pack up en go. I'm agwine down ter Putmon, dat's w'at."

Uncle Remus was accustomed to make this threat several times a day, but upon this occasion it seemed to remind Mr. Huntingdon of something.

" Very well," he said, " I'll come around and help you pack up ; but before you go I want you to tell Sister here how you went to war and fought for the Union.—Remus was a famous warrior," he continued, turning to Miss Theodosia; " he volunteered for one day, and commanded an army of one. You know the story, but you have never heard Remus's version."

Uncle Remus shuffled around in an awkward, embarrassed way, scratched his head, and looked uncomfortable.

" Miss Doshy ain't got no time fer ter set dar an year de ole nigger run on."

" Oh, yes, I have, Uncle Remus ! " exclaimed the young lady ; " plenty of time."

The upshot of it was that, after many ridiculous protests, Uncle Remus sat down on the steps, and proceeded to tell his story of the war. Miss Theodosia listened with great interest, but throughout it all she observed—and she was painfully conscious of the fact, as she afterward admitted—that Uncle Remus spoke from the standpoint of a Southerner, and with the air of one who expected his hearers to thoroughly sympathize with him.

" Co'se," said Uncle Remus, addressing himself to Miss Theodosia, " you ain't bin to Putmon, en you dunner whar de Brad Slaughter place en Harmony Grove is ; but Mars John en Miss Sally, dey bin dar a time er two, en dey knows how de lan' lays. Well, den, it 'uz right 'long in dere whar

Mars Jeems lived, en whar he live now. When de war come 'long he wuz livin' dere longer Ole Miss en Miss Sally. Ole Miss 'wz his ma, en Miss Sally dar 'uz his sister. De war come des like I tell you, en marters sorter rock along same like dey allers did. Hit didn't strike me dat dey wuz enny war gwine on, en if I hadn't sorter miss de nabers, en seed fokes gwine outer de way fer ter ax de news, I'd a 'lowed ter myse'f dat de war wuz 'way off 'mong some yuther country. But all dis time de fuss wuz gwine on, en Mars Jeems, he wuz des eatchin' fer ter put in. Ole Miss en Miss Sally dey tuck on so he didn't git off de fus' year; but bimeby news come down dat times wuz gittin' putty hot, en Mars Jeems he got up, en say he gotter go, en go he did. He got a overseer fer ter look atter de place, en he went en jined de army. En he 'uz a fighter, too, mon, Mars Jeems wuz. Many's en many's de time," continued the old man, reflectively, "dat I hatter tak'n bresh dat boy on accounter his 'buzin' en beatin' dem yuther boys. He went off dar fer ter fight, en he fit. Ole Miss useter call me up Sunday en read w'at de papers say 'bout Mars Jeems, en it hope 'er up might'ly. I kin see 'er des like it 'uz yistiddy.

"'Remus,' sez she, 'dis yer's w'at de papers say 'bout my baby'; en den she'd read out twel she couldn't read fer cryin'. Hit went on dis way year in en year out, en dem wuz lonesome times, sho's you bawn, Miss Doshy—lonesome times, sho. Hit got hotter en hotter in de war, en lonesomer en mo' lonesomer at home; en bimeby 'long come de conscrip' man, en de des everlas'nly scoop up Mars Jeems's overseer. W'en dis come 'bout, Ole Miss, she sont atter me en say, sez she:

"'Remus, I ain't got nobody fer ter look arter

de place but you,' sez she; en den I up'n say, sez
I:

"'Mistiss, you kin des 'pen' on de ole nigger.'
"I wuz ole den, Miss Doshy—let 'lone w'at I is
now; en you better b'leeve I bossed dem han's.
I had dem niggers up en in de fiel' long 'fo' day, en
de way dey did wuk wuz a caution. Ef dey didn't
earnt der vittles dat season den I ain't name
Remus. But dey wuz tuk keer un. Dey had
plenty er cloze en plenty er grub, en dey wuz de
fattes' niggers in de settlement.

"Bimeby one day, Ole Miss, she call me up en say
de Yankees done gone en tuck Atlanty—dis yer
ve'y town; den presently I hear dey wuz a-
marchin' on down todes Putmon, en, lo en beholes!
one day, de fus' news I know'd, Mars Jeems he rid
up wid a whole gang er men. He des sop long nuff
fer ter change hosses en snatch a mouffle er sump'n'
ter eat, but 'fo' he rid off he call me up en say, sez
he:

"'Daddy,'—all Ole Miss's chilluns call me
daddy—'Daddy,' he say, ''pears like dere's gwineter be mighty rough times 'roun' yer. De Yankees,
dey er done got ter Madison en Mounticellar,
en 'twon't be many days 'fo' dey er down yer.
'Tain't likely dey'll pester mother ner sister; but,
daddy, if de wus come ter de wus, I 'speck you to
take keer on um,' sezee.

"Den I say, sez I: 'How long you bin knowin'
me, Mars Jeems?' sez I.

"'Sence I was a baby,' sezee.

"'Well, den, Mars Jeems,' sez I, 'you know'd
't wa'nt no use fer ter ax me ter take keer Ole Miss
en Miss Sally.'

"Den he tuck'n squoze my han' en jump on de
filly I bin savin' fer 'im, en rid off. One time he

tu'n 'roun' en look like he wanter say sump'n', but he des waf' his han'—so—en gallop on. I know'd den dat trouble wuz brewin'. Nigger dat knows he's gwineter git thumped kin sorter fix hisse'f, en I tuck'n fix up like de war wuz gwineter come right in at de front gate. I tuck'n got all de cattle en hosses tergedder en driv' um to de fo'mile place, en I tuck all de corn en fodder en w'eat, en put em in a crib out dar in de woods; en I bilt me a pen in de swamp, en dar I put de hogs. Den, w'en I fix all dis, I put on my Sunday cloze en groun' my axe. Two whole days I groun' dat axe. De grinestone wuz in sight er de gate en close ter de big 'ouse, en dar I tuck my stan'.

"Bimeby one day, yer come de Yankees. Two un um cum fus, en den de whole face er de yeath swarm'd wid um. De fus' glimpse I kotch un um, I tuck my axe en march inter Ole Miss settin'-room. She done had de side-bode move in dar, en I wish I may drap if twuzn't fa'rly blazin' wid silver— silver cups en silver sassers, silver plates en silver dishes, silver mugs en silver pitchers. Look like ter me dey was fixin' fer a weddin'. Dar sot Ole Miss des ez prim en ez proud ez ef she own de whole county. Dis kinder hope me up, kaze I done seed Ole Miss look dat away once befo' w'en de overseer struck me in de face wid a w'ip. I sot down by de fier wid my axe 'tween my knees. Dar we sot w'iles de Yankees ransack de place. Miss Sally, dar, she got sorter restless, but Ole Miss didn't skasely bat 'er eyes. Bimeby, we hear steps on de peazzer, en yer come a couple er young fellers wid strops on der shoulders, en der sodes a-draggin' on de flo', en der spurrers a-rattlin'. I won't say I wuz skeer'd," said Uncle Remus, as though endeavouring to recall something he failed to remember, "I won't say I wuz

skeer'd, kaze I wuzent; but I wuz took'n wid a
mighty funny feelin' in de naberhood er de gizzard.
Dey wuz mighty perlite, dem young chaps wuz ; but
Ole Miss, she never tu'n 'er head, en Miss Sally,
she look straight at de fier. Bimeby one un um
see me, en he say, sezee :

" ' Hello, ole man, w'at you doin' in yer ? ' sezee.

" ' Well, boss,' sez I, ' I bin cuttin' some wood
fer Ole Miss, en I des stop fer ter wom my han's a
little,' sez I.

" ' Hit is cole, dat's a fack,' sezee.

" Wid dat I got up en tuck my stan' behime
Ole Miss en Miss Sally, en de man w'at speak, he
went up en wom his han's. Fus' thing, you know,
he raise up sudden, en say, sezee :

" ' W'at dat on yo' axe ? '

" ' Dat's de fier shinin' on it,' sez I.

" ' Hit look like blood,' sezee ; en den he laft.

" But, bless yo' soul, dat man wouldn't never
laft dat day ef he'd know'd de wukkins er Remus's
mine. But dey didn't bodder nobody ner tech
nuthin', en bimeby dey put out. Well, de Yankees
dey kep' passin' all de mawnin,' en it look like ter
me dey wuz a string un um ten mile long. Den dey
commence gittin' thinner en thinner, en den atter
w'ile we hear skummishin' in de naberhood er
Armer's fe'y, en Ole Miss 'low how dat wuz Wheeler's
men makin' persoot. Mars Jeems wuz wid dem
Wheeler fellers, en I know'd ef dey wuz dat close
I wa'n't doin' no good settin' 'roun' de house toas'n
my shins at de fier, so I des tuck Mars Jeems's
rifle fum behime de do' en put out ter look atter my
stock.

" Seem like I ain't never see no raw day like dat,
needer befo' ner sence. Dey wa'n't no rain, but
de wet des sifted down ; mighty raw day. De leaves

on de groun' 'uz so wet dey don't make no fuss, en I got in de woods, en w'enever I year de Yankees gwine by, I des stop in my tracks en let um pass. I wuz stan'in' dat away in de aidge er de woods lookin' out 'cross a clearin', w'en—*piff !*—out come a little bunch er blue smoke fum de top er wunner dem big lonesome-lookin' pines, en den—*pow !*

"Sez I ter myse'f, sez I : 'Honey, you er right on my route, en I'll des see w'at kinder bird you got roostin' in you'; en w'iles I wuz a lookin' out bus' de smoke—*piff !* en den *bang !* Wid dat I des drapt back inter de woods, en sorter skeerted 'roun' so's ter git de tree 'twixt me en de road. I slid up putty close, en wadder you speck I see? Des ez sho's you er settin' dar lissenin' dey wuz a live Yankee up dar in dat tree, en he wuz a-loadin' en a-shootin' at de boys des ez cool ez a cowcumber in de jew ; en he had his hoss hitch out in de bushes, kaze I year de creetur tromplin' 'roun'. He had a spy-glass up dar, en w'iles I wuz a-watchin' un 'im, he raise 'er up en look thoo 'er, en den he lay 'er down en fix his gun fer ter shoot. I had good eyes in dem days, ef I ain't got um now, en 'way up de big road I see Mars Jeems a-comin'. Hit wuz too fur fer ter see his face, but I know'd 'im by de filly w'at I raise fer 'im, en she wuz a-prancin' like a school gal. I know'd dat man wuz gwineter shoot Mars Jeems ef he could, en dat wuz mo'n I could stan'. Many 's en many 's de time dat I nuss dat boy, en hilt 'im des arms, en toted 'im on dis back; en w'en I see dat Yankee lay dat gun 'cross a lim' en take aim at Mars Jeems I up wid my old rifle, en shet my eyes en let de man have all she had."

"Do you mean to say," exclaimed Miss Theodosia, indignantly, "that you shot the Union soldier, when you knew he was fighting for your freedom ?"

"Co'se, I know all about dat," responded Uncle
Remus, "en it sorter made cole chills run up my
back ; but w'en I see dat man take aim, en Mars
Jeems gwine home ter Ole Miss en Miss Sally, I
des disremembered all 'bout freedom en lammed
aloose. En den atter dat, me en Miss Sally tuck
en nuss de man right straight along. He los' one
arm in dat tree bizness, but me en Miss Sally we
nuss 'im en nuss 'im twel he done got well. Des
'bout dat time I quit nuss'n 'im, but Miss Sally
she kep' on. She kep' on," continued Uncle Remus,
pointing to Mr. Huntingdon, " en now dar he is."

"But you cost him an arm ! " exclaimed Miss
Theodosia.

"I gin 'im dem," said Uncle Remus, pointing to
Mrs. Huntingdon, "en I gin 'im deze "—holding
up his own brawny arms. "En ef dem ain't nuff
fer enny man, den I done los' de way."

HIS SAYINGS

I

JEEMS ROBER'SON'S LAST ILLNESS

A JONESBORO negro while waiting for the train to go out, met up with Uncle Remus. After the usual "time of day" had been passed between the two, the former inquired about an acquaintance.

"How's Jeems Rober'son?" he asked.

"Ain't you year 'bout Jim?" asked Uncle Remus.

"Dat I ain't," responded the other; "I ain't hear talk er Jem sence he cut loose fum de chaingang. Dat w'at make I ax. He ain't down wid de biliousness, is he?"

"Not dat I knows un," responded Uncle Remus, gravely. "He ain't sick, an' he ain't bin sick. He des tuck'n say he wuz gwineter ride dat ar roan mule er Mars John's de udder Sunday, an' de mule, she up'n do like she got nudder ingagement. I done bin fool wid dat mule befo', an' I tuck'n tole Jim dat he better not git tangle up wid 'er; but Jim, he up'n dat he wuz a hoss-doctor, an' wid dat he ax me fer a chaw terbarker, en den he got de bridle, en tuck'n kotch de mule en got on her—— Well," continued Uncle Remus, looking uneasily around, "I speck you better go git yo' ticket. Dey tells me dis yer train goes a callyhootin'."

" Hole on dar, Uncle Remus ; you ain't tell me 'bout Jim," exclaimed the Jonesboro negro.

" I done tell you all I knows, chile. Jim, he tuck'n light on de mule, and de mule she up'n hump 'erse'f, and den dey wuz a skuffle, an' w'en de dus' blow 'way, dar lay de nigger on de groun', an' de mule she stood eatin' at de troff wid wunner Jim's gallusses wrop 'roun' her behime-leg. Den atterwuds, de ker'ner, he come 'roun', an' he tuck'n gin it out dat Jim died sorter accidental like. Hit's des like I tell you : de nigger wern't sick a minnit. So long ! Bimeby you won't ketch yo' train. I got ter be knockin' long."

II

UNCLE REMUS'S CHURCH EXPERIENCE

THE deacon of a coloured church met Uncle Remus recently, and after some uninteresting remarks about the weather, asked :

" How dis you don't come down ter chu'ch no mo', Brer Remus ? We'er bin er having some mighty 'freshen' times lately."

" Hit's bin a long time sence I bin down dar, Brer Rastus, an' hit 'll be longer. I done got my dose."

" You ain't done gone an' unjined, is you, Brer Remus ? "

" Not zackly, Brer Rastus. I des tuck'n draw'd out. De members 'uz a blame sight too mutuel fer ter suit my doctrines."

" How wuz dat, Brer Remus ? "

" Well, I tell you, Brer Rastus. W'en I went ter dat chu'ch, I went des ez umbill ez de nex' one.

I went dar fer ter sing, an' fer ter pray, an' fer ter wushup, an' I mos' giner'lly allers had a stray shinplarster w'ich de ole 'oman say she want sont out dar ter dem cullud fokes 'cross de water. Hit went on dis way twel bimeby, one day, de fus' news I know'd der was a row got up in de amen cornder. Brer Dick, he 'nounced dat der wern't nuff money in de box; an' Brer Sim said if dey weren't he speck Brer Dick know'd whar it disappeared ter; an' den Brer Dick 'low'd dat he won't stan' no 'pro-busness, an' wid dat he haul off an' tuck Brer Sim under de jaw—*ker blap!*—an' den dey clinched an' drapped on de flo' an 'fout under de benches an' 'mong de wimmen.

"'Bout dat time Sis Tempy, she lipt up in de a'r, an' sing out dat she done gone an' tromple on de Ole Boy, an' she kept on lippin' up an' slingin' out er' han's twel, bimeby—*blip!*—she tuck Sis Becky in de mouf, an' den Sis Becky riz an' fetch a grab at Sis Tempy, an' I 'clar' ter grashus ef didn't 'pear ter me like she got a poun' er wool. Atter dat de revivin' sorter het up like. Bofe un um had kin 'mong de mo'ners, an' ef you ever see skufflin' an' scramblin' hit wuz den an' dar. Brer Jeems Henry, he mounted Brer Plato an' rid 'im over de railin', an' den de preacher he start down fum de pulpit, an' des ez he wuz skippin' onter de flatform a hyme-book kotch 'im in de bur er de year, an' I be bless ef it didn't soun' like a bungshell'd busted. Des den, Brer Jesse, he riz up in his seat, sorter kereless like, an' went down inter his britches atter his razer, an' right den I know'd sho' nuff trouble wuz begun. Sis Dilsey, she seed it herse'f, an' she tuck'n let off wunner dem hallyluyah hollers, an' den I disre-member w'at come ter pass.

" I'm gittin' sorter ole, Brer Rastus, an' it seem like de dus' sorter shet out de pannyrammer. Fuddermo', my lim's got ter akin, mo' speshully w'en I year Brer Sim an' Brer Dick a snortin' and a skufflin' under de benches like ez dey wuz sorter makin' der way ter my pew. So I kinder hump myse'f, an' scramble out, and de fus' man w'at I seed was a p'leeceman, an' he had a nigger 'rested, an' de fergiven name er dat nigger wuz Remus."

" He didn't 'res' you, did he, Brer Remus ? "

" Hit's des like I tell you, Brer Rastus, an' I hatter git Mars John fer to go inter my bon's fer me. Hit ain't no use fer ter sing out chu'ch ter me, Brer Rastus. I done bin an' got my dose. W'en I goes ter war, I wanter know w'at I'm a-doing. I don't wanter git hemmed up 'mong no wimmen and preachers. I wants elbow-room, an' I'm bleedzd ter have it. Des gimme elbow-room."

" But, Brer Remus, you ain't——"

" I mout drap in, Brer Rastus, an' den ag'in I moutn't ; but w'en you duz see me sa'nter in de do', wid my specs on, youk'n des say to de conger-gashun, sorter familious like, ' Yer come old man Remus wid his hoss-pistol, an' ef dar's much uv a skuffle 'roun' yer des evenin' youer gwineter year fum 'im.' Dat's me, an' dat's what you kin tell um. So long ! 'Member me to Sis Abby."

————

III

UNCLE REMUS AND THE SAVANNAH DARKEY

THE notable difference existing between the negroes in the interior of the cotton States and those on the seaboard—a difference that extends to habits and opinions as well as to dialect—has given rise to certain ineradicable prejudices which are quick to display themselves whenever an opportunity offers. These prejudices were forcibly, as well as ludicrously, illustrated in Atlanta recently. A gentleman from Savannah had been spending the summer in the mountains of north Georgia, and found it convenient to take along a body-servant. This body-servant was a very fine specimen of the average coast-negro, sleek, well-conditioned, and consequential—disposed to regard with undisguised contempt everything and everybody not indigenous to the rice-growing region—and he paraded around the streets with quite a curious and critical air. Espying Uncle Remus languidly sunning himself on a corner, the Savannah darkey approached.

"Mornin', sah."

"I'm sorter up an' about," responded Uncle Remus, carelessly and calmly. "How is you stannin' it?"

"Tanky you, my helt mos' so-so. He mo' hot dun in de mountain. Seem so lak man mus' git need[1] de shade. I enty fer see no rice-bud in dis pa'ts."

"In dis w'ich?" inquired Uncle Remus, with a sudden affectation of interest.

"In dis pa'ts. In dis country. Da plenty in Sawanny."

"Plenty whar?"

"Da plenty in Sawanny. I enty fer see no crab an' no oscher; en swimp, he no stay 'roun'. I lak some rice-bud now."

"Youer talkin' 'bout deze yere sparrers, w'ich dey er all head, en 'lev'm un makes one mouffle,[2]

---

[1] Underneath.   [2] Mouthful.

I speck," suggested Uncle Remus. "Well, dey
er yer," he continued, "but dis ain't no climate
whar de rich-birds flies inter yo' pockets en gets
out de money an' makes de change derse'f; an'
de isters don't shuck off der shells en run over you
on de street, an' no mo' duz de s'imp hull derse'f
an drap in ya' mouf. But dey er yer, dough. De
scads'll fetch um."

"Him po' country fer true," commented the
Savannah negro; "he no like Sawanny. Down
da, we set need de shade an' eaty de rice-bud, an'
de crab, an' de swimp tree time de day; an' de
buckra man drinky him wine, an' smoky him seegyar
all troo de night. Plenty fer eat an' not much fer
wuk."

"Hit's mighty nice, I speck," responded Uncle
Remus gravely. "De nigger dat ain't hope up
'longer high, feedin' ain't got no grip. But up yer
whar fokes is gotter scramble 'roun' an' make der
own livin', de vittles w'at's kumerlated widout any
sweatin' mos' allers gener'lly b'longs ter some yuther
man by rights. One hoecake an' a rasher er middlin'
meat las's me fum Sunday ter Sunday, an' I'm
in a mighty big streak er luck w'en I gits dat."

The Savannah negro here gave utterance to a loud
contemptuous laugh, and began to fumble somewhat
ostentatiously with a big brass watch-chain.

"But I speck I struck up wid a payin' job las'
Chuseday," continued Uncle Remus in a hopeful
tone.

"Wey you gwan to?"

"Oh, I'm a-waitin' on a culled gemmun from
Savannah—wunner dese yer high livers you bin
tellin' 'bout."

"How dat?"

"I loant 'im two dollars," responded Uncle

Remus grimly, " an I'm a-waitin' on 'im fer de money. Hit's wunner deze yer jobs w'at las's a long time."

The Savannah negro went off after his rice-birds, while Uncle Remus leaned up against the wall and laughed until he was in imminent danger of falling down from sheer exhaustion.

IV

TURNIP SALAD AS A TEXT

As Uncle Remus was going down the street recently he was accosted by several acquaintances.

" Heyo ! " said one, " here comes Uncle Remus. He look like he gwine fer ter set up a bo'din-house."

Several others bantered the old man, but he appeared to be in a good humour. He was carrying a huge basket of vegetables.

" How many er you boys," said he, as he put his basket down, " is done a han's turn dis day ? En yit de week's done commence. I year talk er niggers dat's got money in de bank, but I lay hit ain't none er you fellers. Whar you speck you gwinter git yo' dinner, en how you speck you gwineter git 'long ? "

" Oh, we sorter knocks 'roun' and picks up a livin'," responded one.

" Dat's w'at make I say w'at I duz," said Uncle Remus. " Folks go 'bout in de day-time an' makes a livin', an' you come 'long w'en dey er res'in' der bones an' picks it up. I ain't no han' at figgers, but I lay I k'n count up right yer in de san' en number up how menny days hit'll be 'fo' you er cuppled on ter de chain-gang."

"De ole man's holler'n now, sho', " said one of the listeners, gazing with admiration on the venerable old darkey.

"I ain't takin' no chances 'bout vittles. Hit's proned inter me fum de fus' dat I got ter eat, en I knows dat I got fer ter grub fer w'at I gits. Hit's ag'in de mor'l law fer niggers fer ter eat w'en dey don't wuk, an' w'en you see um 'pariently fattenin' on a'r, you k'n des bet dat ruinashun's gwine on some'rs. I got mustard, en poke salid, en lam's quarter in dat baskit, en me en my ole 'oman gwineter sample it. Ef enny you boys git a invite you come, but ef you don't you better stay 'way. I gotter muskit out dar w'at's used ter persidin' 'roun' whar dey's a cripple nigger. Don't you fergit dat off'n yo' mine."

V

A CONFESSION

"W'at's dis yer I see, great big niggers gwine 'lopin' 'roun' town wid cakes'n pies fer ter sell ? " asked Uncle Remus recently, in his most scornful tone.

"That's what they are doing," responded a young man : "that's the way they make a living."

"Dat w'at make I say w'at I duz—dat w'at keep me grum'lin' w'en I goes in cullud fokes' s'ciety. Some niggers ain't gwine ter wuk nohow, an' hit's flingin' 'way time fer ter set enny chain-gang traps fer ter ketch um."

"Well, now, here ! " exclaimed the young man, in a dramatic tone, "what are you giving us now ? Isn't it just as honest and just as regular to sell pies as it is to do any other kind of work ? "

"Tain't dat, boss," said the old man, seeing that he was about to be cornered; "'tain't dat. Hit's de nas'ness un it w'at gits me."

"Oh, get out!"

"Dat's me, boss, up an' down. Ef dere's ruin-ashun ennywhar in de known wurril, she goes in de comp'ny uv a hongry nigger w'at's a-totin' pies 'roun'. Sometimes w'en I git kotch wid emptiness in de pit er de stummuck, an' git ter fairly honin' arter sump'n' w'at got substance in it, den hit look like unto me dat I kin stan' flat-footed an' make more cle'r money eatin' pies dan I could if I wuz ter sell de las' one twixt dis an' Chris'mus. An' de nigger w'at k'n trapes 'round wid pies and not git in no alley-way an' sample um, den I'm bleedzd ter say dat nigger outniggers me an' my fambly. So dar now!"

VI

UNCLE REMUS WITH THE TOOTHACHE

WHEN Uncle Remus put in an appearance one morning recently, his friends knew he had been in trouble. He had a red cotton handkerchief tied under his chin, and the genial humour that usually makes his aged face its dwelling-place had given way to an expression of grim melancholy. The young men about the office were inclined to chaff him, but his look of sullen resignation remained unchanged.

"What revival did you attend last night?" inquired one.

"What was the colour of the mule that did the hammering?" asked another.

"I always told the old man that a suburban chicken-coop would fall on him," remarked some one.

"A strange pig has been squealing in his ear," suggested some one else.

But Uncle Remus remained impassive. He seemed to have lost all interest in what was going on around him, and he sighed heavily as he seated himself on the edge of the trash-box in front of the office. Finally some one asked, in a sympathetic tone:

"What is the matter, old man? You look like you'd been through the mill."

"Now you'er knocking at de back do', sho'. Ef I ain't bin thoo de mill sence day 'fo' yistiddy, den dey ain't no mills in de lan'. Ef wunner deze yer scurshun trains had runned over me I couldn't er bin wuss off. I bin trompin' 'roun' in de low-groun's now gwine on seventy-fi' year, but I ain't see no sich times ez dat w'at I done spe'unst now. Boss, is enny er you all ever rastled wid de toof-ache?"

"Oh, hundreds of times! The toothache isn't anything."

"Den you des play'd 'roun' de aidges. You ain't had de kine w'at kotch me on de underjaw. You mout a had a gum-bile, but you ain't bin boddered wid de toofache. I wuz settin' up talkin' wid my ole 'oman, kinder puzzlin' 'roun' fer ter see whar de nex' meal's vittles wuz a gwine-ter cum fum, an' I feel a little ache sorter crawlin' long on my jaw-bone, kinder feelin' his way. But de ache don't stay long. He sorter hankered 'roun' like, en den crope back whar he cum fum. Bimeby I feel 'im comin' ag'in, an' dis time hit look like he come up closer—kinder skummishin' 'roun' fer ter see how de lan' lay. Den he went off. Present'y I feel 'im comin', an' dis time hit look like he kyar'd de news unto Mary, fer hit feel like der wuz anudder wun wid 'im. Dey crep' up an' crep' 'roun', an' den dey crope off. Bimeby dey come back, an' dis time dey come like dey wuzen't 'fear'd er de s'roundin's, fer dey trot right up unto de toof, sorter zamine it like, an' den trot all roun' it, like deze yer circuous hosses. I sot dar mighty ca'm, but I spected dat sump'n' wuz gwine ter happ'n."

"And it happened, did it?" asked some one in the group surrounding the old man.

"Boss, don't you fergit it," responded Uncle Remus, fervidly. "W'en dem aches gallop back dey galloped fer ter stay, an' dey wuz so mixed up dat I couldn't tell one fum de udder. All night long dey racked an' dey galloped, an' w'en dey got tired er rackin' an' gallopin', dey all cloze in on de ole toof an' thumped it an' gouged at it twel it 'peared unto me dat dey had got de jawbone loosened up, an' wuz tryin' fer ter fetch it up thoo de top er my head an' out at der back er my neck. An' dey got wuss nex' day. Mars John, he seed I wuz 'stracted, an' he tole me fer ter go roun' yere an' git sump'n put on it, an' de drug man he 'lowed dat I better have 'er draw'd, an' his wuds wuzent more'n cole 'fo' wunner deze yer watchyoumaycolluns—wunner deze dentis' mens—had retched fer it wid a pa'r er tongs w'at don't tu'n loose w'en dey ketches a holt. Leas'-ways dey didn't wid me. You oughter seed dat toof, boss. Hit wuz wunner deze yer fo'-prong fellers. Ef she'd a grow'd wrong een' out'ard, I'd a bin a bad nigger long arter I jin'd de chu'ch. You year'd my ho'n!'"

VII

THE PHONOGRAPH

"Unc. Remus," asked a tall, awkward-looking negro, who was one of a crowd surrounding the old man, " wat's dis 'ere w'at dey calls de fonygraf— dish yer inst'ument w'at kin holler 'roun' like little chillun in de back yard ? "

" I ain't seed um," said Uncle Remus, feeling in his pocket for a fresh chew of tobacco, " I ain't seed um ; but I year talk un um. Miss Sally wuz a-readin' in de papers las' Chuseday, an' she say dat's it's a mighty big watchyoumaycollum."

" A mighty big w'ich ? " asked one of the crowd.

" A mighty big w'atzisname," answered Uncle Remus, cautiously. " I wuzent up dar close to whar Miss Sarah was a-readin', but I kinder geddered in dat it was one er deze 'ere w'atzisnames w'at you hollers inter one year an' it comes out er de udder. Hit's mighty funny unter me how deze folks kin go an' prognosticate der eckoes inter one er deze yer i'on boxes, an' dar hit'll stay on twel de man comes 'long an' tu'ns de handle an' lets de fuss come pilin' out. Bimeby day'll git ter makin' sho' nuff fokes, an' den dere'll be a racket 'roun' here. Dey tells me dat it goes off like one er deze yer torpedoes."

" You year dat, don't you ? " said one or two of the younger negroes.

" Dat's w'at dey tells me," continued Uncle Remus. " Dat's w'at dey sez. Hit's one er deze yer kinder w'atzisnames w'at sasses back w'en you hollers at it."

" W'at dey fix um up fer, den ? " asked one of the practical negroes.

"Dat's w'at I wanter know," said Uncle Remus, contemplatively. "But dat's w'at Miss Sally wuz a-readin' in de paper. All you gotter do is ter holler at de box, an dar's yo' remarks. Dey goes in, an' dar dey er tooken and dar dey hangs on twel you shakes de box, an' den dey draps out des ez fresh ez deze yer fishes w'at you git fum Savannah, an' you ain't got time for ter look at dere gills, nudder."

VIII

RACE IMPROVEMENT

"DERE'S a kind er limberness 'bout niggers dese days dat's mighty cu'us," remarked Uncle Remus yesterday, as he deposited a pitcher of fresh water upon the exchange table. "I notisses it in de alley-ways an' on de street-cornders. Dey er rackin' up mon deze yer cullud fokes is."

"What are you trying to give us now?" inquired one of the young men, in a bilious tone.

"The old man's mind is wandering," said the society editor, smoothing the wrinkles out of his lavender kids.

Uncle Remus laughed. "I speck I is a-gittin' mo' frailer dan I wuz fo' de fahmin days wuz over, but I scos wid my eyes an' I years wid my years, same ez enny er deze yer youno bucks w'at goes a-gallopin' 'roun' huntin' up devilment; an' w'en I sees de limberness er deze yer cullud people, an' w'en I sees how dey er dancin' up, den I gets sorter hopeful. Dey er kinder ketchin' up wid me."

"How is that?"

"Oh, dey er movin'," responded Uncle Remus. "Dey er sorter comin' 'roun'. Dey er gittin' so dey b'leeve dat dey ain't no better dan de w'ite fokes. W'en freedom come out de niggers sorter got dere humps up, an' dey staid dat way, twel bimeby dey begun fer ter get hongry an' den dey begun fer ter drap inter line right smartually; an' now," continued the old man, emphatically, "dey er des ez palaverous ez dey wuz befo' de war. Dey er gittin' on solid groun', mon.'

"You think they are improving, then?"

"Youer chawin' guv'nment now, boss. You slap de law onter a nigger a time er two, an' larn 'im dat he's got fer to look atter his own rashuns an' keep out'n udder fokes's chick'n-coops, an' sorter coax 'im inter de idee dat he's got ter feed 'is own chilluns, an' I be blessed ef you ain't got 'im on risin' groun'. An', mo'n dat, w'en he gits holt er de fack dat a nigger k'n have yaller fever same ez w'ite folks, you done got 'im on de mo'ners' bench; an' den ef you come down strong on de p'int dat he oughter stan' fas' by de folks w'at hope him w'en he wuz in trouble de job's done. W'en you does dat, ef you ain't got yo' han's on a new-made nigger, den my name ain't Remus, an' ef dat name's bin changed I ain't seen her abbertized."

IX

IN THE RÔLE OF A TARTAR

A CHARLESTON negro who was in Atlanta on the Fourth of July made a mistake. He saw Uncle

Remus edging his way through the crowd, and thought he knew him.

"Howdy, Daddy Ben?" the stranger exclaimed. "I tink I nubber see you no mo'. Wey you gwan? He hot fer true, ain't he?"

"Daddy who?" asked Uncle Remus, straightening himself up with dignity. "W'ich?"

"I know you in Charl'son, an' den in Sewanny. I speck I dun grow way frum 'membrance."

"You know'd me in Charlstun, and den in Savanny?"

"He been long time, ain't he, Daddy Ben?"

"Dat's w'at's a-pesterin' un me. How much you reckon you know'd me?"

"He good while pas'; when I wer' pickaninny. He long time ago. Wey you gwan, Daddy Ben?"

"W'at does you season your recollection wid fer ter make it hole on so?" inquired the old man.

"I dunno. He stick hese'f. I see you comin' 'long 'n I say 'Dey Daddy Ben.' I tink I see you no mo', an' I shaky you by de han'. Wey you gwan? Dey no place yer wey we git wine?"

Uncle Remus stared at the strange darkey curiously for a moment, and then he seized him by the arm.

"Come yer, son, whar dey ain't no folks an' lemme drap some Jawjy 'intment in dem years er yone. Youer mighty fur ways fum home, an' you wanter be a-lookin' out fer yo'se'f. Fus' and fo'mus, youer thumpin' de wrong watermillion. Youer w'isslin' up de wrong chube. I ain't tromped roun' de country much. I ain't bin to Charlstun, an' needer is I tuck in Savanny; but you couldn't rig up no game on me dat I wouldn't tumble on to it de minnit I laid my eyeballs on you. W'en hit come ter dat I'm ole man Tumbler, fum Tumblers-

ville—I is dat. Hit takes one er deze yer full-
blooded w'ite men fer ter trap my jedgment. But
w'en a nigger comes a-jabberin' 'roun' like he got
a mouf full er rice straw, he ain't got no mo' chance
'long side er me dan a sick sparrer wid a squinch-
owl. You gotter travel wid a circus 'fo' you gits
away wid me. You better go 'long an' git yo'
kyarpet-sack and skip de town. Youer de freshest
nigger w'at I seen yit."

The Charleston negro passed on just as a policeman came up.

" Boss, you see dat smart Ellick ? "

" Yes ; what's the matter with him ? "

" He's one er deze yer skurshun niggers from
Charlstun. I seed you a-stannin' over agin de
cornder yander, an' ef dat nigger'd a-drawd his
monty kyards on me, I wuz a gwineter holler fer
you. Would youer come, boss ? '

" Why, certainly, Uncle Remus."

" Dat's w'at I 'lowd. Little more'n he'd a-bin
aboard er de wrong waggin. Dat's w'at he'd a-bin."

X

A CASE OF MEASLES

" YOU'VE been looking like you were rather under
the weather for the past week or two, Uncle Remus,"
said a gentleman to the old man.

" You'd be sorter puny, too, boss, if you'd er
bin whar I bin."

" Where have you been ? "

" 'Pear ter me like eve'ybody done year 'bout dat.

Dey ain't no ole nigger my age an' size dat's had no rattliner time dan I is."

"A kind of picnic ? "

"Go 'long, boss ! w'at you speck I be doin' sailin' 'roun' ter deze yer cullud picnics ? Much mo' an' I wouldn't make bread by wukkin fer't, let 'lone follerin' up a passel er boys an' gals all over keration. Boss, ain't you year 'bout it, sho' nuff ? "

"I haven't, really. What was the matter ? "

"I got strucken wid a sickness, an' she hit de ole nigger a joe-darter 'fo' she tu'n 'im loose."

"What kind of sickness ? "

"Hit look sorter cu'ous, boss, but ole an' steddy ez I is, I tuck'n kotch de meezles."

"Oh, get out ! You are trying to get up a sensation."

"Hit's a nat'al fack, boss, I declar' ter grashus ef 'tain't. Dey sorter come on wid a cole, like— leas'ways dat's how I commence fer ter suffer, an' den er koff got straddle er de cole—one deze yer koffs w'at look like hit goes ter de foundash'n. I kep' on linger'n' 'roun' sorter keepin' one eye on de rheumatiz an' de udder on de distemper, twel, bimeby, I begin fer ter feel de trestle-wuk give way, an' den I des know'd dat I wuz gwineter gitter racket. I slipt inter bed on Chuseday night, an' I never slip out no mo' fer mighty nigh er mont'.

"Nex' mornin' de meezles'd done kivered me, an' den ef I didn't git dosted by de ole 'oman I'm a Chinee. She gimme back rashuns er sassafac tea. I des nat'ally kankered an' get hongry atter water, an' eve'y time I sing out fer water I got b'ilin' hot sassafac tea. Hit got so dat w'en I wake up in de mornin' de ole 'oman'd des come 'long wid a kittle er tea an' fill me up. Dey tells me 'roun' town dat chilluns don't git hurted wid de meezles, w'ich ef dey don't I wanter be a baby de nex' time dey hits dis place. All dis yer meezles bizness is bran'-new ter me. In ole times, 'fo' de wah, I ain't heer tell er no seventy-fi'-year-ole nigger grapplin' wid no meezles. Dey ain't ketchin' no mo', is dey, boss?"

"Oh, no—I suppose not."

"'Kaze ef dey is, youk'n des put my name down wid de migrashun niggers."

XI

THE EMIGRANTS

When Uncle Remus went down to the passenger depôt one morning recently, the first sight that caught his eye was an old negro man, a woman, and two children sitting in the shade near the door of the baggage-room. One of the children was very young, and the quartet was altogether ragged and forlorn-looking. The sympathies of Uncle Remus were immediately roused. He approached the group by forced marches, and finally unburdened his curiosity:

"Whar is you m'anderin' unter, pard?"

The old negro, who seemed to be rather suspicious, looked at Uncle Remus coolly, and appeared to be considering whether he should make any reply. Finally, however, he stretched himself and said:

"We er gwine down in de naberhoods er Tally-poosy, an' we ain't makin' no fuss 'bout it, nudder."

"I disrember," said Uncle Remus, thoughtfully, "whar Tallypoosy is."

"Oh, hit's out yan," replied the old man, motioning his head as if it was just beyond the iron gates of the depôt. "Hit's down in Alabam. When we git dar, maybe we'll go on twel we gits ter Massasip."

"Is you got enny folks out dar?" inquired Uncle Remus.

"None dat I knows un."

"An' youer takin' dis 'oman an' deze chillun out dar whar dey dunno nobody? Whar's yo' perwisions?" eyeing a chest with a rope around it.

"Dem's our bed-cloze," the old negro explained, noticing the glance of Uncle Remus. "All de vittles what we got we e't 'fo' we started."

"An' you speck ter retch dar safe an' soun'? Whar's yo' ticket?"

"Ain't got none. De man say ez how dey'd pass us thoo. I gin a man a fi'dollar bill 'fo' I lef' Jonesboro, an' he sed dat settled it."

"Lemme tell you dis," said Uncle Remus, straightening up indignantly: "you go an' rob somebody an' git on de chain-gang, an' let de 'oman scratch 'roun' yer' an' make 'er livin'; but don't you get on dem kyars—don't you do it. Yo' bes' holt is de chain-gang. Yo kin make yo' livin' dar w'en you can't make it nowhars else. But don't you git on dem kyars. Ef you do, youer gone nigger. Ef you ain't got no money fer ter walk back wid, you better des b'il' yo' nes' right here. I'm a-talkin' wid de bark on. I done seed deze yer Arkinsaw emmygrants come

lopein' back, an' some un 'em didn't have rags
nuff on 'em fer ter hide dere nakidness. You
leave dat box right whar she is, an' let de 'oman
take wun young un an' you take de udder wun,
an' den you git in de middle er de big road an'
pull out fer de place whar you come fum. I'm
preachin' now."

Those who watched say the quartet didn't take
the cars.

XII

AS A MURDERER

UNCLE REMUS met a police officer recently.

"You ain't hear talk er no dead nigger nowhar
dis mawnin', is you, boss?" asked the old man,
earnestly.

"No," replied the policeman, reflectively. "No,
I believe not. Have you heard of any?"

"'Pears unter me dat I come mighty nigh gittin'
some news 'bout dat size, and dats w'at I'm a-
huntin' fer. Bekase ef dey er foun' a stray nigger
layin' 'roun' loose, wid 'is bref gone, den I wanter
go home an' git my brekfus, and put on some clean
cloze, an' 'liver myse'f up ter wunner deze yer
jestesses er de peace, an' git a fa'r trial."

"Why, have you killed anybody?"

"Dat's w'at I'm a'quirin' inter now, but I
wouldn't be sustonished ef I ain't laid a nigger out
some'rs on de subbubs. Hit's done got so it's
agin de law fer ter bus' loose an' kill a nigger, ain't
it, boss?"

"Well, I should say so. You don't mean to tell me that you have killed a coloured man, do you?"

"I speck I is, Boss. I speck I done gone an' done it dis time, sho'. Hit's been sorter growin' on me, an' it come ter a head dis mawnin', less my name ain't Remus, an' dat's w'at dey bin er callin' me sence I wuz ole er nuff fer ter scratch myse'f wid my lef' han'."

"Well, if you've killed a man, you'll have some fun, sure enough. How was it?"

"Hit wuz dis way, boss : I wuz layin' in my bed dis mawnin' sorter ruminatin 'roun', when de fus news I know'd I year a fus 'mong de chickens, an' den my brissels riz. I done had lots er trubble wid dem chickens, an' w'en I years wun un um squall my ve'y shoes comes ontied. So I des sorter riz up an' retch fer my ole muskit, and den I crope out er de back do', an' w'atter you reckin I seed?"

"I couldn't say."

"I seed de biggest, blackest nigger dat you ever laid eyes on. He shined like de paint on 'im was fresh. He hed done grabbed fo'er my forwardes' pullets. I crope up nigh de do', an' hollered an' axed 'im how he wuz a-gittin' on, an' den he broke, an ez he broke I jammed de gun in de small er his back and banged aloose. He let a yell like forty yaller cats a-courtin', an' den he broke. You ain't seed no nigger hump hisse'f like dat nigger. He tore down de well shelter an fo' pannils er fence, an' de groun' look like wunner deze yer harrycanes had lit dar and fanned up de yeath."

"Why, I thought you killed him?"

"He bleedzed ter be dead, boss. Ain't I put de

gun right on 'im ?   Seem like I feel 'im give way
w'en she went off."

" Was the gun loaded ? "

" Dat's w'at my ole 'oman say. She had de
powder in dar, sho', but I disrember wedder I put
de buckshot in, er wedder I lef' um out. Leas'-
ways, I'm gwineter call on wunner deze yer jestesses.
So long, boss."

XIII

HIS PRACTICAL VIEW OF THINGS

" BRER REMUS, is you heern tell er deze doin's
out yer in de udder eend er town ? " asked a coloured
deacon of the church the other day.

" W'at doin's is dat, Brer Ab ? "

" Deze yer signs an' wunders whar dat cullud
lady died day 'fo' yistiddy. Mighty quare goin's
on out dar, Brer Remus, sho's you bawn."

" Sperrits ? " inquired Uncle Remus, sententiously.

" Wuss'n dat, Brer Remus. Some say dat jedgment day ain't fur off, an' de folks is flockin' 'roun'
de house a-hollerin' an' a-shoutin' des like dey
wuz in er revival. In de winder glass dar you
kin see de flags a-flyin', an' Jacob's lather is dar,
an' dar's writin' on de pane w'at no man can't read—
leas'ways dey ain't none read it yit."

" W'at kinder racket is dis youer givin' un me
now, Brer Ab ? "

" I done bin dar, Brer Remus ; I done see um

wid bofe my eyes. Cullud lady what wuz in-
tranced done woke up an' say de ain't much time
fer ter tarry. She say she meet er angel in de road,
an' he p'inted straight fer de mornin' star, an' tell
her fer ter prepar'. Hit look mighty cu'us, Brer
Remus."

"Cum down ter dat, Brer Ab," said Uncle Remus,
wiping his spectacles carefully, and readjusting
them—"cum down ter dat, an' dey ain't nuthin'
dat ain't cu'us. I ain't no 'spishus nigger myse'f,
but I 'spizes fer ter year dogs a-howli n' an' squinch-
owls havin' de ager out in de woods, an' w'en a
bull goes a-bellerin' by de house den my bones git
cole an' my flesh commences fer ter creep; but
w'en it comes ter deze yer sines in de a'r an' deze
yer sperrits in de woods, den I'm out—den I'm
done. I is, fer a fack. I bin livin' more'n seventy
year, an I year talk er niggers seein' ghos'es all
times er night an' all times er day, but I ain't
never seed one yit; an' deze yer flags an' Jacob's
lathers, I ain't seed dem, nudder."

"Dey er dar, Brer Remus."

"Hit's des like I tell you, Brer Ab. I ain't
'sputin 'bout it, but I ain't seed um, an' I don't
take no chances deze days on dat w'at I don't see,
an dat w'at I sees I got ter 'zamine mighty close.
Lemme tell you dis, Brer Ab: don't you let deze
sines onsettle you. W'en old man Gabrile toot
his ho'n, he ain't gwineter hang no sine out in de
windor-panes, an' when ole Fadder Jacob lets down
dat lather er his'n you'll be mighty ap' er te hear
de racket. An' don't you bodder wid jedgment
day. Jedgment day is lierbul fer ter take keer un
itse'f."

"Dat's so, Brer Remus."

"Hit's bleedzed ter be so, Brer Ab. Hit don't

bodder me.   Hit's done got so now dat w'en I
gotter pone er bread, an' a rasher er bacon, an nuff
grease fer ter make gravy, I ain't keerin' much
w'edder fokes sees ghos'es er no."

XIV

THAT DECEITFUL JUG

UNCLE REMUS was in good humour one evening
recently when he dropped casually into the editorial
room of "The Constitution," as has been his custom for the past year or two.   He had a bag slung
across his shoulder, and in the bag was a jug.   The
presence of this humble but useful vessel in Uncle
Remus's bag was made the occasion for several
suggestive jokes at his expense by the members of
the staff, but the old man's good humour was proof
against all insinuations.

"Dat ar jug's bin ter wah, mon.   Hit's wunner
deze yer ole timers.   I got dat jug down dar in
Putmon County w'en Mars 'Lisha Perryman wuz a
young man, an' now he's done growed up, an' got
ole an' died, an' his chilluns is growed up an' dey
kin count dere gran'-chilluns, an' yit dar's dat jug
des ez lively an' ez lierbul fer ter kick up devilment
ez w'at she wuz w'en she come fum de foundry."

"That's the trouble," said one of the young
men.   "That's the reason we'd like to know
what's in it now."

"Now youer gittin on ma'shy groun'," replied Uncle Remus. "Dat's de p'int. Dat's w'at make me say w'at I duz. I bin knowin' dat jug now gwine on sixty-fi' year, an' de jug w'at's more 'seetful dan dat jug ain't on de top-side er de worrul. Dar she sets," continued the old man, gazing at it reflectively, "dar she sets dez ez natchul ez er ambertype, an' yit whar's de man w'at kin tell w'at kinder confab she's a-gwineter carry on w'en dat corn-cob is snatched outen 'er mouf? Dat jug is mighty 'seetful, mon."

"Well, it don't deceive any of us up here," remarked the agricultural editor, dryly. "We've seen jugs before."

"I boun' you is, boss; I boun' you is. But you ain't seed no 'seetful jug like dat. Dar she sets a-bellyin' out an' lookin' mighty fat an' full, an' yit she'd set dar a-bellyin' out ef dere wuzent nuthin' but win' under dat stopper. You knows dat she ain't got no aigs in her, ner no bacon, ner no grits, ner no termartusses, ner no shellots, an' dat's 'bout all you duz know. Dog my cats ef de 'seetfulness er dat jug don't git away wid me," continued Uncle Remus, with a chuckle. "I wuz comin' 'cross de bridge des now, an' Brer John Henry seed me wid de bag slung onter my back, an de jug in it, an' he ups an' sez, sezee:

"'Heyo, Brer Remus, ain't it gittin' late for water-millions?'

"Hit wuz de 'seetfulness er dat jug. If Brer John Henry know'd de colour er dat water-million, I speck he'd snatch me up 'fo' de cunfunce. I 'clar' ter grashus ef dat jug ain't a caution!"

"I suppose it's full of molasses now," remarked one of the young men, sarcastically.

"Hear dat!" exclaimed Uncle Remus, triumphantly—"hear dat! W'at I tell you? I sed dat jug wuz 'seetful, an' I sticks to it. I bin knowin' dat——"

"What has it got in it?" broke in some one; "molasses, kerosene, or train-oil?"

"Well, I say she's loaded, boss. I ain't shuk her up sence I drapt in, but I lay she's loaded."

"Yes," said the agricultural editor, "and it's the meanest bug-juice in town—regular sorghum skimmings."

"Dat's needer yer ner dar," responded Uncle Remus. "Po' fokes better be fixin' up for Chris'-mus now w'ile rashuns is cheap. Dat's me. W'en I year Miss Sally gwine 'bout de house w'isslin' 'W'en I k'n Read my Titles Cler,'—an' w'en I see de martins swawmin' atter sundown—an' w'en I year de peckerwoods confabbin tergedder deze moonshiny nights in my een' er town—den I knows de hot wedder's a-breakin' up, an' I knows it's 'bout time fer po' fokes fer ter be rastlin' 'roun' and huntin' up dere rashuns. Dat's me, up an' down."

"Well, we are satisfied. Better go and hire a hall," remarked the sporting editor, with a yawn. "If you are engaged in a talking match you have won the money. Blanket him, somebody, and take him to the stable."

"An' w'at's mo'," continued the old man, scorning to notice the insinuation, "dough I year Miss Sally w'isslin', an' de peckerwoods a-chatterin', I ain't seein' none er deze yer loafin' niggers fixin' up fer ter 'migrate. Dey kin holler Kansas all 'roun' de naberhood, but 'ceppin' a man come 'long an' spell it wid greenbacks, he don't ketch none er deze yer town niggers. You year me, dey ain't gwine."

"Stand him up on the table," said the sporting editor; "give him room."

"Better go down yer ter de calaboose, an' git some news fer ter print," said Uncle Remus, with a touch of irony in his tone. "Some new nigger mighter broke inter jail."

"You say the darkeys are not going to emigrate this year?" inquired the agricultural editor, who is interested in these things.

"Shoo! dat dey ain't! I done seed an' I knows."

"Well, how do you know?"

"How you tell w'en crow gwineter light? Niggers bin prom'nadin' by my house all dis summer, holdin' dere heads high up an de w'ites er dere eyeballs shinin' in de sun. Dey wuz too biggity fer ter look over de gyardin' palin's. 'Long 'bout den de wedder wuz fetchin' de nat'al sperrits er turkentime outen de pine-trees an' de groun' wuz fa'rly smokin' wid de hotness. Now dat it's gittin' sorter airish in de mornin's, dey don't 'pear like de same niggers. Dey done got so dey'll look over in de yard, an' nex' news you know dey'll be tryin' fer ter scrape up 'quaintance wid de dog. W'en dey passes now dey looks at de chicken-coop an' at de tater-patch. W'en you see niggers gittin' dat familious, you kin 'pen' on dere campin' wid you de ballunce er de season. Day 'fo' yistiddy I kotch one un um lookin' over de fence at my shoats, an' I sez, sez I.

"'Duz you wanter purchis dem hogs?'

"'Oh, no,' sezee, 'I wuz des lookin' at dere p'ints.'

"'Well, dey ain't p'intin' yo' way,' sez I, 'an, fuddermo,' ef you don't bodder 'longer dem hogs dey ain't gwineter clime outer dat pen an' 'tack you, nudder,' sez I.

"An' I boun'," continued Uncle Remus, driving the corn-cob stopper a little tighter in his deceitful jug and gathering up his bag—"an' I boun' dat my ole muskit'll go off 'tween me an' dat same nigger yit, an' he'll be at de bad een', an' dis 'seetful jug'll 'fuse ter go ter de funer'l."

XV

THE FLORIDA WATER-MELON

"Look yer, boy," said Uncle Remus yesterday, stopping near the railroad crossing on Whitehall Street, and gazing ferociously at a small coloured youth; "look yer, boy, I'll lay you out flat ef you come flingin' yo' water-million rimes under my foot—you watch ef I don't. You k'n play yo' pranks on deze yer w'ite fokes, but w'en you come a-cuttin' up yo' capers roun' me you'll lan' right in de middle uv er spell er sickness—now you mine w'at I tell you. An' I ain't gwine fer ter put up wid none er yo' sassness nudder—let 'lone flingin' water-million rimes whar I kin git mixt up wid um. I done had nuff water-millions yistiddy an' de day befo'."

"How was that, Uncle Remus?" asked a gentleman standing near.

"Hit wuz sorter like dis, boss. Las' Chuseday, Mars John he fotch home two er deze yer Flurridy water-millions, an' him an' Miss Sally sot down fer ter eat um. Mars John an' Miss Sally ain't got nuthin' dat's too good fer me, an' de fus news I know'd wuz Miss Sally a-hollerin for Remus. I done smelt de water-million on dea'r, an' I ain't got no better sense dan fer ter go w'en I years w'ite fokes a-hollerin—I larnt dat w'en I wa'n't so high. Leas'ways I galloped up ter de back po'ch, an' dar sot de water-millions des ez natchul ez ef dey'd bin raised on de ole Spivey place in Putmon County. Den Miss Sally, she cut me off er slishe—wunner deze yer ongodly slishes, big ez yo' hat, an' I sot down on de steps an' wrop myse'f roun' de whole blessid chunk, 'cepin' de rime." Uncle Remus paused and laid his hand upon his stomach as if feeling for something.

" Well, old man, what then ? "

" Dat's w'at I'm a-gittin' at, boss," said Uncle Remus, smiling a feeble smile. " I sa'ntered roun' 'bout er half'n'our, an' den I begin fer ter feel sorter squeemish—sorter like I done bin an' swoller'd 'bout fo' poun's off'n de ruff een' uv er scantlin'. Look like ter me dat I wuz gwineter be sick, an' den it look like I wuzent. Bimeby a little pain showed 'is head an' sorter m'andered roun' like he wuz a-lookin' fer a good place fer ter ketch holt, an den a great big pain jump up an' take atter de little one an' chase 'im roun' an' 'roun', an' he mus' er kotch 'im, 'kaze bimeby de big pain retch down an' grab dis yer lef' leg oo an' haul 'im up, an' den he retch down an' grab de udder one an' pull him up, an' den de wah begun, sho' 'nuff. Fer mighty nigh fo' hours dey kep' up dat racket, an' des ez soon ez a little pain 'ud jump up de big un 'ud light onter it an' gobble it up, an' den de big un 'ud go sailin' roun' huntin' fer mo'. Some fokes is mighty cu'us, dough. Nex' mawnin' I hear Miss Sally a-laughin' an' singin' an' a-w'isslin' des like dey want no water-millions raise in

Flurridy. But somebody better pen dis yer nigger boy up w'en I'm on de town—I kin tell you dat."

XVI

UNCLE REMUS PREACHES TO A CONVERT

"DEY tells me you done jine de chu'ch," said Uncle Remus to Pegleg Charley.

"Yes, sir," responded Charley, gravely, "dat's so."

"Well, I'm mighty glad er dat," remarked Uncle Remus, with unction. "It's 'bout time dat I wuz spectin' fer ter hear un you in de chaingang, an', stidder dat, hit's de chu'ch. Well, dey ain't no tellin' deze days whar a nigger's gwineter lan'."

"Yes," responded Charley, straightening himself up and speaking in a dignified tone, "yes, I'm fixin' to do better. I'm preparin' fer ter shake worldliness. I'm done quit so'shatin' wid deze w'ite town boys. Dey've been a-goin' back on me too rapidly here lately, an' now I'm a-goin' back on dem."

"Well, ef you done had de 'speunce un it, I'm mighty glad. Ef you got 'lijjun, you better hole on to it 'twell de las' day in de mornin'. Hit's mighty good fer ter kyar' 'roun' wid you in de day time an' likewise in de night-time. Hit'll pay you mo' dan politics, an' ef you stan's up like you oughter, hit'll las' longer dan a bone-fellum. But you wanter have one er deze yer ole-time grips, an' you des gotter shet yo' eyes an' swing on like wunner deze yer bull-tarrier dogs."

"Oh, I'm goin' to stick, Uncle Remus. You

kin put your money on dat. Deze town boys can't play no more uv dere games on me. I'm fixed. Can't you lend me a dime, Uncle Remus, to buy me a pie ? I'm dat hongry dat my stomach is gittin' ready to go in mo'nin'."

Uncle Remus eyed Charley curiously a moment, while the latter looked quietly at his timber toe. Finally, the old man sighed and spoke :

"How long is you bin in de chu'ch, son ? "

"Mighty near a week," replied Charley.

"Well, lemme tell you dis, now, 'fo' you go enny fudder. You ain't bin in dar long nuff fer ter go 'roun' takin' up conterbutions. Wait ontwell you gits sorter seasoned like, an' den I'll hunt 'roun' in my cloze an' see ef I can't run out a thrip er two fer you. But don't you levy taxes too early."

Charley laughed, and said he would let the old man off if he would treat him to a water-melon.

XVII

AS TO EDUCATION

As Uncle Remus came up Whitehall Street recently, he met a little coloured boy carrying a slate and a number of books. Some words passed between them, but their exact purport will probably never be known. They were unpleasant, for the attention of a wandering policeman was called to the matter by hearing the old man bawl out :

"Don't you come foolin' longer me, nigger. Youer flippin' yo' sass at de wrong colour. You k'n go roun' yer an' sass deze w'ite people, an' maybe

dey'll stan' it, but w'en you come a-slingin' yo'
jaw at a man w'at wuz gray w'en de fahmin' days
gin out, you better go an' git yo' hide greased."

"What's the matter, old man?" asked a sympathizing policeman.

"Nothin', boss, 'ceppin I ain't gwineter hav'
no nigger chillun a-hoopin' an' a-hollerin' at me
w'en I'm gwine 'long de streets."

"Oh, well, school-children—you know how
they are."

"Dat's w'at make I say w'at I duz. Dey better be home pickin' up chips. W'at a nigger
gwineter l'arn outen books? I kin take a bar'l
stave an' fling mo' sense inter a nigger in one
minnit dan all de school-houses betwixt dis en
de State er Midgigin. Don't talk, honey! Wid
one bar'l stave I kin fa'rly lif' de vail er ignunce."

"Then you don't believe in education?"

"Hit's de ruination er dis country. Look at
my gal. De ole 'oman sont 'er ter school las'
year, an' now we dassent hardly ax 'er fer ter kyar
de washin' home. She done got beyant 'er bizness. I ain't larnt nuthin' in books, 'en yit I kin
count all de money I gits. No use talkin', boss.
Put a spellin'-book in a nigger's han's, en right
den en dar' you loozes a plow-hand. I done had
de 'speunce un it."

XVIII

A TEMPERANCE REFORMER

"YER come Uncle Remus," said a well-dressed
negro, who was standing on the side walk near
James's bank recently, talking to a crowd of

barbers. " Yer come Uncle Remus. I boun' he'll
sign it."

" You 'll fling yo' money away ef you bet on it,"
responded Uncle Remus. " I ain't turnin' nothin'
loose on chu'ch 'scriptions. I wants money right
now fer ter git a pint er meal."

" 'Tain't dat."

" An' I ain't heppin fer ter berry nobody. Much's
I kin do ter keep de bref in my own body."

" 'Tain't dat, nudder."

" An' I ain't puttin' my han' ter no rekommends.
I'm feared fer ter say a perlite wud 'bout myse'f,
an' I des know I ain't gwine 'roun' flatter'n up
deze udder niggers."

" An' 'tain't dat," responded the darkey, who
held a paper in his hand. " We er gittin' up a
Good Tempeler's lodge, an' we like ter git yo'
name. "

" Eh-eh, honey! I done see too much er dis
nigger tempunce. Dey stan' up mighty squar'
ontwell der dues commence ter cramp up an' dey
don't stan' de racket wuf a durn. No longer'n
yistiddy I seed one er de head men er one er deze
Tempeler's s'cieties totin' water fer a bar-room.
He had de water in a bucket, but dey ain't no
tellin' how much red licker he wuz a-totin'. G'long,
chile—jine yo' s'ciety an' be good ter yo'se'f. I'm
a-gittin' too ole. Gimme th'ee er fo' drams
endurin' er de day, an' I'm mighty nigh ez good
a tempunce man ez de next un. I got ter scuffle
fer sump'n t'eat."

XIX

AS A WEATHER PROPHET

Uncle Remus was enlightening a crowd of negroes at the car-shed yesterday.

" Dar ain't nuthin'," said the old man, shaking his head pensively, " dat ain't got no change wrote on it. Dar ain't nuthin' dat ain't spotted befo' hit begins fer ter commence. We all 'speunces dat p'overdence w'at lifts us up fum one place an' sets us down in de udder. Hit's continerly a-movin' an' a-movin'."

" Dat's so ! " " Youer talkin' now ! " came from several of his hearers.

" I year Miss Sally readin' dis mawnin'," continued the old man, " dat a man wuz comin' down yer fer ter take keer er de wedder—wunner deze yer Buro mens w'at goes 'roun' a-puttin' up an' pullin' down."

" W'at he gwine do 'roun' yer ? " asked one.

" He's a-gwineter regelate de wedder," replied Uncle Remus, sententiously. " He's a-gwineter fix hit up so dat dere won't be so much worriment 'mong de w'ite fokes 'bout de kinder wedder w'at falls to dere lot."

" He gwine dish 'em up," suggested one of the older ones, " like man dish out sugar."

" No," answered Uncle Remus, mopping his benign features with a very large and very red bandanna. " He's a-gwinter fix um better'n dat. He's a-gwineter fix um up so you kin have any kinder wedder w'at you want widout totin' her home."

" How's dat ? " asked some one.

" Hit's dis way," said the old man, thoughtfully. "In co'se you knows w'at kinder wedder you wants. Well, den, w'en de man comes 'long, w'ich Miss Sally say he will, you des gotter go up dar, pick out yo' wedder, an' dere'll be a clock sot fer ter suit yo' case, an' w'en you git home, dere'll be yo' wedder a-settin' out in de yard waitin' fer you. I wish he wuz yer now," the old man continued. "I'd take a p'ar er frosts in mine, ef I kotched cold fer it. Dat's me!"

There were various exclamations of assent, and the old man went on his way, singing "Don't you Grieve Atter Me."

XX

THE OLD MAN'S TROUBLES

"WHAT makes you look so lonesome, Brer Remus?" asked a well-dressed negro, as the old man came shuffling down the street by James's corner yesterday.

"Youer mighty right, I'm lonesome, Brer John Henry. W'en a ole nigger like me is gotter paddle de canoe an' do de fishin' at de same time, an' w'en you bleedzd ter ketch de fish and dassent turn de paddle loose fer to bait de hook, den I tell you, Brer John, youer right whar de mink had de goslin'. Mars John and Miss Sally, dey done bin gone down unto Putmon County fer ter see dere kinfokes mighty nigh fo' days, an' you better b'leeve I done bin had ter scratch roun' mighty lively fer ter make de rashuns run out even."

"I wuz at yo' house las' night, Brer Remus,"

remarked Brer John Henry, "but I couldn't roust you outer bed."

"Hit was de unseasonableness er de hour, I speck," said Uncle Remus, dryly. "'Pears unto me dat you all chu'ch deacons settin' up mighty late deze cole nights. You'll be slippin' round arter hours some time er nudder, an' you'll slip bodaciously inter de calaboose. You mine w'at I tell you."

"It's mighty cole wedder," said Brer John Henry, evidently wishing to change the subject.

"Cole!" exclaimed Uncle Remus; "hit's got pas' cole on de quarter stretch. You oughter come to my house night 'fo' las'. Den you'd a-foun' me 'live an' kickin'."

"How's dat?"

"Well, I tell you, Brer John Henry, de cole wuz so cole, an' de kiver wuz so light, dat I thunk I'd make a raid on Mars John's shingle pile, an' out I goes an' totes in a whole armful. Den I gits under de kiver an' tells my ole'oman fer ter lay 'em onto me like she was roofin' a house. Bimeby she crawls in, an' de shingles w'at she put on her side fer ter kiver wid, dey all drap off on de flo'. Den up I gits an' piles 'em on agin, an' w'en I gits in bed my shingles draps off, an' dat's de way it wuz de whole blessid night. Fus' it wuz me up an' den de ole 'oman, an' it kep' us pow'ful warm, too, dat kinder exercise. Oh, you oughter drapt roun' 'bout dat time, Brer John Henry. You'd a-year'd sho' nuff cussin'?"

"You don't tell me, Brer Remus?"

"My ole 'oman say de Ole Boy wouldn't a-foun' a riper nigger, ef he wer' ter scour de country fum Ferginny ter de Alabam!"

XXI

THE FOURTH OF JULY

UNCLE REMUS made his appearance recently with his right arm in a sling and his hand bandaged to that extent that it looked like the stick made to accompany the Centennial bass-drum. The old man evidently expected an attack all around, for he was unusually quiet, and fumbled in his pockets in an embarrassed manner. He was not mistaken. The agricultural editor was the first to open fire :

"Well, you old villain ! what have you been up to now ? "

"It is really singular," remarked a commencement orator, "that not even an ordinary holiday—a holiday, it seems to me, that ought to arouse all the latent instincts of patriotism in the bosom of American citizens—can occur without embroiling some of our most valuable citizens. It is really singular to me that such a day should be devoted by a certain class of our population to broils and fisticuffs."

This fine moral sentiment, which was altogether an impromptu utterance, and which was delivered with the air of one who addresses a vast but invisible audience of young ladies in white dresses and blue sashes, seemed to add to the embarrassment of Uncle Remus, and at the same time to make an explanation necessary.

"Dey ain't none er you young w'ite men never had no ocasion fer ter strike up wid one er deze Mobile niggers ? " asked Uncle Remus. " 'Kaze ef you iz, den you knows wharbouts de devilment come in. Show me a Mobile nigger," continued the old man, "an' I'll show you a nigger dat's marked for de

chain-gang. Hit may be de fote er de fif' er July, er
it may be de twelf' er Jinawerry, but w'en a Mobile
nigger gits in my naberhood right den an' dar trubble sails in an' 'gages bode for de season. I speck
I'm ez fon' er deze Nunited States as de nex' man
w'at knows dat de Buro is busted up; but long
ez Remus kin stan' on his hine legs no Mobile nigger can't flip inter dis town longer no Wes' P'int
'schurshun an' boss 'roun' 'mong de culled fokes.
Dat's me 'up an' down, an' I boun' dere's a nigger
some'rs on de road dis blessid day dat's got dis put
away in his 'membunce."

"How did he happen to get you down and maul
you in this startling manner?" asked the commenc-
ment orator, with a tone of exaggerated sympathy
in his voice.

"Maul who?" exclaimed Uncle Remus, indignantly. "Maul who? Boss, de nigger dat
mauled me ain't bornded yit, an' dey er got ter
have anudder war 'fo' one is bornded."

"Well, what was the trouble?"

"Hit wuz sorter dis way, boss. I wuz standin'
down dere by Mars John Jeems's bank, chattin'
wid Sis Tempy, w'ich I ain't seed 'er befo' now
gwine on seven year, an' watchin' de folks trompin'
by, w'en one er deze yer slick-lookin' niggers, wid
a bee-gum hat an' a brass watch ez big ez de head uv
a beer-bar'l, come 'long an' bresh up agin me—so.
Dere wuz two un um, an' dey went 'long gigglin'
an' laffin' like a nes'ful er yaller-hammers.
Bimeby dey come 'long ag'in an' de smart Ellick
brush up by me once mo'. Den I say to myse'f,
'I lay I fetch you ef you gimme anudder invite.'
An', sho' 'nuff, yer he come ag'in, an' dis time he
rub a piece er water-million rime under my lef'
year."

"What did you do?"

"Me? I'm a mighty long-sufferin' nigger, but he hadn't no mo'n totch me 'fo' I flung deze yer bones in his face." Here Uncle Remus held up his damaged hand triumphantly. "I sorter sprained my han', boss, but dog my cats if I don't b'leeve I spattered de nigger's eyeballs on de groun', and w'en he riz his count'nence look fresh like beef-haslett. I look mighty spindlin' an' puny now, don't I, boss?" inquired the old man, with great apparent earnestness.

"Rather."

"Well, you des oughter see me git my Affikin up. Dey useter call me er bad nigger long 'fo' de war, an' hit looks like ter me dat I gits wuss an' wuss. Brer John Henry say dat I oughter supdue my rashfulness, an' I don't 'spute it, but tu'n a Mobile nigger loose in dis town, fote er July or no fote er July, an', me er him, one is got ter lan' in jail. Hit's proned inter me."

THE END